Poison by Punctuation

Chalkboard Outlines: Book 2

Kelley Kaye

Unlocking New Worlds

Poison by Punctuation
Chalkboard Outlines™: Book 2
A Red Adept Publishing Book
Red Adept Publishing, LLC
104 Bugenfield Court
Garner, NC 27529
http://RedAdeptPublishing.com/

First Ebook Edition: April 2018

Cover Art by Streetlight Graphics

This book is dedicated to the late Frederick Ramsey, a mentor and friend. I know how you felt about atheists who still believe in angels, so I never told you I was one of those nutcases myself. You understand it now, don't you? Yes, I know.

Rest in peace, Fred, except when you're doing your own seraph work, and then you're just gonna have to suck it up and watch over things.

Invest me in my motley; give me leave
To speak my mind, and I will through and through
Cleanse the foul body of th'infected world,
If they will patiently receive my medicine.

—*As You Like It,* 2.7.58-61

Prologue
Thursday, September 17

Kisten Hollis sat on a bench in the locker room, clutching her stomach with one hand and holding out the other to ward off sudden vertigo. The growing pain in her midsection pulsed, an unfamiliar feeling not usually associated with her illness. She shook it off and opened her gym locker. Cheerleading practice had been held before school today because the homecoming game was almost here. Double practice time was needed to prepare for their halftime routine.

As the smallest girl on the squad, Kisten perched on the top of the pyramids and was thrown through the air like a rag doll on a regular basis. She loved the way it felt to be tossed freely into the sky, to feel her long blond hair ballooning out like a parachute, to pirouette and fall safely into the arms of her teammates. Well, usually into their arms. *There was last week, when Sara Harper reached down to slap at a mosquito and missed me, but otherwise...*

Everyone else had left already, but Kisten preferred to be alone when pricking her finger and testing her blood. All her friends knew she was diabetic, but something about the way they averted their eyes after she purposely drew blood on her index finger or after she injected insulin into her stomach made this a ritual best performed alone.

She wondered, for a split second, if her real mother or father had also had diabetes. Maybe knowing her medical history would've gotten her diagnosed earlier. But she couldn't think of how that would have been helpful. She might've started jamming a needle into her belly three years earlier, and that was no fun.

No, Kisten couldn't see the point of having known this information any sooner. She was being foolish and daydreamy, which happened more and more these days whenever the subject of her real parents came up. Thoughts of "What if?" and "Why me?" took over. *But maybe—*

Stop. You've got terrific parents. They help you more than anyone else ever could. Start each day with a grateful heart, dummy! Kisten shook her head and expertly pricked her index finger then watched the small blood drop swell as it appeared.

Ugh. She really felt awful. Besides a vague nausea, she sensed some tingling in her fingertips and stomach, and her head nodded and swayed with inexplicable drowsiness. It was like she'd taken NyQuil before practice, and it was just now starting to hit her. She'd had an insulin shot before breakfast, so her blood sugar shouldn't be low enough to cause any symptoms. *What's going on?*

Kisten read the paper strip that documented her blood sugar level. It was only a little low, so she took what she called her "drug paraphernalia" out of her backpack to prepare another injection. Like an efficient factory worker at an assembly line, she laid out an alcohol swab, an insulin vial, and a syringe. She jabbed the needle into the vial and drew out the proper dosage. Tapping the syringe to clear out any bubbles, she pulled up the Thomas Jefferson High School T-shirt to expose her middle. The morning's injection site appeared red and inflamed, which hadn't happened in years, not since she had gotten comfortable with the injections. *Strange.* She poked at the round cherry spot and winced at the pain.

She thought of going to the nurse then dismissed the thought immediately. No way was the nurse here this early, anyway. Plus, Kisten knew more about diabetes than almost anyone around her. She had wanted to understand it, her body, and what it was doing to her body. Her mom had learned along with her, so maybe before class started, she could give her mom a call. Moms always seemed to know what to do.

The act of looking down at her stomach made her dizzy all over again. She had to hurry so she could tackle some more of that upcoming English paper. Schoolwork was piling up because the homecoming game had been keeping Kisten distracted. She found a space on her belly that didn't have any faded skin discolorations from previous shots, pinched some skin, and jabbed the needle in.

Kisten stood from the locker room bench and walked toward the showers, still clutching her middle. Maybe a quick, cool shower would clear her head. Maybe she'd hit a nerve or something with her syringe. It would all be better in a minute. *Start each day with a grateful heart.*

O, when she is angry she is keen and shrewd.
She was a vixen when she went to school,
And though she be but little, she is fierce.

—*A Midsummer Night's Dream,* 3.2.323-5

Chapter 1
Sunday, September 13

Emma Lovett hunched over the computer in her minuscule office, located in the little kitchen in the back of her very tiny home in Pinewood, Colorado, pounding away at the keyboard. She was writing a letter to the members of the Pinewood School District, with every intention of forwarding it to the *Pinewood Daily* and every television and radio station for hundreds of miles, respectively. She was fired up. Well, not fired up enough to ruin her weekend over it, which was why she was writing it on a Sunday evening, but by the grace of all that was holy, she was determined to make—

Her internal soapbox monologue was silenced by the doorbell.

"Yoo-hoo! Are ya decent?"

Emma heard the voice through the open windows of the dining room, which snuggled up to the kitchen of her precious little home. She clicked Save on her computer and walked toward the door just in time to see a blond coif poke its way through the previously unlocked, now open, door.

Shoot, I probably should have locked that. One would think her confrontation with two murderers in the first week of her first teaching job the previous year would have left remnants of concern for her safety.

She reached the door and pulled it all the way open as Leslie Parker strode past her.

"You really should lock that," Leslie chided.

Emma blew a stray lock of brown hair off her forehead. "Yep, that thought occurred to me as you walked right on in. No, I am not feeling too decent, Miss Leslie. Am I naked? No. Indecently annoyed and frustrated? You bet. I. am."

Leslie's demeanor went from brazen to concerned as she brushed another stray piece of hair off Emma's face in an uncharacteristically maternal gesture. Although she was more than a decade older than Emma's twenty-seven years, the idea of Leslie and motherhood went together like coffee and prune juice.

"What's wrong? I thought you were spending the weekend with Hunter in Aspen. Oh no. Did he pull a guy thing? Did he pull a homebody thing and refuse to do something exciting with you? He is a little unimaginative. What? Tell me. Scared of commitment? Not enough sex? Keeping his options open? That bastard." Leslie stopped talking when she saw Emma shaking her head violently.

"No, no. It's nothing like that. Hunter and I had a wonderful weekend. I'm still trying to get him to go home to Holly Hills with me, though, to meet my momma. I have no idea why he's balking."

"Maybe he's had a bad experience with mothers," Leslie said. "My mother-in-law may have been the least significant of my marital problems, but she wasn't number one on my speed dial, either. So what is it, then?"

Emma's shoulders drooped. "It's the blasted school board. I swear, Leslie, if that group ever had a good idea, it'd die of loneliness. I'm writing them a letter about their current Band-Aid for the gaping wound our society is dealing with. There's that Bullyproofing seminar scheduled for teachers on Tuesday, which is just the type of thing we might be able to use in our classrooms. But that's the only thing they're doing! Bullying is a societal problem, and one little seminar for just us, with no connections or follow-ups, and no other groups involved, equals... what? Nowhere near a solution, that's what. Wednesday comes, and—blammo!—we are right back to the same old, same old, and nothing's any better."

Leslie furrowed her brow. "Bullyproofing *what*? What are you talking about?"

Emma rushed over to the small green couch in her itty-bitty living room, picked up a piece of paper from the coffee table in front of it, and brandished it at her friend. "Good grief, Leslie. You really should read the stuff that comes in your school mailbox once in a while. It's not all spam. You might miss something, like this seminar. The school board is paying umpteen thousand dollars to bring someone, some 'expert,' to the district office to teach us the latest trends in how to fight bullying. It's a good idea for refreshing the knowledge of those of us fighting in the trenches. Professional growth is important. But it's not enough. Not even close."

Leslie grabbed the paper. "I'm confused. There are some real bullying buttmunches in that high school. You saw how they treated Adam Butler last year. They did everything but duct-tape him into a locker. And cyberbullying—that horrible, anonymous nonsense that now seems to be every corner douchebag's soup du jour—is rampant. So what is the problem with the seminar?"

"The problem, missy, is that the school district is once again trying to mandate somethin' they don't understand. How many of those board members used to be teachers? None, that's how many. Have any of them seen a kid dump another kid into a trash can? Or sat in the girls' bathroom, comforting a crying girl who just got a text calling her a whore? Where is the money for the on-site school psychologist? Where're the workshops to teach the students to treat each other with respect? Why aren't we helping the community understand and confront the problem? I sent a letter to the superintendent last year when we met Adam Butler, remember? You helped me write it. I never heard one thing back."

Emma drew in a huge, shaky breath and squeezed her fists, nails digging into her palms. "Remind me to tell you sometime about a suicide contagion I experienced in junior high school. Those boys were bullied, and the community didn't know how to help. I couldn't help. It's not enough, Leslie. Not by a long shot."

Emma stopped and looked at her friend curiously. "Why am I not hearing more complaining from you? Remember last year when they made us do that team-building in-service, and you had to hug Charlie Foreman? I thought you were gonna go ballistic. That didn't help you build a team; it just made you both madder than a whole 'team' of wet hens."

Sir Toby and Trinky, her Sheltie and calico, gathered at Leslie's feet, their body language clearly demanding some loving. She complied, bending gracefully at the waist, like a ballerina doing a stretch, to reach down and scratch their heads.

Emma shook out her long brown ponytail and smoothed her pink sweatpants, suddenly conscious of her messy hair and slouchy Sunday attire. Leslie wore a Metallica T-shirt and faded denim shorts, which somehow did not undermine her perfect blond bob. *I swear, Leslie could dress in burlap and win a mud-wrestling competition and still come out looking like a debutante.* It was infuriating, especially when the classy look and snarky attitude hid someone with a giant heart.

"Yes, my dear," Leslie cooed. "Outsiders, though well-intentioned, sometimes miss the mark." She straightened her T-shirt, grabbed its front with both fists, and cocked her elbows like a Revolutionary head of state. "'It shows a will most incorrect to heaven, a heart unmortified, a mind impatient, an understanding simple and unschooled.'"

Emma shook her head in frustration. "Yes, yes. *Hamlet.* Got it. You're dodging the question. I know why I am interested in this seminar. Even if it is a measly Band-Aid, it's better'n nothin'. Why are *you* interested?"

"Oh, I don't know. It might not be so bad to refresh myself on some techniques other than whacking them upside the head." Leslie had a personal war going against PDAs—public displays of affection—in the hallways, which she combated by lightly tapping the offenders on the backs of their heads. "What else do you think we should do to address the problem to a more widespread audience, Grasshoppah?" She'd asked, but she didn't really seem concerned about the answer. Her glance roamed all over the wall, the plants, the animals—everywhere but at Emma's eyes.

"Leslie, what is up with you? C'mon. Spill."

Leslie collapsed onto the striped loveseat and started picking at cat and dog hairs that had landed there. A couple of the hairs stuck to her fingertips, and she blew them into the air. "Weeeelll, there's a teacher over at the junior high. Shawn something. I saw him at Old Chicago the other night, and..."

With thoughts of the in-service abandoned, Emma started jumping up and down. "An interest. You have an interest! Well, it's about time. I thought you'd never get over ol' Rainshadow. Is this Shawn half your age or younger?"

Leslie shook her head along with one hand, trying to dislodge the last hair from her fingertip. "I think he's in his thirties, just like me, smarty-pants." She sighed. "I don't know. We'll see what happens. It's been hard, ya know? I really dug Rain. I miss him."

Rainshadow Thornberry—his friends called him Rain—was the twentysomething son of Emma's hippie neighbor, Delilah. He and Leslie had had a mad fling during the summer, until he'd up and gone into the Peace Corps one hot July day. He was now spending the next who-knew-how-many years in a distant third-world country, teaching the citizens how to farm or sanitize water or maybe even build schools—hopefully schools without bullies or with ambitious people who had problem-solving ideas to add to a teacher in-service.

Leslie had wanted him to stay here so she could continue teaching him the arts of love, but Rainshadow was the save-the-Earth type, and the Earth called. She'd always referred to him as her boy toy, but apparently, there was more to it than she'd let on. Emma had only known Leslie for a year, but there'd never been more than a week or so between her dates. Until Rain. Emma loved her neighbor Delilah, and Rain had certainly brought out a softer side of Leslie. This was the first time Emma had heard her friend say anything vulnerable since he'd left.

"Oh, all right then. For the sake of potential love, or at least potential monkey business, I'll let you go to the in-service unscathed." Emma ran over to her tiny kitchen then ran back out with a lint roller. "But hey! Does that mean you knew about the seminar already? You obviously hadn't read the notice."

Leslie allowed Emma to lint-roll her palm and the sleeve of her shirt. "I hadn't. I'd been trying to figure out a way to talk to this guy other than putting on my phone-sex voice and calling him out of the blue. The in-service just provided it, baby."

Emma went back into her little office, which was really a breakfast nook, and continued typing. Leslie meandered in behind her.

"Glad to be of help," Emma said. "I'm still sending the letter, even if, as usual, it changes nothing. You're right, though. Maybe I should add more positive suggestions to the letter, as opposed to just ranting." She held the back of her hand to her forehead and struck a pose. "Ah'm afrayd it's mah lot in life to be undermahned and underappreciated."

A small white refrigerator squatted next to the doorway to the living room, not even two steps from the nook. Leslie opened it and started rooting through. She pulled out a Coke, popped the top, and started chugging. "Oh, spare me the sweet Southern swooning baloney. You know the school board can't be bulldozed into changing a decision once it's made, much less charmed or—heh heh—bullied into it."

"Come on, Les. We were born to root for the underdog, fight the good fight, solve mysteries, and all that."

Leslie swished Coke from cheek to cheek and gave the can to Emma to share. "Champion lost causes?"

Emma took a sip and set the can down next to the keyboard. She had intended to stop buying sodas and stock up on something healthier, but her shopping arm hadn't caught up to her good intentions yet. "Yup. Your crusade against public displays of affection is a lost cause if ever I saw one, yet you persist in smacking offenders upside the head in the hopes of curing the terminally hormonal. Did you know my next lost cause is getting Pinewood to ban plastic bags at all the grocery stores?"

Leslie snorted. "Yeah, don't'cha know *that* will happen after we've won the war against terrorism."

Emma swiveled the computer chair around to face Leslie in the kitchen. "Do you know what terrorizes me? The fact that our not-so-distinguished chief of detectives, Carl Niome, needed the help of two English teachers to figure out who killed Melvin McManus. He'd probably believe the terrorists when they told him they were double agents and invite 'em over for beer and a game of pool." She altered her Southern drawl slightly to adopt a doofier style. "We don't want them evil terrorists gettin' hold of some-a them nookyoular-type weapons, now do we?"

Leslie snatched the can back and chugged the rest then let out a huge burp that somehow, coming from her, always sounded sexy. Emma wondered how she did that and thought of some of her friend's other unusual talents as Leslie spoke.

"'And still he smiled and talked, and as the soldiers bore dead bodies by, he called them untaught knaves, unmannerly, to bring a slovenly unhandsome corpse betwixt the wind and his nobility.'"

Quoting Shakespeare to fit any occasion was one of those unusual talents. Emma had yet to figure that one out, either. "That has to be one of the Henrys," she mused. "Which Henry is it?"

Emma relieved her friend of the empty can. She stepped through the back doorway into the small pantry then down two small steps to the basement door and the door to the backyard. She tossed the can into a canvas recycle bag hanging from the door to the basement. Back up the steps and through the pantry, Emma returned to her breakfast table-slash-office desk, which took up a kitchen corner in her cozy little house. She loved it so dearly. It was another example of the new, independent life she'd created for herself since her divorce.

"*Henry IV,*" Leslie said. "Hey, do you want to go get some dinner? I don't have anything to eat in my house."

"You never have anything to eat in your house." Emma grabbed her letter off the printer then stuck it in an envelope, scribbled an address on it, and walked out the front door to drop it into the mailbox, which hung from a pillar on the porch. She called back to Leslie, "You don't cook, so what's new? Anyway, can't go. I've got papers to grade for my Advanced Composition class."

Leslie came to the front of the house, stood at the edge of the porch, and turned around, hands on her hips. "Aw, shucks. We've only been in school for three weeks. When did you collect those papers?"

"Friday."

Leslie swished away an imaginary pile of papers. "Emma," she clucked. "Emma, Emma, Emma. You are well aware they can sit in a pile for another two weeks before the kids will start asking for them. They know the rule. If it takes *them* two weeks to write one paper, you should have at least two weeks to grade thirty."

Emma gazed at the fictional papers Leslie had swished away, now littering the porch like fallen soldiers of student effort. "Sure, sure. I know. But it's a big pile, and they just... stare at me. I have to start them tonight. I always eat too much when I'm out with you, anyway. I have to watch my girlish figure." She posed in her doorway, arms on either side of the doorframe.

Walking gingerly backward down the three red stairs off the porch, Leslie spoke. "Yeah, you want to make sure *Hunter* keeps watching your girlish figure. He'll keep watching, and you know it. He's a big drooling puppy dog for you." She continued her backward trek toward her little red convertible and twinkled red nails at Emma. "Okeydokey, artichokee. If you've got no love for my dinner idea, I'll see you at school tomorrow. Toodles."

"See you tomorrow." Emma closed the door, let out a big sigh, and settled down on the couch. When she'd moved clear across the country to learn to be a teacher, she hadn't counted on all the emotional issues she'd have to face. They daunted her because each time she thought of people in pain, it hurt her heart too. She was quickly figuring out that "teaching" might include teaching others to heal.

But not right now. Right now is about teaching descriptive essays. She patted the dog and cat on either side of her and thought really hard about how she could better combat bullies and about starting in on that monster stack of papers.

I shall despair. There is no creature loves me;
And if I die, no soul will pity me.
Nay, wherefore should they, since that I myself
Find in myself no pity to myself?

—*Richard III*, 5.3.201-4

Chapter 2
Monday, September 14

Thomas Jefferson High School was established in 1906, although at that time, it was simply called the Pinewood School. It served kindergarten through high school and was located in a one-room schoolhouse on the north side of town. TJ High, where Emma taught, was a mammoth building on the south side of town, surrounded by pine trees—many of which were used to hide kids sneaking a smoke or a kiss between classes—and serving over fifteen hundred students.

This made for way too many people in one place for Emma, who'd actually attended a one-room schoolhouse in her hometown of Holly Hills, South Carolina. Her graduating class had had a total of thirty-three students. She noted many more students than that as she drove into the teachers' parking lot. Students spilled into the courtyard as they poured around the corner from their lot in the back. *Looks like an ant farm. Holy smokes.*

Speaking of her graduating class, Emma dreaded next summer's ten-year reunion, not because she didn't have friends in her class, but because of the one former classmate who'd broken her heart—her ex-husband, Ronald Talicky, the man who put the "rogue" in the term "devilishly handsome rogue." His infidelities had put an end to their brief marriage and forced Emma to begin a new and independent life.

Maybe it was wishful thinking that he'd skip the reunion. *Oh yeah. Ronald missing an opportunity to socialize, aka flirt, with any female showing signs of a pulse? Would never happen.*

Thank goodness for sweet and straightforward Hunter, who never made her feel uncertain. She calculated the time she had this morning before her first-hour class and regretted that she'd be unable to see him before lunchtime.

Emma's first year of teaching had been intimidating and overwhelming in more ways than one. Besides finding a dead body the first week of school and then catching the killer, Emma had to navigate halls crammed with tall, squirming bodies—halls that, every day, appeared to be one of those stunts in which one stuffed as many people as possible into a phone booth. She also had to successfully navigate the atmosphere in a room of thirty or more adolescents, people with opinions and outlooks forming or already formed, rotating through her classroom every seventy-two minutes, expecting education or maybe entertainment, depending on the student. This kind of navigation was hard to do.

It had gotten easier, though. This year, many of the students remembered her from the previous year, and frequent greetings anywhere from "Hiya, Ms. Lovett" to the slightly less appropriate "Yo, Miz Lovett. S'up?" increased her comfort level.

She received and reciprocated many of these greetings on her way to her classroom, room 104 in the English wing.

Leslie was waiting for her. Looking chic and unruffled, as always, in a sleeveless white smock paired with flowy oriental-print satin pants, she acted more flustered than she looked as she gestured Emma over. "You've got to come with me and see what's been done to the gym."

"New gym or old gym?" Emma felt the disgusted look crossing her face as she revisited yet another school board argument. Should the district have spent millions of dollars on a new gymnasium when the old one was perfectly large and functional? Or should they have done something about the disgraceful auditorium-slash-theatre that only seated two hundred kids in hard, plastic seats? *Guess which one they picked.*

"New gym. They've got it closed off to kids right now, but I think Abigail will let us in." Leslie pulled at Emma's arm. "Nice dress, by the way. I don't think I've ever seen you in a solid color. That's a charming blue. Makes your brunette locks shine from your shoulders like... oh, I dunno. Like a shiny wooden boat on a lake. C'mon. Hustle!"

Emma followed Leslie, using a staccato hop to catch up to her long-legged and faster friend. "Oh for Pete's sake. What's wrong? Did the backboard refuse to come down? I don't have all day to lollygag. Its seven twenty, and you know my creative writers are excited to start writing creatively."

"Shush." They approached the large double doors to the new gym, otherwise known as the Wildcat Pride gym. A curmudgeonly old townsman had actually given beaucoup bucks to the district to have it called the Hatch Complex—after himself, of course—but he was the only one who actually called it that.

Abigail Patterson, the school secretary—who, in reality, ran the school—stood sentinel. "Hello, ladies," she whispered. A small, frail-looking woman with gray curls and glasses, Abigail looked and sounded like a harmless Aunt Bea. But when she barked orders over the PA system or kept kids and teachers in line, she transformed like Bruce Banner into the Incredible Hulk or Jekyll into Hyde. Emma had only witnessed it in person once, but once was enough. Now, every time the commanding voice exploded over the PA, she tried to match it to Abigail. She failed every time.

"Abigail, may we please go in?" Leslie asked. "I think Emma should see what horrible thing has been done to our magnificent new gym."

Emma barely kept her snort silent. Abigail nodded and pushed the door open.

The Wildcat Pride gym had blue bleachers to match the school colors, with only the set on the right extended. Rows of blue-and-white championship banners lined the walls along the top, mostly for basketball, although Pinewood had had a state champion wrestler the previous year. Lights from each corner spotlighted that banner.

Two janitors worked at either end of the back wall, trying to wash out the huge black letters defacing it from end to end. "You all need to fail" was what Emma was pretty sure it had said, although the *y* and the *l* were already scrubbed out, so now it said "Ou all need to fai." And strangely enough, the letters were sprawled across the wall fairly close to the ground, no more than five feet up, Emma thought.

She shrugged at Leslie. "What do you think it means? Who are the 'you all'? All students? All athletes? It can't mean all freshmen. Quite a few of those are failing already, three weeks into the semester. It's a little close to the ground. Maybe a short freshman could have done it."

Leslie grabbed Emma's arm and thrust it toward the wall, fingertips reaching the same height as the tops of the graffiti. "You could've done it, Short Stuff. Are you feeling put out about something?" Leslie shook her head. "Just kidding, Pollyanna. I don't know who did it. Maybe it's not telling students that they need to fail in the future. Maybe it's someone who's *already* failing who wants to get back at the teachers and administrators. Like, 'Hey, I'm failing. Now it's your turn.'" She threw her head back and cackled like the Wicked Witch of the West. "Muah ha ha ha ha!"

Emma shivered. "Okay, my pretty. Stop that evil laughter 'cause it gives me the willies. Maybe it's just your typical angry, pointless vandalism. Let's get back to class before the kids claim that ridiculous rule."

Some kid had heard, probably from an older brother or sister in college, that if the teacher hadn't shown up after fifteen minutes, that meant class was canceled. It had gotten to the point that students called the fifteen-minute rule after about two minutes of teacher absence.

Emma and Leslie nodded to Abigail and headed back to their rooms.

Kids were milling around but still present when Emma arrived. Hunter Wells sat at her desk, and as she smiled his way and went to greet him, catcalls and whistles followed her. Hunter and Emma were very careful to avoid the dreaded PDAs anywhere on school grounds or where they might see kids. But kids weren't stupid. They only had to look at the smiles that lit the pair's faces when they saw each other to know there was a "thing" happening.

"Hey," he whispered. "Did you see the gym? These kids are all talking about it, although I don't think any of them actually saw it. Either that or they're having fun creating their own threatening sayings. My favorite so far is 'You all should get hit in the head with a pail.'" He grinned, and that dimple Emma loved so much creased his cheek. "I already started the early birds on that brain barfing you do for your journal writing." He gestured to the whiteboard, on which he'd written "Brain Barf," and to the enthusiastic creative writers with their heads already down, scribbling away.

Hunter's first year as an actual teacher started this year, although he had spent time at Thomas Jefferson the previous year as a spy for the Colorado High School Sports Association, trying to infiltrate the coaches' group—otherwise known as the Lounge Lizards—to unravel a grade-changing scandal. The scandal had been resolved with no significant criminal roundup, but Hunter had succeeded in catching a few other things, including Emma's eye and maybe even her heart.

His experience pretending to be a teacher made him really want to be one, so he'd taken out his history degree—formerly abandoned as being interesting but useless—and dusted it off. Besides having a fun summer getting to know Emma, Hunter had also completed student-teaching classes for his teacher's certificate. The principal,

Nathan Farrar, had done an amazing job schmoozing the Department of Education to get the previous year approved as his student-teaching experience. *And what an experience it was, murders and all!*

"Hmm," Emma mused. "'You all should get hit in the head with a pail.' That's a good one. Maybe it's Jack threatening revenge on Jill." She grinned and winked at Hunter.

His sparkly-blue-eyed return wink, accompanied by a wide smile and that adorable dimple, for crying out loud, made Emma's heart flutter.

Hunter gestured in the direction of the gym. "This is my planning hour, so I told Abigail I'd help them clean up. What are your plans for lunch?"

"Well, Mr. Wells," she whispered, "first things first. I would really like to know who had this defacing party of negativity on our walls. Maybe I'll investigate a little. Mrs. Albert is making us vegetarian lasagna. Want to join?"

Hunter's face screwed up in distaste. "Vegetarian? Uh-uh. Thanks anyway. I'll grab a hamburger with some of the guys."

She threatened to clunk him over the head with her Shakespeare paperweight. "Neanderthal."

He winked again. "Granola." He came around the side of her desk and headed up one of the aisles of student desks, high-fiving a male and a female student. No slave to gender stereotypes was he. She tried to watch him leave the classroom without making her ogling obvious. Oh, how she loved to watch him go.

Emma took roll and, after their journal entries were complete, gave the class a free period to work on a story for their creative writing unit. Soft music played on her computer in an effort to promote the flow of creative juices. Glancing about the room, she took in the fake but nice plants in the corners and the beanbag area cluttered with her personal library, which had been repurposed to help students fall in love with words like she had. She tried to remember which books were in there that might relate to the message on the gymnasium wall.

Why do people wish suffering on others? The Shakespeare bust didn't answer. She made a quick list of students she might be able to question, kids she knew were part of the beating heart of school action. Maybe they'd learned of someone who was mad or felt slighted, more so than the usual teenage angst.

She stared absently at the pile of Advanced Composition essays that she had brought from home but found herself doodling instead. When she looked down, she discovered that she had written *You all need to fail* over and over. Disturbed, she crinkled up the paper and threw it in the wastebasket.

Chapter 3

Emma and Leslie decided to eat in the big teachers' lounge in the main office to meet the three new teachers. They stood in the doorway to the lounge, gazing across the floor and gearing up for intros. Leslie liked to wait until new people got comfortable before showing up to introduce herself to them. Since she didn't look anything like a regular teacher and oozed confidence, Emma imagined this display of hand-pumping enthusiasm made the new teachers uncomfortable all over again. But Leslie just wanted to let them acclimate for a bit. She had no real sense of her intimidation factor.

"Hey, Parker! Want a hug?" called Charlie Foreman, a gym teacher, football coach, and superintendent's son. Leslie despised him, and Emma was learning to. He'd been a prime suspect in the custodian's murder the previous year, and Emma was a little upset that he'd ended up being guilty of only stupidity, sexism, and maybe some misogyny. Certainly cluelessness.

His comment was rewarded by titters from the rest of the table, a group of coaches and sports fanatics who called themselves the Lounge Lizards. Their required lunchtime topics, every single day, were sports or sex. Hunter had sat with this group the previous year to spy on them. He had been the only one not regularly pounding the others on the back and high-fiving their juvenile antics. That was the reason Emma had noticed him. Well, not the only reason.

Incredibly, Leslie ignored him. Usually, anytime Charlie opened his mouth, she took the opportunity to belittle him with a Shakespearean insult he'd never understand. Sometimes she did this even when he hadn't said a word. But today, she ignored the loud table along the back wall and set her yellow lunch tray down at a table on the right, which was surrounded by three new faces.

"Hiya!" She grinned. "I'm Leslie Parker, English teacher extraordinaire and crusader against PDAs in the hallways. And this is Emma Lovett. She knows her English pretty well too."

"Hi, I'm Emma." Emma shook hands with a tall, beefy man in overalls, a woman of indeterminate age with big teeth and short brown hair going gray, and a heavy brunette who wore what could be politely described as a muumuu but that Leslie, in a snarky moment, might call a tent.

The overall-clad giant spoke first. Emma could tell from his freckles that he had once been called Carrot Top. His still-thick, short hair was now a yellow-white-peppered gray. He shifted the apron of his overalls and extended a beefy paw. "Hi, Emma. I'm Otto Henry, the new ag teacher. This is Diane Seymour, a new business and A-plus Program teacher, and Rhiannon Pressman, who's monitoring all the study halls."

"I'm afraid I'm not familiar with the Ag Department," said Emma, shaking Otto's hand with enthusiasm. "We have an Ag Department? And what's the A-plus Program? I know about the Business Department, of course." She nodded toward Diane, the short-haired woman, feeling stupid. *Of* course *I know the Business Department? Conversationalist extraordinaire, that is I. Sheesh.*

Otto Henry chuckled. "That's Agriculture Department. By your accent, I'd say you came from somewhere down south. Not a whole lot of farming and ranching in the middle of the swamp, but here we've got plenty. I'm teaching Vet Science, Plant Science, Ag Welding, and good ol' Ag 1 and 2." He paused to take a breath, hooking a thumb in one overall strap and spinning a brass pin on its post with the other. "Thomas Jefferson always has a ton of kids win 4-H awards every year, and I'm real excited to be a part of it. See this pin? This one is an adult leadership pin, but if you see students with the student version, you'll know they worked long and hard for it."

That's it! He looks like Opie Taylor from The Andy Griffith Show *at fifty years old. 4-H? Ag Welding?* Emma felt a little scared to ask. "Um, that sounds great. I bet you're really proud."

He reached over and shook Leslie's hand too. "Yep. It's gonna be a great year. Speakin' of 4-H and the like, I hate to eat and run, but I need to get back to my room. Angie Painter's coming in, trying to choose between a blue or belted pig, and I've gotta approve it."

Before Leslie could say anything Shakespearean about sows—Emma thought that was the Old English word for pigs—Otto hurried from the lounge. Diane watched him go, and Rhiannon watched Diane. She sensed a vibe between the three newbies that seemed more attached than simply three new teachers together in unfamiliar surroundings. Maybe they'd taught together before.

Swine? Could be the quote would be about swine, not sows. Emma smiled at the picture in her head of blue pigs and pigs with big cowboy belt buckles around their middles. *Completely non-Shakespearean image.*

Leslie focused on Diane. "I'm afraid I'm not familiar with the A-plus Program, either." Then she appraised Rhiannon. "Are you named after the song? I love Stevie Nicks."

"Ooh, me too!" Emma gushed. "Who sings that one again? Wait, don't tell me. I know it starts with an *F*." She addressed the table of newbies. "Don't you think this is weird? I forget the names of things, sometimes. Okay, lots of times." She smiled. "But I can always remember the first letter of whatever it is I forgot. Isn't that weird? I think it's a syndrome." *Now I'm just babbling.*

The two women stared.

Leslie made a face. "*Pfftt!* It's Fuh-leetwood Mac, young'un." She broke into a little rendition of the classic rock song, pitchy but recognizable, while they waited for either woman to respond.

The two ladies sat at a square table typical to office lounges, with a faux wood grain on its surface. Emma took the seat Otto had just vacated and set her brown-bag lunch—tuna on wheat—down. Diane shrugged, picked up the napkin next to her lunch tray, and started folding it into smaller and smaller squares, thin fingers bending and smoothing. Leslie had finished the whole song and taken a bow before anyone said anything.

Rhiannon twitched as if someone had just materialized from thin air and said "Boo!" But she finally spoke. "Uh, the A-plus Program is a computer remediation program. Diane runs the lab off of the courtyard, and teachers send kids in to work on the computers in areas where they, um, struggle." Rhiannon had curly brown hair that didn't really lie down on her head as much as it exploded from her scalp. She wore no makeup, and her hand clutched at the flower print of the muumuu.

Leslie nodded. "I've seen those programs. They're neat." She explained it for Emma. "They have them for math and science and English. They teach lessons to the kids, sometimes with video-game-type practices, and then quiz them, giving their scores back immediately." Since her song had ended with no applause, Leslie sat down as well, looking expectant.

A strained silence followed, Diane folding and smoothing, Rhiannon clutching the muumuu like a lifeline. Suddenly, Rhiannon blurted out, "I don't know who I'm named for. I'm not even a real teacher. I just babysit them while they study."

Emma reached over and patted her hand. "Rhiannon, kids need time to study, and it's good you're there to help if they get stuck."

Rhiannon ducked her head and started taking big bites from her brown-bag ham sandwich. Diane kept frenetically folding her napkin without eating anything.

It was the most awkward situation Emma had ever been a part of, and she'd been in some doozies. Diana kept folding and smoothing her napkin, and Rhiannon chewed sandwich bits without saying anything else.

Leslie shot a quizzical look at Emma then rose from her seat, taking her tray and grabbing Emma's brown bag and sandwich mid-bite. "So nice meeting you all. My friend and I have a few things to do before fourth hour."

"Oh really? Like what?" These were the first real words from Diane, and they came out sounding sharp and judgmental, like maybe Emma and Leslie wanted to leave campus for a smoke break.

Emma finished chewing her food. Neither of them was prepared for an actual account of their whereabouts. "Well," said Emma. She hadn't actually solidified any grading or lesson plans just yet but longed to leave the table ASAP. *I'm not usually this uncomfortable around new people. My Southern hospitality has flown the coop, like a chicken with an eagle's wings.*

"Well," said Leslie. "We're going to check out preparations for the science fair. Yeah, that's right, isn't it, Emma? You wanted to learn more about our great scientific minds here at TJ High?"

"Sure!" Emma nodded like a bobblehead doll. "I wanted to see if anyone was... building a rocket! Yes, a rocket or... or maybe one of those models of the universe. See y'all at the in-service tomorrow." Emma had already moved halfway out the door, with Leslie backing out and waving.

"Those two are kinda short, right?" Emma whispered as they hurried down the steps and through the main office, passing the front counter and bursting into the commons. "Otto 'Opie Taylor' Henry is tall, but one of those gals could've made the graffiti."

A couple of students sat across the way, eating lunch in front of the gym doors, but otherwise, they crossed an empty expanse of shiny brown tiles.

"Ugh. I certainly feel like I've failed after that train wreck. If one of them did the graffiti, she is on her way to successfully making me feel like a loser." Leslie wiped imaginary sweat from her brow. "Maybe I shouldn't be so keen on welcoming the new guys every year. I don't think I've ever felt such stress over keeping a conversation afloat."

"Afloat? I almost broke out a joke to avoid complete radio silence. Let's stop on our way and check that graffiti again for a clue."

Leslie pulled Emma through the doors of the new gym to look at the vandalism. All the spray-painted words were gone, and the gymnasium smelled of fresh paint. Both women inspected the entire wall and the floor under the one extended set of bleachers to look for clues, without success. They continued toward the smaller gym.

"Oh no. Not your jokes," Leslie said, continuing their conversation and patting Emma's shoulder. "I'm still trying to recover from the one you told at the first-day faculty meeting about the snail riding on the turtle. And rockets? We built rockets and model universes in the fifth grade here in Colorado. I don't know how advanced you all were in good ol' Holly Hills, but here, they're probably doing genetic experiments and making virtual-reality gloves so they can grope an imaginary girl and get their jollies."

Emma pursed her lips. "Eww. Do you really think...? Never mind. I don't want to know. Let's check it out. Maybe someone working on a project in there saw someone heading into the new gym with nefarious destruction-of-property purposes? Wouldn't hurt to ask. I don't believe I've ever been to a science fair before."

Leslie grinned. "Hence your fifth-grade memories of rockets and model universes." They went through the girls' locker room to the old gym since, apparently, the new gym couldn't be wasted on something as inconsequential as science. Emma hoped no one had graffitied or destroyed any of the science projects.

The old gym appeared organized and untouched. Long cafeteria tables sprouted up from the floor of the basketball court at odd angles and were covered with even odder charts, doohickeys, thingamabobs, and other scientifically named experiments. Each table had a busy student scientist working away, but Emma and Leslie were the only observers. *Must still be preparation time.* As they meandered from table to table, they nodded like they understood perfectly whatever theory or premise was being presented.

"This is the *real* science fair," whispered Leslie, pointing at a display labeled "Combatting the global food crisis: Diazotroph bacteria as a cereal crop growth promoter." "See? No rockets or model universes here. We of the word-loving persuasion can maybe figure out what *diazotroph* means." She looked expectantly at Emma.

Emma nodded. "Of course, being the queens of the English language that we are." *Great Caesar's ghost! Prefixes, suffixes, and bears. Oh my!* Emma stared at the word. "I think *dia* means 'passing through'?"

Leslie bobbed her head up and down. "Yup. And I think *troph* is something Greek. 'To nourish'? Nourishing." Her voice got louder. "So that would make diazotroph bacteria..."

"Bacteria that nourishes you as it passes through you." Now Emma's voice rose as the excitement caught on. "So we eat nourishing bacteria to solve the global food crisis! Wow. Sounds gross, but anything to solve the crisis. Now that's an amazing science fair project. That possum is *on the stump*! I had no idea."

Leslie sniggered. "On the stump, yes indeedy. These are the kids who worked on this stuff all summer while everyone else went out to the lake. The fair at the end of the year has experiments from *all* of the science classes, and those kids are required to take those classes to graduate. So there's not near as much... enthusiasm at that one," she said. "It's probably okay that you missed last spring. I think one of the Earth Science kids did his experiment to show that an earthworm's poop looked the same as the food going into the earthworm."

Emma flipped through a notebook filled with charts about which countries had the biggest food shortages and photographs of the different bacteria. "Heck. So sorry I missed that one."

"That's okay. I only went because they had some recycling display that Rain wanted to see." She sighed. "Damn that Peace Corps, anyway, and all their tree-hugging, save-the-planet ideals."

Emma elbowed her friend as they reached a table in the far corner. "Look at this one." A tall, lanky boy with thin blond hair stood behind his display table next to a computer monitor, wearing a glove that had thin wires attached to all the fingers.

Leslie cocked her head. "Is that a virtual-reality glove? This reality not enough for you, my good sir?"

The boy flushed and shifted his weight from foot to foot. "No, ma'am. It's a sign-language glove."

Leslie grinned. "So you *sign* your displeasure at this reality?"

This time, Emma's elbow to the ribs was intended to hurt. "Ignore Ms. Parker," said Emma. "Embarrassing students is her goal in life. Tell us how it works."

"The wires send a signal to this computer, see." He turned a screen toward Emma and gestured to it. "Then, whoever's wearing the gloves can sign the words. The computer recognizes the symbols as real words and types them on the screen."

Emma nodded, impressed. "That's really great. But why would you need to have a deaf person sign the words to create the letters? Deaf people can type."

The boy smiled, starting to warm up, and nodded at them both. He took the glove off and handed it to Emma. "Yeah, sure they can. But this way, a person could sign someone's speech, say, and then it could be written on the computer and simultaneously transferred onto big screens so people who don't know sign language can read it like subtitles. Or you know, there are computer programs that translate the written word into braille, so blind people could read the braille after it's signed. I think there are probably lots more applications. I, uh, just haven't worked them all out yet."

"That is truly amazing," said Emma, donning the glove and wiggling the wired fingers. "Don't you think so, Ms. Parker?"

But Leslie had wandered over to another display table.

Emma chuffed. "Excuse that rude Ms. Parker. Her curiosity takes over her manners sometimes." She smiled at the boy and handed him the glove. "Just really quickly before I leave—did you hear about the graffiti on the walls of the other gym?"

"I heard something when we started working this morning. Big black letters, right? My friend Rosalie told me it had something to do with someone wanting all of us to eat kale. Seems like a weird thing to write on walls."

Emma laughed. "That's not *exactly* what it said, but it's close enough. Have you heard anyone talking or bragging about tagging those walls?"

He shook his head. "I would tell someone if I knew. If you see something, say something, right?"

"Right as rain. Hey, great project. I hope you win a ribbon." Emma excused herself and found Leslie in front of a huge terrarium. *Isn't that what fish tanks are called when there's no fish in them?*

"Look," Leslie said. "Poisonous frogs." She gestured to the student at the table. "That's Blake Candelar. He was in my mythology class. Look, it's poisonous frogs." She seemed to be locked in a death stare with one of the small amphibians crouched on a piece of driftwood in the front corner.

Emma shook the student's hand. "Hello, Blake. Good to know you. Why are you experimenting on poisonous frogs? Aren't they dangerous?"

A short boy with a shock of black hair that stood straight up off his forehead, Blake Candelar had large brown eyes that made his bulbous nose look not so bulbous. He wore baggy jeans and a black T-shirt that said "Chicks dig short guys with big feet." He didn't look like what Emma thought of as a stereotypical science student, but here he was at the heavy-duty, real science fair. *You'd think I'd have learned not to stereotype by now.*

"This is a wild Australian frog," Blake said, pointing to the one Leslie stared at. "And this"—he walked over to the back end of the tank to indicate a brightly colored one—"is a poison dart frog. I'm studying them because they manufacture their own poisons, and a lot of people don't know how or why. The Australian one is, like, totally fascinating because the poisons are made in the alkaloids on its skin."

Leslie finally stood up from her big frog stare-down. "So what's the project? Are you gonna teach people how to manufacture stuff in their skin?" She lifted her arm and posed it. "'Yet I'll not shed her blood, nor scar that whiter skin of hers than snow, and smooth as monumental alabaster, yet she must die.'" She dropped her arm with a flourish. "*Othello*, of course."

Blake laughed. "Sure, big advances in biochemical warfare, Ms. Parker. You always did like the crazy death stuff in mythology. No, I found some cool research about how the poisons in these frogs could be extracted and used for medicines. Lots of drugs come from plant alkaloids, so I'm trying to find some new or improved ways animal alkaloids could have medical benefits too. Maybe a better sort of painkiller that's not addictive, a faster-moving local anesthetic, or whatever."

He ran a hand over his spiky hair. It popped right back up. "Alkaloids have something called nicotinic receptors, which play a major role in things like pain perception and could even help protect from stroke." He shrugged. "You know, stuff doesn't happen in nature for no reason. If an organism is making it, it must have value for life."

Emma and Leslie stood quietly, staring at the frogs.

"Wow, Blake," said Emma finally. "I can't even wrap my head around that idea, and here you are showing ways it could be used. I'm amazed. You could smart the dew right off the honeysuckle!"

Blake shrugged again and shoved both hands deep into his baggy pockets.

The two women fawned over him for as long as he could stand it, then they left to check out the rest of the fair. "Blake is short," murmured Emma as they wound up their visit. "His T-shirt even said something about it."

"Yes, but did you hear anything from any of these kids that sounded like they felt upset or slighted?" Leslie asked. "If the graffiti had happened after the ribbons were handed out, then maybe I could see it. It doesn't really make any sense for it to happen right now, if it's one of them, I mean. Right?"

"No, you're right," Emma said, running her fingers over the edge of a table displaying pinwheels, all moving at different rates. She wondered how that experiment worked. "Those hateful words screamed like something someone had been holding back for a long time. The dripping black paint..." She shivered. "I'd sure like to know who feels that way. Maybe we could help."

Leslie took Emma by the arm. "Sure, Pollyanna. As long as we're helping from a safe place. Maybe with your pink stun gun handy." They continued toward the exit. None of the other displays equaled the three they had stopped at, but at least they didn't find anything comparing earthworm food and earthworm poop.

Here are a few of the unpleasant'st words
That ever blotted paper!

—*The Merchant of Venice*, 3.2.190

Chapter 4
Tuesday, September 15

"The activity is called Wrinkled Wendy. It's a physical representation of how people feel during and after being bullied."

Emma and Leslie stood in a large conference room at the Pinewood School District office building, known to teachers as the Head Shed. The over two hundred middle and high school teachers in the district were divvied up into groups at the beginning of the day and had to rotate through different rooms with varied activities in each room. Since comfort was key for events like these, Emma wore shorts and tennis shoes with her favorite, most comfortable pink T-shirt, and Leslie sported linen shorts and a brown shirt with a picture of Shakespeare on the chest. It said, "I'd challenge you to a battle of wits, but I see you are unarmed."

Emma and Leslie were not grouped with Hunter or Shawn Clingman from Pinewood Middle School—the guy Leslie wanted to make time with—and so far this morning, they'd had to attend two interactive workshops called "Who Are The Real Victims Of Bullying?" and "Bullying Should Not Be An After-School Activity," neither of which seemed to Emma like new or useful information. Emma questioned the instructors, trying to get some more practical tips, with no success. For these reasons, she and Leslie were sulking.

Emma thought the seminar fell short of what needed to be done to fight bullying, and she was pretty sure Leslie just wanted to be making time with the hunky middle school teacher. Emma knew that she'd personally come around to finding at least a little value in the seminar, but the jury was still out for Leslie.

Eight other people stood around the room, including Charlie Foreman and the three newbies, Diane, Rhiannon, and Otto. Charlie had been surreptitiously checking sports highlights on his phone all morning, Rhiannon had been following Diane around like a duckling followed its mother, and Otto had spent the morning socializing with the ag teacher from the middle school, a Danny DeVito doppelgänger who also taught wood shop.

Emma tried once to catch Diane or Rhiannon's eye to at least wave hello, but the awkward feelings from yesterday's lunch seemed to have stuck around. Diane just glared, first at her and then Leslie, who had folded into a yoga pose called Standing Forward Bend and therefore didn't notice. Rhiannon met her eye but dropped her head before Emma could react. *Better be thinking about new ways to make friends, girlie. Your old ways aren't working at all.*

Now the group convened for a session called "Changing Paradigms: Wrinkled Wendy Vs. Wondrous Wendy."

"Well," Leslie whispered to Emma, "I know the paradigm of ignoring the problem in the hopes it'll go away doesn't work, so..." She gave a long-suffering sigh. "Since we can't go find Shawn and Hunter until the 'Lunch On Your Own' session, let's give Wrinkled Wendy our best front-row attitudes!"

She handed Emma a marker that had been in a Take Me jar at the front of the room and smiled a toothpaste-commercial smile. Emma giggled at her friend's goofy faces until the speaker called the group to attention.

Emma checked out their new location while she listened. Long tables, which usually held conferees, were pushed along the walls, with chairs stacked in corners. A giant trash can held court from the center of the room, and several white pieces of paper had been spread on the floor around it like serfs of the kingdom.

About three feet long and maybe two feet wide, the pieces were shaped like the female symbol on the door of a public restroom. Emma gazed over the shapes lying across the floor like fallen subjects of the trash can's dominion, and she had a moment of sadness, remembering the white chalk outline of Melvin McManus's body marking the place in the main office where he'd been bludgeoned to death the previous year. She straightened her back and brushed off the feeling. *They're just pieces of paper. They're not bodies.*

The woman talking to the room had introduced herself as Sasha Paulsen. Sporting a brunette pixie haircut and wearing a tank top and running shorts, Sasha had the kind of lean muscles Emma associated with tennis players or runners. She held a jumbo-sized pad of paper under one toned arm. "Our job is fighting bullies, right?" the woman enthused, bouncing on her feet like someone getting ready to race. "So we're gonna fight them by using some fun! And some thinking and pondering. And then we'll talk about how you can use these methods in your classrooms, okay?"

Sasha took stock of the silent group. "Okaaay?"

"Woot, woot!" Leslie chirped.

Emma remembered they were sporting front-row attitudes. "Go, bullyproofing!" she called, pumping her fist in the air. Then she just felt stupid.

Otto Henry winked her way, pumping his own fist, and that made it better.

Sasha smiled at them both. "Yeah. Woot, woot! Go, bullyproofing! That's what I'm talking about. Thank you, ladies. Okay!" Sasha took the notepad from under her arm, set it down, and picked up one of the shapes from the floor. She held it against her chest. "This here is Wendy. There is a Wendy shape for every two of you, so I'd like you to grab a partner, take your markers to one of the shapes, and cover Wendy with phrases of negativity. Think about the worst things you've ever experienced somebody saying about you or somebody else, and write those statements down." She looked around the room. "Don't be shy. Anything rude or disrespectful or hurtful you can think of, cover our friend Wendy with it. I know it's a little strange, but there's a good reason, I promise."

Emma felt very uncomfortable with this idea. It went against her momma's most basic and often repeated admonishment, "If you can't say something nice, don't say anything at all." Surely learning *new* ways to bully someone wasn't useful in fighting bullying? She started toward her shape, halting just in time to see a gleam lighting her friend's eyes. Leslie's eyebrows waggled in her signature Groucho Marx face, and suddenly, Emma understood the sneaky glow. They clicked their markers together and sat down at the nearest Wendy shape. The rest of the room followed suit, and pretty soon, chatty whispers filled the air as each duo laid out their nastiest thoughts.

"Poisonous, bunch-backed toad," Leslie whispered gleefully, filling in one of Wendy's legs. "Canker-blossomed, beetle-headed, flap-eared knave!" she hissed, scribbling the words onto Wendy's front.

"Lump of foul deformity!" Emma giggled. "Thou art a boil! A plague-sore! A mountain of mad flesh! A... a..." She paused, stuck, trying to finish covering Wendy's head with another Shakespearean insult.

"A bolting hutch of beastliness!" Leslie cackled quietly. She finished Wendy's other leg with a flourish. "Not so much brain as ear wax!"

She and Emma bumped fists.

"The thing is," Emma said, "nobody truly knows how insulting these really are. Charlie never knows."

"Yeah, well..."

Speaking of Charlie, his whispers had grown in volume as he sat in the corner, filling his Wendy shape next to Otto Henry, who'd ended up with Charlie as his partner since the Danny DeVito look-alike partnered with his middle-school colleague. Otto and Charlie filled in their shape while whispering insults until the rhythm of negativity seemed to build up in Charlie's system, and he had to say the words out loud.

The litany of words stayed at a normal level until Charlie couldn't hold it in any longer. "Pantywaist!" he finally bellowed. "Reject!" He breathed heavily, like the bullyproofing exercise was actual exercise. Otto sized up his partner like he was a particularly sad farm animal and bent to fill in an empty space. Charlie ended his rant with a last, definitive yelp. "Fat, ugly looooo-ser!" Then he collapsed over the Wendy shape like a deflated balloon.

Emma, Leslie, and the rest of the room watched the corner in alarm. Sasha Paulsen spoke up from the other corner. "Um, well. Okay. That's the first step in the Wrinkled Wendy activity. Now, I'd like you to take your Wendy shape, crinkle it up, and toss it into the garbage can. Go ahead. Crush her up! Throw her away."

Charlie Foreman struggled to right himself from his prone position, scooped up the paper shape, and crunched it together with relish.

He winked at his reluctant partner, Otto, and flung the mashed-up Wendy through the air. "Buh-bye, Wendy!"

The ball hit the edge of the can and skittered across the floor, coming to a stop in front of Leslie. Leslie shook her head as she crushed their Shakespearean Wendy doll and picked up Charlie's to take them both over to the garbage can, muttering, "'What's here? The portrait of a blinking idiot, presenting me a schedule...'" as she deposited them both.

Charlie started to comment, probably to make an excuse about the missed shot, when Sasha came forward from her corner to stand over the garbage can. "That's right. Good job, everyone! Now, I know that was harder for some of you than for others"—she glanced meaningfully in Charlie's direction—"but here's where it's going." She gestured over the top of the can. "First, here's poor Wendy, sad Wendy, broken and bent and destroyed, feeling like a piece of garbage from all the ugliness that's covered her."

Emma briefly remembered her heart shattering when she found out Ronald had cheated, really the only time in her incredibly fortunate young life when the term *broken* might have applied to her. *Oh, I am such a lucky, lucky ducky.* She surveyed the room. *Is there somebody at TJ High who wants me to fail, because I'm so lucky?*

Sasha reached down into the can and mixed up all the Wendy dolls. "This is the way your students feel when those kinds of words are used against them, whether they are words used in person or, worse, from the cowardly anonymity of the internet." When she finished mixing, she pulled one out. She opened it and smoothed it across the tops of her legs, straightening it as best as she could, and contemplated the phrases that had been inked there. "Let's see: bitch, slut, whore, trash. Pretty typical shaming phrases. Wow. Sinner? Kind of an old-fashioned slur." Emma hadn't heard those words in the first year of her teaching profession. Kids these days had more slangy, but just as damaging, ways to shame.

"But all in all, these are pretty typical bullying words, so I'm going to white them out," Sasha said. "I'll cover them up so they don't exist anymore, which is often what happens in the home or in the classroom, I think. We might cover up the bad things going on, or we whitewash their significance. We teach everyone the 'sticks and stones' phrase, or we pull out our other favorite adages—'Boys will be boys' or 'That's just kid stuff. Everyone goes through it'—and we feel this solves the issue. Maybe we don't even see it as an issue."

Emma almost shouted, *No, no, that's what I'm talking about. We need to do more, not less!*

Sasha took a deep breath and blew it out. "So what's the problem with whitewashing? I'm doing my job, making sure my students never do it again. Why haven't I solved the problem?"

Emma raised a hand. *Do teachers have to raise their hands at in-services?* "Because look at Wendy. She's still all wrinkled and bent." She saw Diane Seymour, two people over, hold one finger to the corner of her eye like people do to stop a tear from falling.

"Those words stuck around," Leslie said. "Wendy is emotionally broken from the bullying."

"Exactly!" crowed Sasha. "Who said teachers make terrible students?"

"Teachers say it," Leslie responded, "all the time. We are terrible students because we sometimes pass notes at meetings and giggle worse than fifth graders watching a health video."

"Well, you are totally right this time and *great* students!" Sasha pulled the long notepad from under her arm. "This is what the title of the workshop means. We have to change the paradigm of covering up what really qualifies as bullying or trying to downplay the significance of hateful words. We have to start from the beginning." She opened the long paper pad and tore out a new, clean Wendy shape. "We have to teach students how to begin again."

Whew. Okay, guess I almost spoke too soon. This workshop is turning out better than I thought. Now, if we can just figure out how to expand it to the kids and the whole community, we might make it so no one feels the need to paint their hate and fear on the walls. Emma nodded her approval toward the instructor.

Sasha strode around the room, pulling out smooth white Wendy shapes and handing one to each pair. "Now, I'd like you to get one of the crumpled Wendys from the can and smooth it out as best you can. Then, I want you to cover your new Wondrous Wendy with positive and loving phrases." She stopped in front of Charlie and handed him a shape. "Try to have as much fun with this as you did with the first Wendy."

Charlie rolled his eyes but took the shape to hand over to Otto.

She turned to the rest of the group, holding forth the last shape in the book. "Then read your positive words to your partner and attach the Wrinkled Wendy to the back. You can take the whole thing home as an example if you want, or you can create your own activity. The point is teaching kids the power of their words and a new way to talk to others and to themselves."

She glanced at her watch. "You have ten minutes before lunch on your own. Please take this portion of the activity as seriously as you took the first one." Again, she looked right at Charlie as she returned to her original corner.

Emma saw Diane patting Rhiannon Pressman's shoulder as they sat down to unwrinkle the Wendy they took out of the garbage. They got Emma and Leslie's Wendy. Emma smiled. *I wonder what they'll think of all that Shakespearean bullying.*

Leslie had already taken a shape from the garbage can. She smoothed it out as Emma sat down. "I kinda like this exercise, Grasshoppah. Whaddya think?

"I think she's got the right idea, especially the part about helping kids talk to each other."

"Maybe face-to-face instead of through the screens on their cell phones, right?" Leslie waved her marker in the air. "I think we should use regular phrases for this part. Even though ol' Willy Shakespeare makes some of the most incredible portraits of positivity, I just..."

"I know what you just." Emma smiled at her friend.

She bent over the shape and wrote "You Are Strong" across Wendy's arm. Leslie wrote "You Are Smart" on Wendy's head. They both had the same thought at the same time and wrote "You Matter" down Wendy's legs.

"Maybe if we use this in some lessons this week, we can figure out a way to introduce a question or two about ways people might react to bullies by... I don't know... tagging gym walls." Emma said. "Hey, let's see how many positive comments we can fill her up with before we meet up with Hunter and your newest conquest."

"Yeah. That's a competition I could go for," Leslie said. "'Virtue is bold, and goodness never fearful.' *Measure for Measure*."

"Amen, sista," said Emma, and they filled every possible white space on their Wondrous Wendy until Hunter came looking for them.

Rightly to be great
Is not to stir without great argument,
But greatly to find quarrel in a straw
When honour's at the stake.

—*Hamlet*, 4.4.53-6

Chapter 5
Wednesday, September 16

School on Wednesday morning seemed normal. At least, there were no vandalized walls to be seen. The chatter at the beginning of Emma's first three periods was normal chatter. Students had apparently forgotten all about the vandalism during their Tuesday off. Either that or Homecoming plans took precedence.

Emma thought the latter, especially after she had to confiscate a note being passed back and forth from Brooke Martin to Janna McNeil during her lecture on the post-modernist era in American Lit. The note didn't hold anything conversational, just a list of colors that Emma assumed were of dresses and flowers and some rough sketches of said dresses.

Emma didn't really mind if they passed notes. She recalled her own gossipy messages to her best friend, Hannah, in high school, mostly about her future-now-ex-husband, Ronald Talicky. But it was *not* okay to pass notes while Emma spoke to the class. That was just rude. It wasn't as if she talked all period. *And come on. Kurt Vonnegut is an interesting guy!*

In Creative Writing, students worked on a partner-led review of poetry terms, so her mind could be free to wander, which it did, mostly back to questions about the graffiti on the gym wall. *Maybe this relates to the homecoming dance, since it's almost here? Somebody could've tried to ask someone to the dance and been rejected, or maybe* hoped *someone would ask them but never did? Those feelings, at that age, seem so end-of-the-world serious.*

She ended the period by deciding the dance might be the perfect place to ask some subtle questions of students.

AFTER THEIR STICKY experience with the new teachers on Monday, Emma and Leslie decided to have lunch in their usual small lounge off the library. Hunter agreed to eat with them, as did the librarian, Edward Dixon. When the bell rang, they all gathered at the front of the library counter, except for Edward, who must've been finishing some last-minute paperwork behind his desk.

Edward had actually been a suspect in the murder they'd solved the previous year, but he had turned out to be a good, albeit strange, man. *For that matter,* Emma thought, *Hunter was a suspect too—all that sneaking around to spy on the coaches.* When Hunter entered the library and gave her a dimpled grin, she was so glad he hadn't killed anyone.

"Edward, where is your banned list?" asked Leslie. One of Edward's peculiarities was a tendency to ban students from the library if they committed anything he perceived as an offense against literature, from bringing sodas in while they read to writing notes in the margins of *Moby Dick* or other classics, making fun of the title. The long banned list usually unfolded accordion-like from the corkboard to the floor whenever Edward added another name. Now, the corkboard showed a plain expanse of cork.

A tall, gangly fellow in tweed high-water pants and a bow tie, Edward bore a strange resemblance to Alfalfa of *The Little Rascals* fame, although he had no hair spike. "Leslie. Emma. Hunter." He bowed slightly to the two women and nodded to Hunter. "I've decided to fight the problem of literary insensitivity from the trenches, as it were. I'd like to *redeem* those who disrespect literature. From the soda spillers to those who graffiti inside the hallowed covers of the classics." His voice rose now. "I'm going to *teach* them the error of their ways right here in my little library. I'm going to *show* them how to behave properly, or by God, I'll—"

His face started turning red, and he stopped talking only after Leslie reached across the desk to rest her hand on his forearm. "Little jerks," he muttered.

"I think that's a terrific idea, Edward," said Emma. "Rehabilitate 'em! But for now, boys and girl, let's just eat our lunch." The corner of the desk held four trays of food, typical yellow school trays that smelled anything but typical. "Aw, looky here. Mrs. Albert made us chicken cacciatore."

They all made appreciative noises and followed her into the lounge that nestled behind the library office. The topic of conversation at lunch was the homecoming dance. Emma and Leslie were scheduled to chaperone together, but when Hunter offered to be Emma's escort, she raised pleading eyes toward Leslie. Leslie met her gaze, and Emma thought she saw a flash of something like pain. *She must be thinking of Rain, and how ironic that those two words rhyme. Rain... pain. Good grief.* Emma opened her mouth to tell her they'd go to the dance like they planned.

But Leslie blotted the corners of her mouth, patted her perfect blond bob, and turned to Edward. "How about it, Edward? Ya wanna paint the town, or should I say the gymnasium, red with me this Saturday?"

Edward's face flushed, and his eyes bulged like they might pop out. "Wh-Why, Leslie," he stammered. "I'd be... that would be... I mean... goodness." He hadn't finished with his clumsy acceptance when they heard yelling from the library. Edward, ready to rehabilitate, charged out. The others followed.

"I know it was you, you bitch! Why don't you admit it so I can kick your ass!" This came from the mouth of a girl Emma knew from the previous year, Alexa Champlain. Beautiful and trendy, with expensively highlighted hair and short shorts paired with high-heeled sandals, Alexa was not made more attractive by her potty mouth. She waved a piece of paper toward a girl Emma didn't recognize right away, but she recognized the blue-and-white cheerleading outfit the girl wore.

The girl edged backward, ducking Alexa's waving hands. "I didn't send that note, Alexa, and you know it! Why would I send notes to all my friends on the squad? Why would I send one to myself?" She whirled around to a table and started rummaging in her backpack.

Edward grabbed Alexa's arm and held onto it while Leslie took the piece of paper she'd been brandishing. The cheerleader pulled an identical piece of paper from the backpack, and Emma put out her hand for it. With a grateful expression, the girl handed the note over to Emma.

"Maybe you're throwing us off track by sending us all a note, you nightmare in a cheerleader skirt!" Alexa yelled.

Other students began ducking out the door.

"You've already proven how sneaky you are by stealing Steve!" Alexa escaped Edward's grasp and lunged for the girl again, but Hunter stepped between them, grabbing both her wrists.

"I didn't *steal* anything," said the girl. "Steve asked me to Homecoming because he's tired of your head games. Everyone's tired of them, Alexa."

"Bite me." Alexa tried to charge again, but Hunter held on.

Emma found it so interesting to watch him in action. Most teachers would be knee-deep in lecture mode right now, but his silent stance seemed to ease the tension a little. *I do like a strong, silent type.*

"Ladies, ladies. Let's look at these notes, shall we?" Leslie unfolded the one Alexa had been holding, and Emma followed suit.

They placed them side by side on the table. Each was printed on ordinary computer paper, with a font made to look like an elementary student's writing. Alexa's note said only, "You're all the same, and your actions will kill you." The cheerleader's note was slightly more extensive. "Don't you see? You don't have problems, but you are the problem. You don't deserve her love, and your pridefulness will send you straight to hell."

"Well," said Emma. "I hope these aren't the kinds of notes you pass back and forth in class. I think death threats will get you more than lunch detention." She faced the cheerleader. "You were in my speech class for a little while last year, right? I'm sorry, but I've forgotten your name."

The girl was almost crying. Her nose was red, and small tufts of hair escaped her perky blond ponytail. "Kisten. Kisten Hollis. And I would never give someone a note like this. Not... not even *her*. Someone shoved it into the vents in my locker. I found it after third period. My best friend, Caitlin Bauer, has the locker next to mine. She got one too." Kisten sniffed. "A really mean one in this"—she gestured to the font—"this gross little-kid writing that said her attitude was gonna kill her."

Kisten ran a hand over her head, trying to smooth the wisps that had escaped. She sniffed again. "I think mine is the meanest, though. It sounds like something they'd say at my church. My parents drag me there, and Pastor Barrows is all fire and brimstone. He says I'm gonna burn in hell because of my short skirts and... and..." She hiccupped and plopped down at the table, putting her head down and curling her arms over it.

Emma reached over the table to pat her shoulder. "I believe you, Kisten. Do you have any ideas about who might have sent them? Anyone you've had trouble with lately?"

Kisten inclined her head toward Alexa. "Besides her going crazy right now? No. My friends and I have just been so busy getting ready for the game and the dance that we've barely had time for school, and then these notes show up for no reason."

Leslie asked Alexa, "And where did you find yours?"

Alexa hadn't taken her fierce glare from Kisten. "Someone put it right in the pages of my open textbook. It sat right here at this table while I was in the bathroom. You were here, witch. It could have been you."

Alexa swore again. Hunter still stood between Kisten and Alexa, arms crossed. The two students who'd stayed to rubberneck were parked over by the computers on the back wall, safe from Alexa's flying arms and foul mouth.

Leslie spoke. "All right, Alexa. Dispense with the language, please. It makes you sound tacky. Did you see anyone close to your table before you left or when you came back in?"

"No. There was a class here when I got here, but they left, I guess. I dunno when. You were here, like, for a long time, you—"

Leslie held up a "stop talking or else" hand. "Kisten, have you been here for a while?"

"Y-Yes. I used the computer over there." She pointed to the row on the far-left wall, close to the two rubberneckers. "I have a business paper due next period."

"Nothing like procrastination to make you miss lunch," Leslie remarked.

"Did you see anything unusual?" asked Emma.

"No. I didn't see anything. I was typing so fast. I really should get back to my paper. Am I in trouble?" Her chin trembled. "Oh please. The homecoming game..."

"Of course you're not in trouble," said Leslie. She glared at Alexa. "*You* might be in trouble if you don't watch your mouth." She took the notes and folded them up. "But for now, you two must split up. And stay away from each other!"

After one last evil stare, Alexa flounced from the library, if one could call the way she walked in those heels *flouncing*. Emma wondered what would possess someone to do that kind of damage to her feet. But she remembered cramming herself into some painfully tight jeans to impress Ronald Talicky.

She took the notes from Leslie. "What are we gonna do with these? Should I take them to Principal Nate?" The font was one of those picked from the long list in a word processing program. This one, Emma remembered, was called Scribble because it was supposed to resemble a child practicing writing. While usually very cute, the font combined with the hateful words it spelled out just seemed creepy.

Leslie sighed. "I don't know. Looks like the work of SSP rivals. Probably nothing to worry about. But yes, you might as well take them to Nate. Following protocol is our friend, right? When it suits us to have it so." She grinned.

"SSP?" asked Hunter.

"Senior Snot Posse," Leslie said. "Senior Snoot, Senior Snit, Senior Sh—you get the picture—Posse."

Edward really looked ready to faint.

"They don't call themselves that, I don't think. It's not like the Lounge Lizards. It's just something kids say to characterize those really pretty, often cruel and catty older girls who walk around like they rule the school, which I guess maybe they do, in a way."

"Okay, I'll run these to the main office," said Emma. "I bet Principal Farrar ends up giving them to Abigail, secretary extraordinaire, though. She seems much more in charge. If anyone might know what to do with them, it's Abigail." She thought for a moment. "What do you call those senior boys afflicted with senioritis and I'm-too-cool-to-go-to-classes-anymore-I'd-rather-just-scam-on-freshmen-girls?"

The corners of Hunter's mouth twitched. "STP? Senior Testosterone Posse?"

Even Edward was laughing now. "I say. How about SBOTLTS? Senior Boys On The Loose To Scam?"

Silence from the room.

"Ahem," said Leslie. "Mnemonic devices should *aid* your memory, Edward, not frazzle it up even more."

"I really have to go plan something this hour," said Emma. "And I'm still not done with those essays from Advanced Comp. Leslie, I'll talk to you later?"

Leslie nodded.

Emma made her voice playful. "And Hunter, I'll talk to *you* later?"

He grinned and winked. Edward, looking embarrassed about his long acronym, had melted back into the stacks.

As Emma wound her way through the halls and back to her classroom, she thought about the notes the girls had received. She thought about the graffiti on the gymnasium wall. They were angry messages, and to her, it seemed more than just teen angst. But Leslie was probably right. She had been teaching a lot longer than Emma. *Maybe I'll make copies of the notes before I take 'em in to Abigail, though, just in case.* A hat rack, where Emma kept her purse, stood next to the little student library in the corner. She pulled out her cell phone to snap pictures of the icky notes.

With the notes in one hand, Emma headed toward her desk. The Shakespeare paperweight she loved dearly lay on its side. *Strange.* A piece of white notebook paper rested on top of the desk. She picked it up just as Leslie burst in with a piece of paper in her hand.

"I got one too!" she shouted. "What the heck is going on?"

Emma flipped her piece of paper over to read a message in large black block letters.

You are the problem. You should all fail. You should die.

Chapter 6

What in the Sam Hill is happening here?

After comparing their notes with each other's and the ones that were sent to the students, Emma handed off her mission of taking the student notes to the principal. She was really frazzled. Leslie took them all to give to Principal Nate Farrar so he could take the notes to Chief Detective Carl Niome of the Pinewood Police Department. Leslie's history with the detective meant she didn't want to do it, and though Emma hadn't known the man for long, she agreed.

The row in the library had been upsetting, but these notes made Emma feel like a butterfly pinned to an entomologist's display board. *Why would Leslie and I be targets? It doesn't make sense. We're not SSP rivals. We're not* anybody's *rivals.* She wandered to her little library in the corner of the room, picked up a book, and put it down. She paced back to the bookshelf behind her desk to straighten a display that didn't need straightening, and she still had ten minutes left of lunch and her whole seventy-two-minute planning period to think about it.

Righting her poor Shakespeare bust, Emma placed it carefully back in its corner of the desk. She placed her phone next to the computer and pulled up pictures of the notes to look up the word combinations. The most unusual one—the one sent to Kisten Hollis about pridefulness sending her to hell—was the only one with any hits, and those didn't seem unusual, mostly about pride being the foremost of the seven deadly sins in the bible, the gateway to all the other sins. *That makes sense, I guess. Leslie always talks about the "hubris" lessons in her mythology class, and how the Greek gods hated pride the most too. But Kisten didn't seem arrogant to me at all.*

She straightened the pile of Advanced Composition essays, which she fully intended to finish this hour. She only had five left. *I need to focus on educating my students. This will all work itself out. No hubris for me, only optimism. Yup, I am as happy as a dead pig in sunshine. Sure.* After a couple of deep breaths, she reached for the first essay, only to realize that she really needed to pee.

She put the essay down, patted the Shakespeare bust on the head, and left room 104 for the nearest bathroom, a staff toilet nestled between the library and the main office. She wasn't sure why she hadn't stopped on the way out of the library the first time. Being upset usually made her bladder *more* twitchy, not less. Maybe the adrenaline from the confrontation between Alexa and Kisten had put her innards into a kind of shock. *I swear, I don't remember ever being in a situation like that with another girl wanting to beat me up, although I know girls sure can be catty. I guess I should go talk to Nate a little more to see what we can do to make sure Alexa stays in her own lane.*

Emma thought briefly about the two girls and her experiences with them in the classroom the previous year. She'd had Alexa for American Lit and remembered the beautiful clothes and trendy hair as not representing the girl herself. The same with the attitude—her whole stuck-up-higher-than-a-light-pole demeanor seemed forced. When she deigned to take part in a discussion, Emma sensed a yearning underneath the carefully constructed façade. For acceptance? Maybe. For love? Surely. Alexa acted like a person who didn't hear the words *I love you* very often. Emma found no confidence underneath the bossy behavior at all, even though she'd behaved like the queen bee back then and now in her senior year. It didn't look as though anything had changed.

Kisten was only in Emma's speech class for the first two weeks, and Emma's memory of that time was a complete mishmash of hazy impressions. Between the terror of her first year of teaching and the horrifying murder of sweet Melvin, she felt lucky to even be able to place her. Kisten was a nice girl, though. Emma remembered that much.

She unlocked the women's staff bathroom and peered around the door, taking in the new cluster of girly bathroom products on the counter, set out for teachers to share. She saw the can of linen-smelling air freshener and smiled at the lingering scent in the air. *Lord love a duck, we certainly couldn't take the chance of leaving a stink as we leave the bathroom, where someone might see and know it was us, now could we? The world might end.*

She opened the door to the first stall. She'd read somewhere that the first stall was actually the cleanest because everyone thought other people would go to that one, and therefore, everyone skipped the first stall and went down to the end. As she slid the latch and plopped down, she heard the rustle of keys. Not sure what possessed her, Emma lifted her feet off the ground and propped them on the edge of the porcelain seat.

"I know it wasn't directed at me," someone whispered, "but he just acted so horrible. It's like I was right back there listening to them. Hating them."

Footsteps thumped down to the last stall, and Emma couldn't help but nod at the back of the door. *See? Clear on down to the end. She didn't even try a closer door, thank goodness.*

Another voice seemed to come from in front of the sink. "I know, I know. It's hard." This whisper was slightly louder, closer to speaking volume, and Emma strained her ears to identify it. "That Charlie Foreman is a real piece of work. But he's not them. He's not your stepfather, not your stepbrother." The whisper sounded strident, like a hiss. "And he has no control over you like they did." The toilet flushed. The speaker at the sink waited for the noise to fade before murmuring, "You have to breathe. Just breathe. We're here for you. Promise."

The end stall opened, and footsteps started toward the sink then stopped in front of Emma's stall. She sensed movement beyond her door, like the woman bent to look under the stall. The door rattled. Emma held her breath. The movement continued on past, and it was all she could do to release the air slowly rather than in one relieved and loud whoosh. *Whew.*

When the end-stall woman reached the sink, Emma heard the whoosh of the faucet. "What about those two English teachers?" she whispered. "That tall one, especially." The faucet shut off. "I don't trust either one of them. Too pretty. Too cocky." The *chunk chunk* of the handle on the towel dispenser sounded a few times, then came a rip and a crinkle as she dried her hands. "I bet they never had anyone talk to *them* like that."

"Well, maybe they'll get nicer as time goes on," the first voice purred. "Maybe we won't have to stay much longer. I think we're getting close."

"Maybe. Maybe not. We've been close before and haven't been able to find him."

The bathroom door opened, and the two shuffled out.

Now what was all that about? I'm not cocky! Leslie's not... okay. I'm not cocky, anyway. Emma waited for another three minutes before gently putting her feet to the ground and leaving the women's bathroom. She was so eager to talk to Leslie about what she'd just overheard that she clean forgot to pee.

"GUESS WHO I OVERHEARD in the bathroom?" Emma said as she bounced into room 101. Leslie sat at her shiny black lacquered desk, surrounded by walls that looked to Emma like a New York City studio apartment, not that she'd ever been to one. Black-and-white prints from photographers like Scott Mutter and Ansel Adams perched on the walls at crazy angles, offset by red, purple, or black squares behind them. Emma didn't know how Leslie could set them up all crooked this way and make it look purposeful and artistic when Emma could barely hang her posters straight.

"Hmm," Leslie said. "Alexa Champlain in the bathroom, talking to one of her SSP pals and confessing to the notes and the graffiti. Case solved on day two. Bravo!" She gestured to the left wall. "Hey, check out my new print. Bill Brandt, my new favorite." The black-and-white photo in this frame showed the giant soles of someone's feet. "It's called *Feet Abstraction*. Isn't it fantastic?"

Emma moved to stand directly in front of the print. Behind the giant feet, she could see only an empty apartment. It didn't look like there was a person attached to the feet. Very Leslie. "It is fantastic. Looks like somethin' right up your alley. Sophisticated and cool. It'd just never occur to me to explore the photography of feet."

Emma clasped her hands together and turned back to her friend. "No, I'm pretty sure it was Diane Seymour and Rhiannon Pressman. They were talking about Charlie Foreman and the Wrinkled Wendy activity and how horribly he behaved when saying all those mean things out loud. Weren't they the only other women at that exercise?"

Leslie nodded. "They were. Is that all they said?"

"No. One of them talked about how Charlie sounded just like 'them,' and the other one said, 'He's not your stepfather or your step-brother, and he doesn't control you like they did.'" Emma went back to the lacquered desk to look at Leslie's pile of work. "Then that person told the other person to breathe, and then the first gal started talking about us. She said we're cocky."

"'Hath not old custom made this life more sweet than that of painted pomp?' That's *As You Like it*, Grasshoppah, and I can maybe see how I might be construed as cocky." She grinned and stacked a few papers to set them aside. "Maybe. So who said what?"

"I don't know which one was which. That's the frustrating part. They were whispering. I did see Diane brush off a tear during that in-service, though. Maybe the activity reminded her of whatever experiences she's had that would cause her to vandalize the school." She gestured over Leslie's shoulder. "What are you working on?"

"Oh, we're starting the medieval period," Leslie said. "The boys like it because they get to cover medieval weaponry—you know, mace and quarterstaff, poleaxe and trebuchet. My personal favorite's the flail. A lot of the girls like that part of the unit, too, but some of them like learning about the clothes."

"Ugh." Emma shook her head. "Otherwise known as hot, binding, and heavy?"

"And smelly." Leslie laughed. "Don't forget smelly. I think when we cover the *Canterbury Tales*, I'm gonna have them create their own pilgrimages." She slapped both hands gleefully on the desk. "But they have to write the whole thing in couplets." She twisted her hands together like the Wicked Witch of the West. "Believe it or not, once they get started on projects like these, they really have fun. It's like the learning is accidental. They don't even realize it's happening." She grabbed a pad of sticky notes from her desk and scribbled a note to herself about pilgrimages and couplets. First, she stuck it on her forehead just to make Emma laugh. Then, she put it on her desk and pressed down to make it stick. "So how is it that Diane and Rhiannon didn't know you were there? Did you turn into an actual fly on the wall?"

Emma blushed. "I picked my feet up when I heard someone coming in. I don't know why. I guess just all the craziness of the fight in the library, the graffiti, and now these notes."

Leslie chortled. "And they call me a nosy parker, but that's because my name is actually Parker. You are just your own sneaky little nosy parker, aren't you? So do you think it could be one of them leaving the notes?"

Emma sat down in a student desk. "I don't know. I guess it's possible. The one talked about her stepfather and brother, though not her step*mother* and *sister*. All of these notes were directed at girls. As far as we've seen, anyway." She scraped a fingernail along the edge of the desk. "I don't really think it relates to the notes. I just found it interesting, and then I wanted to tell you we were the subject of the conversation, however briefly."

"I certainly don't think you are cocky, Emma Maria Conchita Alonso Lovett." Leslie smiled. "I do love your growing tendency to be nosy, though."

Emma shrugged. "I figure if there's a mystery to be solved, even a little one, I'm gonna want to solve it. I am my father's daughter, even if the ones he solved were from his beloved books. What did Nate do with the notes?"

"Well, obviously, he gave them to Abigail because we all know she's the one who's really in charge. She tsk-tsked them like only Abigail can and then got on the phone with Carl, aka Chief Detective Chowderhead. It sounded like he wasn't taking them as anything more than kids being kids. Not helpful, as per usual."

"I'd agree with him, except for the fact that the notes are threatening specific people directly, and we are two of those people! It's not like the generality of the graffiti on the gym wall. Everyone goes into that gym." Emma stood and headed for the door. "We must keep trying to figure it out, amongst all of our myriad other teaching responsibilities. I made copies, you know. I tried googling some of the word combinations in the threats, especially that unusual one with religious undertones. What I found related to pride being the worst of the seven deadly sins. How is sweet little Kisten Hollis prideful? She only seemed freaked out there in the library."

"'My high-blown pride at length broke under me and now has left me weary.' *Henry VIII.*" Leslie shrugged. "Just because she doesn't seem prideful doesn't mean the note-sender doesn't see her that way, right?"

"You are absolutely right. Maybe because she's a cheerleader, and they are generally seen as the popular, social type who could be full of themselves. I'll keep looking, my friend. You go ahead and create an amazing medieval project, Leslie Neil Patrick Harris Parker." She stopped at the doorway and laid a swooning hand on her forehead. "I must return to my room and prepare for freshmen."

Leslie waved her out. "May the force be with you."

This world's a city full of straying streets,
And death's the market-place, where each one meets.

–*The Two Noble Kinsmen,* 1.5.15-16

Chapter 7
Thursday, September 17

Emma sprinted into her house, and everything was burning. Flames shot up from the centers of her tiny green couch and fat striped loveseat. All the plants were aflame like the Bible's burning bush. Flames licked their way up the walls and toward the ceiling. The picture window at the back of the house had a message written in blood. "You think you have problems? I'll show you a problem." Emma ran screaming toward the bedroom. She couldn't go that far—it was too hot—but she knew Trinky and Sir Toby were in there. She could hear the plaintive meowing and whimpering behind the door. She fell to her knees, crying for her beloved pets, when she became aware of the sirens in the distance.

She woke to the unpleasant wailing of the alarm clock. Bleary and discombobulated, she smacked the button to see the time. Five thirty a.m. She couldn't conceive that anyone in their right mind would want to be blasted out of bed this early. And by an annoying siren sound? Usually, she set her alarm for music to gently propel her out of bed. *Gently. At a reasonable time.*

Then she remembered. Those notes. Those horrible notes, first to the students then to her and Leslie. After Leslie turned in all those notes, Emma had felt frustrated that nothing really happened. Chief Detective Carl Niome had lived up to his Chowderhead nickname and shrugged off the notes as harmless teenage pranks.

Emma and Leslie had stopped by the main office at the end of the day to express their fears—Emma's fears, anyway. Abigail had patted the English teachers on the shoulders and told them, in that whispery voice, she'd take care of it. The ladies should go home and rest, she'd said, and she'd light a fire under that silly ol' chief. She'd suggested they start swimming in the mornings before school to relieve some stress. Such a nice way to start the day, she'd said.

The funny part was that Emma and Leslie had agreed. Swimming. Yes, that would be nice. Then they'd left the office without even discussing the notes any more, under the calming thrall of Abigail's transparent whisper.

Emma didn't know about Leslie, but she'd personally had enough excitement last year for an entire lifetime. So many horrible things had happened at Thomas Jefferson High School in her first year that it was a wonder she'd returned. It seemed like the strangest, most bizarre events could lead another person to murder. Emma just couldn't understand it—she didn't even kill spiders, much less people.

As she lay sprawled in bed, her thoughts swirled in her head like bubbles, ascending only to burst open and disappear. Melvin McManus, the murderer's first victim in the previous year's tragedy, had been a sweet and unassuming custodian at the school. His penchant for using famous quotes to assess a student situation reminded Emma of her dear, sweet late father, Donald, and this made the discovery of Melvin's body doubly horrific. Emma and Leslie had needed to question and suspect all sorts of people the previous year—good friends, and even Hunter. She for sure never, never wanted to repeat the danger they'd all faced. *Stop obsessing, you ninny. This is a couple of nasty notes, not another murder. Overreactor. Just get outta bed and go get some exercise.*

Emma stared at the ceiling, willing herself to get up, willing the universe to deliver no

more problems, no more nastiness. She couldn't comprehend starting a new year with more trouble. She wanted to date Hunter Wells and inspire students, grade papers and eat the marvelous lunches prepared by Mrs. Albert. That was it. *Swimming, yes. That would be nice.* Hence the ridiculous hour of the morning and the siren alarm clock.

"WHAT ARE WE DOIN' HERE, again?" asked Emma. They sat on the bench in the locker room at six a.m., Leslie sleek in her red Speedo tank suit, even with the blond bob sticking out at crazy angles. Emma hadn't shopped for a suit in a long time, so she wore a faded navy one-piece with pills forming along the material covering her bottom.

"Exercising. Relieving stress. Because Abigail told us to." Leslie yawned and ran her hand through her hair.

"Who do you think sent those notes, Leslie?"

"Aw, heck. I don't know. Probably just some crazy kid who's venting. I'm sure it's nothing to worry about. C'mon. Race you." She ran out of the locker room.

"You're not supposed to be running by the pool!" Emma shouted, but she heard the splash before she could even pull the seat of her suit down over her rear end. She sighed, trotted out, and dove in. *Holy cow! This water is cold enough to make a preacher cuss.* She popped up, shivering, and blew out air in a whoosh, paddling over to Leslie. "I thought they had the heat on all year round."

"They do, ya wuss. It's a balmy eighty degrees in here." Leslie splashed her. "See? Practically a hot tub, this is."

"Maybe I'm still recovering from that frigid fall morning. It's only six a.m., for Pete's sake." Emma splashed back, flicking her fingers as Leslie pushed backward and away from the water drops. "My, those cheerleaders are up early this morning too. I saw a couple of them leaving the football field."

Leslie did a slow-motion jog through the water. "I know. They always have a big routine to perform at halftime of the homecoming game. They must put in extra hours to prepare." She bounced on the soles of her feet. "Marco!"

Emma laughed. "No goofy games. I need to be swimming some laps. I can definitely see cellulite on my backside."

"Cellulite, schmellulite. You look great. But okay, you be a good little girl and get yourself a workout. I'm for the cannonballs."

As Emma started a methodical crawl stroke in one of the lap lanes, she heard Leslie shout "Yippee!" followed by a thunderclap when she hit the water.

EMMA SWAM. LESLIE CAVORTED until almost seven. The morning exercise made Emma feel surprisingly better. Each time she touched the wall and did a flip turn, it became a small stress reliever. *Touch the wall. Pow to the nasty notes! Flip, turn. Shove the stress away with my feet! Sail across the water to a peaceful shore. Repeat.* She came up out of her last lap to find Leslie standing over her, threatening to dunk. She convinced Leslie that dunking would be more fun at a backyard party, and besides, they had to shower and primp a little before classes started at seven forty-five. Leslie, apparently remembering her pale face without makeup, agreed.

They got out and dried off. Emma scooted away from the side of the pool when Leslie started snapping her wet towel. She skidded around the corner of the locker room and stopped short when she saw the foot protruding from the corner of the gym lockers. The foot was encased in a short white sock with a blue paw embroidered on the side. *Oh my God. Oh no. Oh no.*

The foot led to a leg covered by a short blue-and-white cheerleading skirt. The skirt was attached to a Wildcat T-shirt. It was only when Emma saw the blue-tinged skin and slack jaw of the girl who belonged to the tee that she started screaming for Leslie.

"Oh my God! What's going on? Who is that?" Leslie skidded to a stop beside Emma, who had kneeled next to the girl's body to check for a pulse. No pulse she could feel, but the girl's skin was still warm.

"It's Kisten Hollis. My God, Leslie, we just saw her yesterday. Call an ambulance."

Leslie floundered around her bag for her cell phone and dialed 911. Emma was trying to remember steps from the CPR class she'd taken the previous summer. She couldn't remember if it was thirty pumps on the chest for every two breaths, or two pumps followed by thirty breaths. Leslie left the phone on with the dispatcher's tinny voice coming up from the bench.

She joined Emma on the floor and palpated the girl's chest while Emma breathed into her mouth. Kisten lay blue and still on the floor.

Emma started to cry. "I don't know what to do. I don't know if we're doin' it right." She breathed into the girl's mouth again. "Nothing's happening. Oh God, nothing's happening, Leslie!"

When they heard the hollow sounds of official-sounding walkie-talkie clicks and voices and footsteps running across the floor of the pool deck, they stared down at Kisten's lifeless form. Then their eyes met.

"Not again!" Emma wailed.

Chapter 8

Detective Carl Niome was a short, florid, beefy man with a gin-blossom nose and a paunch he often ran his hands over when he was upset or angry, which was pretty much any time he saw Emma and Leslie—especially Leslie. The previous year, she'd revealed to Emma the sordid story of losing her virginity to Carl when they were in high school. Back then, he'd been a star football player who had confidence and muscle tone as opposed to a pregnant man-belly, broken capillaries, and a bad attitude, but Leslie was still humiliated.

After the EMTs pronounced the death of the cheerleader, Carl, chief of detectives, came first to the scene. Emma privately thought the man incompetent to be the commander of an ant farm. Leslie and Emma, the principal, and Abigail Patterson were on the deck outside of the swimming pool. Otherwise, the whole area had been shut down to students and staff.

Emma and Leslie had combined their classes, and Martha Bonaventure, a friend of theirs, had taken over the melded groups during her first-hour planning period.

Emma trudged over to Detective Niome and another man. They stood in the doorway of the swimming pool, holding something in their gloved hands. "What's going on?" she asked. Hiccupped, actually. The ambulance carrying Kisten's sheet-covered body left by eight thirty, and an hour later, Emma finally started feeling the tears trickling to a stop.

"Nothing that concerns you, young lady," Carl said, arching an eyebrow.

Leslie joined the group. "I think it concerns us. We found her. We tried to save her."

The detective set the unencumbered arm across his paunch. "And what about that? This is the third dead body you've been involved with in less than two years. What were you doing here?"

Leslie looked down at her swimsuit and fingered the towel around her waist. "Nothing that concerns you, young man." She nodded toward the detective's hand. "Is that a needle?"

The other guy spoke up. "Yes, and this is a vial. Insulin. She must've been diabetic. My first thought was drug overdose, then we found this vial over in the corner of the locker room."

Abigail joined them as the detective brandished the vial. She wrung her hands and gasped. "Oh my goodness. Kisten *is* a diabetic. Do you think she went into insulin shock? I didn't know that could kill you right away. I thought you went into a coma first. Oh, maybe she's not really dead, just in a coma. We have to..."

She tried to bustle away in Abigail-saves-the-day fashion, but Leslie held her arm. "She's dead, Abigail. I'm so sorry."

Abigail's face fell, and her chin trembled. She appeared light years from the campus force Emma knew her to be.

Niome spoke. "You know who this girl is?"

Abigail nodded.

"We'll need you to come in and identify her. That will save her parents from having to do it."

"Why didn't you ask one of us about this?" said Emma. "We told you who she was. I could do it. She was in my class for a short time last year, and Leslie and I saw her yesterday, after... after she..." She caught Leslie's eye.

Leslie nodded.

"After we stopped another girl from beating her up. Boyfriend troubles. You don't think...?"

Carl practically vibrated and said, "Someone beat her up? Who was it?"

"No one beat anybody up, Carl," Leslie said. She took the towel off her waist and re-wrapped it under her armpits. Her bare feet pressed into the concrete like tree roots. "Kisten and another student, Alexa Champlain, had an altercation in the library yesterday over a boy and some nasty notes."

Abigail's lip quivered. It jiggled the chains of her glasses. "I'll do it. If it will help her poor parents..." The other detective led her through the pool area and out through the locker room.

Poor Abigail. If I thought I could do it any better, I'd insist on being the one. But who am I kidding? I'd probably start bawling all over again. Not helpful.

Niome crossed the deck to Principal Nathan Farrar. The tall, skateboarding administrator—his claim to fame with the students—looked shaken and upset. Emma was pretty sure the deaths of students would be the most stressful thing an administrator could handle. She wondered if Nathan felt responsible. She knew she would if it happened in her school. *Wait. This is my school too. I'm not in charge or anything, but this kind of thing shouldn't be happening on my watch, dang it! My daddy would've told me to fix the problem before the problem fixes me.*

She gestured Leslie over to the weight cage. She didn't understand why all the weights and weight machines were in a cage, like some student might freak out and start launching barbells across the deck, and the cage might be the only thing stopping him, but now she held the frame to keep herself steady. "Do you think this has something to do with those notes or that graffiti? Maybe we should remind them."

"I don't know. Maybe it's an accidental death like Abigail said. Insulin overdose or something."

But Emma was already marching toward the principal and Carl Niome. "It just seems like one is too close to the other. They both smell of violence to me."

Leslie shrugged and followed.

Emma crossed her arms over her chest, suddenly conscious of her lack of clothes. "There're these notes, see. Two girls got them for sure, maybe others. Leslie and I each got one. And then this graffiti—"

Carl held up a hand. "Your principal told me all about the graffiti right after it was found. Listen, ladies. Detective Lichtenberg will take your statement. Then you should just go home. Nate already said that school would be canceled for today. Besides, we don't even know if this is a suspicious death or an accident. The ME will meet us at the morgue."

"Oh, you've called the medical examiner? How very professional of you, Detective," Leslie said.

The detective ran his hands over his stomach and up over the thinning strands of what little hair he still had. "Go. Home."

Leslie flounced away. Emma, defeated, followed her back into the locker room to dress.

"My, he's grouchy, isn't he?" Leslie said as she pulled a shirt over her head. "I am not excited to have to deal with him again."

"Leslie, I can't believe Kisten is dead," Emma said. "She's just a kid. Kids aren't supposed to die. Her parents... oh, Leslie, her poor parents!" Emma's hands trembled as she tried to pull on her old green sweats, the wet seat of her suit bunching up on the varnished wooden bench. "And what about the other kids at school? Oh God, Leslie. She said the other girl who got a note... Caitlin? Kisten said that was her best friend." The sweatpants caught on the swimsuit bottom, and Emma's frustrated and flailing hands ripped a hole in the suit as she tried to shove it down. She groaned and plopped down on the bench.

"Maybe it's best you know now," Leslie spoke softly. "You will lose students, and there's nothing harder as a teacher." She rolled and unrolled the bottom of her T-shirt against her sweatpants. "My fourth year, I lost a student named Peter Maray, a complete and utter daredevil in everything he did—skateboarding, parkour, snowboarding, motorcycling, you name it. And he was the nicest kid you could ever hope to meet. He talked to everyone, smiled all the time, just a delight." She rolled the shirt out violently. "He crashed his three-wheeler into a tree. Total pointless accident. Dead at sixteen." She flattened her hands against the bench and stared at Emma. "I don't know if I'd be able to handle it if Peter were my kid. It was hard enough when he was my student."

She slipped her shoes on and stood to go. "Come on. I'm not in the mood to tussle with Carl the Crabby today."

Emma followed her out.

They were exiting the deck when a man came through the door. He was short, probably five feet seven, and he wore a lab coat over jeans. He smiled at the two ladies and assessed Emma through two of the biggest brown eyes Emma had ever seen, framed by impossibly long eyelashes.

That's so unfair. Girls need those lashes, not guys.

"Um, I got sort of lost, and I know I'm late. Is this the where the body of..." He referred to his clipboard. "Kisten Hollis is?"

"You must be the medical examiner," purred Leslie. She placed her hand in his. "I'm Leslie Parker. This is Emma. We found Kisten's body."

Emma stuck her hand out. "We tried to save her."

"From what the EMTs told me, there was nothing you could do. I'm Will Capshaw. I'd better get in there."

"She's gone," Leslie said. "The ambulance already took her away, probably to you at the morgue, if that's where you examine her, or your office or whatever."

"Wow, I really am late." He gazed across the deck at the pool, like maybe a body would materialize in the shimmer of the water. When none did, he folded the clipboard under his arm. "I guess I'm not organized enough today, to do something so clueless. Nice to meetcha. Gotta go."

He started walking toward the girls' locker room instead of back the way he came. "Whoops," he said and wheeled around to correct himself.

Aw, that's cute. He has no sense of direction. Then Emma mentally slapped herself. "Can we find out how she died?" Emma asked. "I mean, since we tried to save her and all."

Will turned the clipboard around, hugging it to his chest. "I can't share cause of death unless her parents allow me to, unless it's not determined to be accidental. And if that's the case, I'll share my findings with the police." He stared at Emma.

She felt a brief flutter where she wasn't supposed to be fluttering over anyone but Hunter. *Stop that!*

"I'm sure there will be an autopsy. If I'm cleared to share any information with you, it'll be after that. My office is on Seventh and Wellington." He kept gazing right at Emma. "Don't worry. It wasn't your fault."

HUNTER WAS WAITING for Emma when she got back to her classroom. His worried look and fierce hug made her feel even more guilty for noticing the ME. Maybe she'd even flirted. She'd certainly stared into his eyes long enough to remember them.

"Are you okay?" he asked. "I know we're all supposed to go home, but I had to find you. Nate told me you and Leslie found the body."

"Yes, but we didn't know it was a body then. We tried to save her, Hunter, but we couldn't." She collapsed into a chair. "What if we did it wrong? I couldn't remember my CPR properly. Thirty breaths to two pumps, or two breaths to thirty pumps? She'd turned so blue, Hunter. And she was so young. I knew her. I mean, not well, but I knew her." Tears shone in Emma's eyes once again, and she dropped her head down onto the desk. "I'm supposed to be teaching 'em, not finding their bodies."

Hunter stood above her and stroked her hair. "Shh. I'm sure there was nothing you could have done. What did Niome say?"

Emma's muffled voice came up from the desk. "Niome couldn't find his posterior with both hands in his back pockets. You know that. The ME came just as we were leaving." She averted her eyes in an involuntary guilty reaction, which seemed pretty stupid since she was facedown on the desk.

"Yeah? Good. Maybe the ME will know how to find him. You sounded like Leslie there for a minute. What did the ME say?"

Emma lifted her head. "Nah, Leslie would say something Old English for not knowing his butt from his elbow. The ME said he'd know more after the autopsy. We're supposed to check with him later."

"What are you doing for the rest of the day?" He helped her up from her chair and hugged her again.

"I know we don't know whether Kisten's death was an accident, Hunter, but what if it's not? Kisten was one of the students who got those nasty notes. I'd really like to figure out who sent them." Emma rested her head on Hunter's solid shoulder. *Look how well I fit with this sweet man whom I love. Forget big brown eyes and flirtatious gazes, you idiot.*

"How are you going to do that?" Hunter dropped his hand down and grabbed hers.

They stood hand in hand while Emma mulled the question over. "I don't have a clue. Maybe I could research diabetes-related deaths." She sighed. "I have papers to grade too, of course."

Just then, Leslie poked her head in. "Come on out and look. We've become a crusade."

Chapter 9

The students and staff had been sent home amongst a flurry of chatter and rumormongering. But a few kids remained and had been joined in the courtyard by several adults carrying signs. The largest sign was brandished by a wizened little man, probably about seventy years old. He had Don King hair in pure white, and his face was a map of wrinkles. Emma had never seen him before. Although he wore no vestments over his jeans and Oxford shirt, he was obviously the man in charge. His sign said Pinewood Holiness Pentecostal Church.

As Leslie, Emma, and Hunter looked on, he jumped up onto one of the concrete benches that surrounded the huge old trees and gathered his followers around. "Brethren and sistren!" he shouted. "What shall be done on the morn of this terrible tragedy? Are we not Christians?" A murmur of "Amen" came from the crowd. One of the students grabbed another by the wrist and lifted both their hands up into the air.

The preacher started to pace. "'And we are not afraid,'" he said, "'but are quite content to die, for then we will be at home with the Lord!' That's from Second Corinthians, brethren and sistren. That's how we will teach and comfort this constituency!" Each "amen" rose in volume.

"Is that what we are?" Leslie whispered. "A constituency?" The three of them viewed the spectacle from the entrance doors on the west side of the courtyard, the only teachers still there. "I thought we were, you know, a campus."

Emma asked Hunter, "Isn't this illegal? I mean, separation of church and state and all that?" She'd always thought school should be for school, and religion for religion. She'd seen it back in Holly Hills when one of her teachers threw out a school science book and brought her own. *Put the two together, and things get iffy.*

"I think this doesn't count," said Hunter. "Lots of meetings, youth groups, etcetera, meet on school grounds. It's just that it can't be a part of the classroom curriculum or part of an activity sponsored by the school." He gestured to the two students who'd grabbed hands and were now waving them back and forth like seaweed in a tide pool. "This is spontaneous and not sponsored by anyone, as far as I can see."

"Yeah, and this school district doesn't mind splitting hairs over that particular amendment, anyway," Leslie said, swishing a hand across her body in dismissal. The elastic on her sweatpants must've been old because she had to keep hitching them up. "Don't you remember graduation last year? They always open it with a prayer, which completely annoys me. What if I were a Zoroastrian? I've been fighting it for years. I might as well be objecting to the existence of football."

"I get it, my friend. A mash-up of the two worlds never works. I guess if this is outside the classroom, people can choose whether or not to partake. But I understand your point of view. People can feel like it's shoved in their faces, and this isn't the place for it. You *do* object to the existence of football, by the way," said Emma.

"I know," she sighed. "But only because it seems to take precedence over every other thing, including education sometimes. Feels like bashing heads rather than expanding them, ya know?"

Hunter threw an arm around each woman and squeezed their shoulders. "It's the American way, ladies. What can you say?"

"Not much," said Leslie. "Say, I know nothing about this church. What do you think makes the Pentecostals tick?"

"Oh, we had lots of these churches back in South Carolina," Emma said. "They're holy rollers from way back. Speaking in tongues, collapsing on floors, anything you'd picture from a good ol'-fashioned tent revival."

"Great." Leslie smacked herself on the side of the head. "I guess I just have to keep reminding myself that variety is the spice of life. I do like it spicy."

Hunter chuckled but got serious fast when he saw the pained look on Emma's face. "What?"

"Oh, I don't know," Emma sighed. "A lot of people I knew back home, they just hurt, ya know?" she said. "They clung to any comfort that made them feel better. And I knew some of these ministers. They're awe-inspiring, really. Their faith is sincere and genuine. And powerful."

The pastor and his congregants were holding hands and singing some sort of gospel song. When they came to the end of one song, they held up their hands, waved them in the air, and started another song.

Leslie's mouth hung open. "Awe-inspiring."

Emma reached behind Hunter's back and shoved her. "Awe-inspiring, O' Jaded One. I know how you feel about organized religion. I do. And mostly I feel the same way, but about the organization, not about God. I mean, don't you think there's something out there? Bigger than we are?"

Hunter nodded furiously, probably eager for redemption from his inappropriate laughter. "I do. There's too many wild things out there, things science seems unable to touch."

Leslie stared at Emma. "I seem unable to touch your whole train of thought. So maybe I better just go." She stalked toward the parking lot, bumping into some of the Pentecostals on her way out.

"No, Leslie, wait! I just mean..." Leslie was gone. *For Pete's sake. People disagree sometimes. It is okay. Maybe she's more upset about Kisten's death than she lets on.*

"What do you think that was all about?" asked Hunter.

Emma sighed. "I don't know. Everybody has different reactions to a traumatic situation, I guess. Leslie gets argumentative and self-righteous. I tend to get all flustered and overcompensate. Neither one of those things is especially healthy, I guess. Maybe we should both take up prayer."

Hunter shook his head. "I can't see it. I could suggest a healthy alternative, however. More fun than prayer." He waggled his eyebrows.

Emma smiled up at him. "Heathen." She started to kiss him then stopped when she sensed the eyes of some of the group on her. *Bad PDA, bad.* "No, I really have to finish these essays from Advanced Comp. This day off means I'm out of excuses. See you later, alligator?"

He squeezed her hand. "Count on it, crocodile."

He headed to his car in the back parking lot. On the way through the courtyard to her little green Honda parked in front, she paused. Two of the students from the prayer meeting headed toward the street but were interrupted by another, bigger kid. He ran between them, shoving both arms outward and sending them sprawling.

"Stupid Bible thumpers!" he shouted. "Get a life!" Then he reversed direction and ran back toward the street.

"Hey, you!" Emma shouted, stunned. "Hey, come back here!" She started running after the kid but then saw how fast he was going. *I couldn't catch him if I had an engine attached to my ankles.* Instead, she ran toward the other two, a boy and a girl, both of whom were helping each other up. "Oh my gosh, are you okay?" Emma didn't know either one of them. "I am so sorry! Who was that kid?"

The boy looked young, probably a freshman, with brown wispy hair mussed from the fall. "I didn't know him. I've never seen him.

But he must be older. Sarah, did you know him?" The boy stared gravely at Emma. "My sister's a junior."

Sarah also had brown hair, thicker, in a braid hanging down one shoulder. "No, I don't know him." She shrugged. "I know the type, though. We get those intolerant ones 'round here all the time. Not willing to look out for anyone but themselves. Sad." She regarded Emma. "You're Ms. Lovett, right? I've heard all about what you did last year to solve that custodian's murder. You're doing the Lord's work, ma'am."

Emma blushed. "Thank you, Sarah. I just... well, I'm glad I could help. You must've come here to pray for Kisten. I'm so sorry. Did you know her?"

They both shook their heads.

"Not well," Sarah said. "She was real quiet at church. I'm pretty sure she got drug there every week by her adoptive parents because they were so into church and this pastor of theirs, Brother Barrows. She never seemed very interested. It's really sad she died, though. My uncle has diabetes. It's a hard disease."

"As far as that mean boy, though, did you hear about the vandalism on the gym wall?" Emma asked.

They nodded again.

"Do you think he could've done it? Has anyone at your church or in your group of friends talked about who might do something like that? I'm sorry. You said you're Sarah, but I didn't catch your name."

"Sorry. It's Joseph." He shook Emma's hand. "The only thing anybody's said to me was how weird it was to have somebody spray-painting around here. Even the hoodlum kids don't do that."

Sarah's eyebrows rose. "Someone told me the gym wall said something about sending everybody to jail. I think that's wrong. Only criminals should go to jail." Her eyes traveled beyond the parking lot, where the shoving kid had run.

That kid sure acted like a criminal. He should go to jail. Or maybe get conked in the head with a pail and have the sense knocked into him.

Emma faced the two students. "Sarah and Joseph, I am so sorry about what that kid did to you. That was wrong. Even though none of us knows who he is, I'm going back to the school right now to see if there's anything that can be done."

"Thank you, Ms. Lovett," said Joseph, "but I don't think there's much they can do since he was off campus when he shoved us. It happens a lot, you know. People don't understand. We'll pray for him and for you." They smiled at Emma and headed down the road, trailing their signs behind them.

"I'll take that," Emma whispered to their receding figures. "Any day and twice on Sunday." A little bit wistful, she changed course and headed back to the school.

AFTER REPORTING THE shoving kid to Abigail, Emma drove her Honda the measly five minutes it took to get to her house, thinking again how cool small towns were. She lived right in the middle and could get to her school and the mall and any restaurant or bar anywhere in town in the aforementioned measly five minutes. Leslie sometimes groused about seeing students everywhere she went, feeling like teachers lived in such a fishbowl. Emma didn't really mind because she liked interacting with students. *They should know we all don't sleep under our desks.*

She drove into the carport, left the car unlocked—once again, three cheers for small towns—and ambled over her small welcome mat to enter her dollhouse. She still called it that and, after a year and a half of living there, was still overjoyed and awestruck every time she walked through the door. It was one of the first things she'd owned all by herself, and being inside of it felt like nirvana.

Her pets greeted her immediately. Trinculo, the calico, wound her way through Emma's legs, and Sir Toby, the Sheltie, barked and jumped up and down.

"Hello, babies," she cooed. "Did you miss me?" Their affection said yes, but Emma suspected it might also have something to do with her role as keeper of the food. They followed her into the narrow kitchen, Sir Toby's nails sliding across the hardwood floor, halting at the pantry.

Emma kept up a running patter with her pets as she dished out their dinner. "Did you know a girl at the school died today? It's just so awful. I talked to her in the library yesterday, and I had her in class for a couple-a weeks last year. So I didn't know her that well, but Abigail seemed very upset and talked about how nice she was. She had diabetes. Do you think that's what killed her?"

The animals didn't respond. They were busy wolfing their food.

"I hope, I hope her death was an accident, girls, but then these other awful things are going on that make me worry."

Trinky finished her meal and started slaloming around and through Emma's legs.

"Kids are doing horrible stuff. Like just now, some random kid shoved some demonstrators and called them names, but Abigail said since no one knows who the kid is and since he'd already left campus, they can't do anything about it. I even called Detective Niome from the car. He said the same thing, but of course, he would. I think the man has 'Kids will be kids' tattooed on his... on some private place, and he has no idea what that really means or should mean. Sheesh."

She picked up Trinculo and carried her to the couch. "There were some very nasty notes sent to some of the girl students, too, and to me and Leslie. Do you think that could be related?"

No comment. Sir Toby was still wolfing. Emma plopped down on the couch with the remaining Advanced Composition essays. When she finished her dinner, Sir Toby jumped up and joined the party. The pets were all lovey-dovey and slobbering on their momma now that their stomachs were full.

"Oh, sure," she said. "*Now* you want to talk." She pushed them both off. "Later. Must work now." She graded essays for what felt like hours and had just finished the last one when her eyes shut without even consulting her.

EMMA WOKE AT SIX O'CLOCK. *Wow, I napped for three hours.* She shuffled to the kitchen for some dinner of her own. Frozen sandwich pockets were the best she could do tonight. *Aw, who am I kidding?* Frozen sandwich pockets were the height of culinary artistry in Emma's world. It was weird, too, because her mom was the belle of Southern cooking. She knew more about spices than the wisest voodoo priestess. That gene had apparently been by the side of the pool, toweling off, when Emma dove in. Hunter didn't cook much either, so they'd been to all of Pinewood's restaurants. Twice. Emma had taken up running to keep her butt from ballooning.

She stood at the kitchen counter and munched. The cell phone, perched next to the microwave, was silent. Usually, Leslie had called by then, if only to make strange noises into the phone or to try a Joan Rivers or Cher or Eddie Murphy impression. Emma didn't know why Eddie Murphy, but Leslie had that throaty laugh almost down. *Hmm. The religious tiff must really be grating on poor Leslie.*

But Emma meant business. Leslie had the tendency to be a little judgmental sometimes, and Emma really did know some people whose faith was enormous, not something they faked. Emma admired them for that. So she wouldn't call Leslie just yet. *Give her some time to think it over.*

She also thought about Kisten. It seemed like high schoolers only died when they were acting stupid, in a car or on a motorcycle or occasionally when there were drugs involved. Otherwise, they had the constitutions of a Hostess Twinkie—it seemed like they would outlast anything. *I'd really, really like to know how she died. Not sure if that helps anything, but...*

From where she sat in her tiny breakfast nook at the back corner of her tiny kitchen, Emma looked up the number of the ME's office on Seventh and Wellington and dialed.

The line connected after one ring. "Pinewood Medical. Dr. Capshaw."

She almost coughed out a huge bite of sandwich pocket. "Oh! I, um, I wasn't expecting you to be there this late." She chewed mightily and tried to swallow. "I was just going to leave a message. This is Emma Lovett from Thomas Jefferson High School."

"Hi, Emma. I usually don't work this late. But Kisten Hollis's adoptive parents are very upset and want answers."

She swallowed hard. "Understandably."

"Yes, really." Emma heard water running in the background, then it stopped. "Anyway, they wanted the autopsy done as soon as possible so they could begin funeral arrangements. I've been working on her for about five hours."

"Did you find anything? Anything you can talk about? I mean, I'm just curious because we found her and all." Emma didn't want to admit that her curiosity might be more of the morbid-fascination variety than of the teacherly-concern kind. And she absolutely did not remember Will Capshaw's big brown eyes.

After a long stretch of dead air, Will spoke. "I can tell you only one thing because I'm sure it'll be small-town gossip soon enough. Her death is definitely suspicious. Her two most recent insulin punctures look different from how a regular injection site should look. They are like big round bruises but darker. The skin cells around the injection site have gone necrotic."

"What does that mean?"

"It means those cells are dead. An ordinary insulin injection might cause a slight discoloration or light bruising but not necrosis."

Emma noticed a mystery bruise on her own knee, already fading from purple to yellow. "At the risk of sounding like a broken record, what does that mean?"

"It means she was probably poisoned."

Emma covered the bruise on her knee and squeezed it.

"You still there?" he asked.

She jiggled her head as if trying to dislodge something from her brain. "Yes, I'm still here. What kind of poison?"

"I'm running a tox screen. I won't have the results until tomorrow, but really, I can't say any more."

Poison? In her insulin vial? Holy cheese and crackers. "I understand. Thank you so much for your help, Dr. Capshaw."

His voice sounded as if he was smiling. "Please, call me Will."

"I will, Will." *Stop that, you idiot. You're flirting.* Emma reached down to pet Sir Toby, hoping a little dog mothering would keep her from thinking inappropriate thoughts.

"Bye."

She clicked the cell phone off then on again. She poked at Leslie's number on the screen.

Leslie said, "Go."

"Leslie, I think we need to play Nancy Drew again."

A long pause. "I don't know. Are you sure Nancy has adequate *faith*?"

"Argh. You're being silly. Stop it. I just found out Kisten Hollis was probably murdered. Poison."

"And such a deal of skimble-skamble stuff
As puts me from my faith."

—*Henry IV Part I*, 3.1.148–9

Chapter 10
Friday, September 18

Friday morning, Emma came to school right before the bell rang. Early-morning swimming excursions seemed unwarranted, if not downright stupid. Maybe they could get poisoned, too, since they'd all received notes. But she couldn't imagine how, since no one else took injections. *Maybe in the food?* But Emma brought her own food or got it straight from Mrs. Albert, so she didn't think it was a real threat. She and Leslie met at the mailboxes in the teachers' lounge and agreed to call Will Capshaw at lunch to check on the status of his autopsy.

"I don't know, though, Leslie," Emma whispered, pulling the morning mail from her box. "He said he wouldn't be able to tell me anything more than he did." She flipped through the stack.

Leslie glanced at the contents of her mailbox then sent it sailing into the trash can. "Yes, we'll see," she murmured. "You might have to yank out your superhero cape." At Emma's questioning look, she clarified. "You know, Super Southern Belle. That swooning-Scarlett O'Hara accent that can leap men's best intentions in a single bound."

Emma was not sure about the wisdom of using a flirtation tactic to get information. She already felt guilty about his big brown eyes locking with her green ones. *No, thank you kindly. I'll keep both my oars in the water on this front.* "Hmm. We'll see. It didn't sound like there was much he could tell us anyway, even if someone could flirt it out of him." She raised her eyebrows. "Why don't you flirt with him? For that matter, why don't you date him yourself?"

Leslie spoke out of one side of her mouth. "He had no interest in me whatsoever. Wasn't it obvious? Those chocolate drops of eye candy were for your consumption only."

The three new teachers sat at a round table in a whispered conversation of their own. Emma knew Diane and Rhiannon, at least, didn't really like her, but maybe that was because Emma and Leslie hadn't tried hard enough or been welcoming enough. *It's really hard being a new teacher, and we haven't helped the newcomers acclimate at all. Where are our Wondrous Wendy skills now? Plus, maybe I can find out more about who was talking in the bathroom.*

Emma strode across the lounge to greet them. "Hello! Let's see if I've got this—Otto Henry, Rhiannon Pressman, and... I'm sorry, Diane...?"

The three teachers abruptly stopped speaking to look at Emma. "Seymour. My name is Diane Seymour." Her voice dripped like melting icicles.

"Of course, Diane. I'm sorry. How could I forget?"

Otto shifted his considerable bulk in the seat and coughed. Although he'd been friendly the past two times Emma had seen him, right now he seemed lost and uncomfortable. Rhiannon's eyes were riveted to the brown carpet under their feet. *Maybe I interrupted a conflict.*

"I guess I'm all twitterpated from the horrible, sad stuff going on at the school right now. Did any of y'all have poor Kisten in one of your classes? I had her last year for only a few days, but..."

"I didn't know her," Otto said. "She must've not been interested in agriculture. Sometimes it's just..."

His voice trailed off as Leslie marched over. "Hi, colleagues! You're all looking like the mighty educators you are today. Ready to face the hormone hurricane? Great!" Without waiting for a reply, she yanked Emma out of the lounge.

Emma waved to Abigail as Leslie dragged her through the main office. "What'd you do that for? I was investigating Kisten's death. I only got to hear from Otto, so we don't know if either of the other two knew her. I'm probably even less popular with those three now than before."

Leslie stopped once they were back out in the commons. "I'm sorry. I just couldn't wait anymore to talk to you."

"I thought we were fighting about religion." Emma smiled at Nick Luchyky, a fun current and past student of hers, as he walked by. "Aren't you mad at me?" She trotted along the brown tiles, trying to keep up.

Leslie unlocked her classroom door and held it open for Emma to enter first. "I know. I should know... I usually know better than to get into conversations about religion and politics. We just seem to agree about so much that it threw me."

"I'm glad you're not mad and that you're feeling magnanimous." Emma sat down at a student desk that faced Leslie's black lacquered one. "Well, I have never met a group of people I feel so completely stupid in front of. Do you think that's because of what they said in the bathroom? They don't know I overheard them, so why do I still feel so oogy? Do you think that's why they're so antisocial? They've already given up on us?" Emma asked.

Leslie locked the door behind her—apparently not ready to let students lounge in her room—then leaned back against it. "You'll learn there are two types of teachers."

"Oh? Help me see the light, Yoda."

"I prefer to be Obi-Wan. But sometimes I like to stray over to the dark side, especially when there are cute men, good beer, or really fattening foodstuffs involved. Maybe I'm Darth, evil master of hot men and trans fats." She patted her stomach. "Anyway, like I was saying, two types of teachers. No, I take that back. Three. There's the type that really loves kids or wants to change the world or follow a noble calling or whatever. Then there's the type that mostly wants summers off. Sometimes number one becomes number two when they get burned out, but usually, if you like kids, you will always like them."

Emma thought she was the first type, absolutely. "And the third type?"

"The third group is and always has been mysterious to me. There seems to be a kind of teacher who doesn't really like kids at all. They find it extremely difficult to interact socially with almost everybody. I meet these teachers and wonder how on earth they could find any satisfaction in a job that requires interaction with others every second of every day. Unpredictable hormonal teenage others, no less." She stroked her fingertips across the print of the giant foot.

"Maybe that's why the third type do it—because it's easier to feel socially safe when you're around people much younger."

Leslie checked the clock on the opposite wall. "Yeah, well, considering what's going on around here, it's a wonder *anybody* feels safe, socially or physically. Poison? That's what Dr. Will said?"

"In Kisten's insulin vial. But he doesn't know what kind yet."

Leslie opened her door, and the two waiting early birds trickled in. She gave them both fist bumps and went with Emma toward her classroom. "Don't hate me cuz I'm a heathen, 'kay? Let's put our heads together and figure this thing out."

Emma unlocked her door just as the first-period warning bell rang. "Never. I could never hate you! Let's think of some ideas and bring 'em to lunchtime."

Leslie strode backward to her classroom. "On it. Crime-fighting concepts coming up. See you at"—she backed into a big football player, who whirled around, looking mad, but wiped the scowl away when he saw who it was since Leslie could be scary—"lunch."

EMMA ENTERED THE SMALL lounge off the library with heavy steps. All morning, her students had been quiet and reserved, which she might have welcomed any other time. When she asked Chris Summers if he was going to Homecoming on Saturday, he just stared.

Finally, he said, "Do you think there's gonna be any Homecoming? I mean, after..."

She didn't know the answer. *Would they cancel Homecoming?* She sat in silence with the students for the remainder of third period.

"Are they going to cancel Homecoming?" she asked Leslie, who was already munching on a pig in a blanket. Mrs. Albert, the school cook, created special cuisine for Leslie and her friends because Leslie had saved her beautiful daughter from oversexed high-school males, though said daughter probably resented being saved. But Mrs. Albert must not have had the heart to cook anything special today.

"I guess not," Leslie said. "I talked to Nate. He said he thought it would be best if everything went on as scheduled. People would start feeling better faster."

"But she was murdered," Emma groaned. "We're not only talking about the grieving process here. What if it isn't safe?"

Leslie sighed. "Nate assures me Detective Niome has it all under control."

"Detective Niome can't control his own breathing."

"True." Leslie smiled through cheeks stuffed with pigs in blankets. She looked like a demented chipmunk. "Sho what are we going to do about dat?"

"How about we start with our phone call to the good Dr. Capshaw?"

"Cah him Wiw," Leslie said, mush mouthed.

Emma reached across the table and thunked Leslie's puffy cheek. "*You* call him Will."

"Oh, I *will*." Leslie swallowed and went to the phone in the corner of the lounge to ask for Dr. Will. After identifying herself, she listened, throwing in an occasional "Mmm-hmm" and "Oh really?" and ending with a "No, I understand."

She hung up.

"What'd he say? What kind of poison?" asked Emma.

Leslie came back to the round table and sat down. "He said he can't say, but it doesn't even matter because he still doesn't know. He said he ran screens for everything he thought a regular person could get hold of—strychnine, arsenic, cyanide, all your Agatha Christie specials, and some not-so-specials. He got zip."

Emma took a bite of the pig without any blanket, as if that might make it healthier. "So what now?"

"He said he'd keep looking. He's saving a bunch of tissue samples from various organs—"

Emma sucked in a breath. *God, he was talking about pieces of a little girl, a former student's organs.*

"Because her family is coming to pick up the body. I guess the funeral is tomorrow."

"That seems really fast."

"Well, you know, I'm sure they want to start the healing process as soon as possible. How could they start healing while she's still on a slab in the morgue?"

Emma sighed. "I guess you're right. I don't believe in funerals. Did you know that? Or burials, open caskets—none of it."

"Me either," Leslie agreed. "My aunt made me go see my grandma at an open-casket funeral when I was about five. She looked like I always thought a mummy would look, only with lipstick and shellacked hair. It horrified me. I'll never forget it. What about you? I thought, you know, good little Southern girl, steeped in tradition and all."

Emma headed to the phone and started punching buttons without lifting the handset. Facing away from Leslie, she said, "I mentioned this to you when I was writing the letter to the school district.

When I was thirteen, my middle school had what's known as a contagion of suicides. Two eighth-grade boys and one seventh-grade boy, all within six months, all with guns. The seventh grader was my friend George. I've only gone to his funeral, and it was open casket, even though he did it with a *gun*, Leslie!"

She turned now to face her friend. "They had done a good job of coverin' the gunshot, I guess, but he was all yellow and still and small. I had recurring nightmares for years after that, where George would walk into my English class looking like he had in that casket, and he'd tell me he'd been given a second chance, and nobody knew what had happened but me, so I had to keep it a secret. I always woke up shaking, thinking 'How do you keep a secret like that?'"

"Wow," Leslie breathed. "That's awful."

"Anyway, no funeral for me." Emma shrugged. "I want to be cremated and have my ashes scattered over the water at Hilton Head. I want my friends and family to throw a party in memory of me. No one gets to say anything about me until they've shoved five giant marshmallows into their mouths and tried to recite the Pledge of Allegiance, or they've sung an entire goofy song in front of the whole group. Anything like that that makes them relaxed and open. Do ya get it?" Emma patted the phone like it was a pet and returned to the table.

"Got it. Great idea. Me too, only I want my ashes scattered right here in the mountains, or maybe not cremated. Just laid out on the body farm at the college so future CSIs can study my rate of decomposition. And I think they should also take three shots, at least. Whiskey, for sure, or B-52s. And they can sleep under the stars and think about me so nobody's driving under the influence of alcohol and marshmallows."

Emma pressed her palms on the table like she was trying to keep it from taking flight. "So what do we do now? I mean, about the murder?"

Leslie tapped her long red fingernails on the table. "I can't help going back to those threatening notes. Kisten said a bunch of her friends had received notes as well. Didn't she say something about her friend with the locker next to her? Caitlin Bauer?"

Emma stood again, excited to have a strategy. She picked up Leslie's tray, and together, they headed toward the cafeteria. "We have planning periods now. I'm sure Abigail will tell us Caitlin's fourth-hour class, and we can ask if she has any ideas about who sent hers.

Also, if she knows of anyone else who got a note."

"Let's go. Hey, Dr. Will asked about you when I was on the phone with him, by the way."

"Did not!" In a single gesture of betrayal, Emma's heartbeat quickened.

"Did too!" Leslie started singing. "Emma and Wi-ill, sitting in a tree-ee, K-I—"

"Shut up. My gosh, you are embarrassin'. I'm with Hunter, remember? Gorgeous, hides philosophy in his *Sports Illustrated* magazines so coaches don't know he's a philosopher Hunter? Very sweet and wonderful to me Hunter?"

Leslie took the tray from Emma and put it on the conveyor belt that led into the kitchen. The students had pretty much cleared out of the cafeteria and gone to the courtyard to sit in the sun. "Slightly boring Hunter?"

Emma punched her in the shoulder. "He's not boring at all. He's very reliable. Dependable."

Leslie made a snoring sound and received another punch to the shoulder. "All I'm saying is that I saw a spark of danger in the big brown eyes of Dr. Will Capshaw. Sometimes, danger is good, and predictable is bad."

"Sometimes danger is just dangerous."

"Okay, killjoy," said Leslie. "Let's go find Caitlin Bauer."

Chapter 11

They found Caitlin Bauer in Diane Seymour's fourth-hour business class. "Damn," said Leslie. "This might be harder than getting a kid out of Charlie Foreman's Advanced Strategies of Golf class. She doesn't seem to like us very much. Do you think she likes us very much?"

"I think she likes us about as far as she could throw us. And she's very small. Sorta frail. That whole group of new teachers doesn't seem all that interested in making new friends."

Emma and Leslie stood outside of Diane's class. The business wing sat in the far south corner of the school, in the same hallway as home economics. They peeked in the small rectangular window. Diane stood in front of the class, thin nose making a vertical slash as she read from a book while the students clacked furiously on their computers.

Timed typing test? Did they still do that? These kids were so smart with technology that Emma thought the hunt-and-peck method might be fine if they were hacking their way into the Pentagon. *They might have to run fast, but type fast...?*

Diane glanced up from her book and caught them peeping. The look on her face could freeze vodka. Leslie and Emma whipped their heads away from the small window and stood at either side.

"What should we say?" whispered Emma. "Caitlin is wanted in the office? Surely, Diane knows the power of Abigail by now."

"No, I say family emergency. That and female problems seem to be the easiest ways for kids to get out of class without too much trouble. Females, anyway. And don't call me Shirley."

"Got it. Family emergency." They quietly opened the door and slid along the side wall. Diane stared at them all the way. The kids stopped typing and stared too.

Emma felt her face flame until a kid on the other side of the room shouted out, "Yo, Miz Lovett! And Miz Parker. 'Sup?" A student from her speech class last year, Marty Chisolm was a natural public speaker, outgoing and effusive. Emma immediately relaxed until she saw Diane Seymour's face, which still held the alcohol-freezing quality.

"Now that you've interrupted my class, how may I help you?" Diane crossed her arms in front of her chest, which would have been more intimidating except that she couldn't easily get her arms around the huge book she held. Her short, graying hair was teased into a stiff helmet, and she wore a severe navy suit that buttoned all the way up under her chin. She was likely hot and uncomfortable.

"We're so sorry to bother you, ma'am." *Bring on the serious Southern accent.* "But we need to be a'takin' Caitlin Bauer along with us, ma'am. If y'all please. She has a family emergency—just minor, nothin' to worry about, just needs Caitlin's attention. She'll be back here quicker 'n grass through a goose."

Leslie always regarded Emma with amazement when she spoke like a Southerner. She turned that drippy debutante accent on and off at will, sometimes adding a little home-girl sugar or banjo-pickin' twang, depending on the situation. When asked, Emma had explained that the accent served a multitude of purposes, adding seductiveness, sweetness, or if she needed the cover, stupidity, to the perceptions people had of her. Hopefully, her home-girl sugar would make Diane feel like they were all family here, for a second at least.

Diane sighed noisily through her big teeth. "Well, I guess. Caitlin, you have to go with these women now." She glared up at Emma and Leslie. "Don't keep her for long. There's a lot to do."

Caitlin stood up from a computer near the back and met Emma and Leslie as they left. She wasn't wearing a cheerleader outfit, and her blond, perky, game-ready ponytail had been replaced by a subdued braid down her back. She looked sad and deflated.

Safely out in the hall, they stood with Caitlin. Her pink T-shirt said "I put the grrr in girl," and her denim shorts hung low on her waist.

"There's not really a family emergency, Caitlin. We just needed to talk to you. I'm sorry about your friend Kisten," said Leslie.

Her chin quivered. "I know. I can't believe it. Is this about her?"

"Actually," said Emma, "we had some questions about that note you received the other day. Can you tell us more about it?"

Caitlin nodded. "The whole squad got them. Some were in backpacks. Some were shoved into the vents of our lockers, like mine. Mine said something about constant perfection having to bring failure sometime, and I think the other three girls' were all the same as mine. Kisten's sounded religious, which I guess made sense 'cause her adoptive parents are really into that church they always took her to, and it seemed like the pastor—Barrows?—was always checking on her too. People knew all that info, so anyone mighta put it in the note."

Her eyes searched Emma's face. "Do you think *that* has something to do with her death? I thought she went into insulin shock, that it was an accident. I miss her so much. She was quiet, but once you got to know her, she was, I don't know, deep. People thought she was stuck-up because she was so quiet, but she was, like, such a thinker, ya know?" Caitlin clenched her fists. "I thought her death was an accident."

Leslie turned Caitlin around to face her, grasping her shoulders. "Caitlin, this is important. Did anyone else get those notes?"

"I-I don't know. I don't think so. Well, you saw Alexa's. But as far as I know, she's the only non-cheerleader who got one. She's such a bitch that I wouldn't be surprised if she sent one to herself just so she could raise a fuss." Caitlin sniffed. "So you're saying Kisten was... murdered?"

It's interesting that only certain notes seemed more personal—Kisten's and Alexa's. I guess mine and Leslie's too. The rest were pretty generic. "We don't know yet, Caitlin. But you have to promise something. Keep this to yourself, okay? At least until we know more. We don't want to throw anyone into a panic. I know that'll be hard. I know you'll want to talk to your friends. But that could hurt the investigation, okay?"

Caitlin nodded and raised her chin. "I won't say *anything*. I promise. Are you doing the investigation? I heard how you caught the killer of that janitor last year. That's just savage."

Leslie arched her eyebrows. "No, honey. The authorities have it all under control. That was an accident last year, our involvement. We wouldn't *dream* of purposely obstructing the investigation of qualified police personnel. Just stay savage yourself, okay? And be careful."

Caitlin hugged them both and went back into her business classroom.

"Is it completely embarrassing that I feel like a famous person when these kids know and like what we did last year to find Melvin's killer? And what was all that about?" asked Emma. "You lie like a no-legged dog. We wouldn't dream of obstruction, huh? We live to obstruct."

Leslie grinned. "I said obstructing *qualified* police personnel."

"Okay, O' Queen of Semantics. What are we going to not obstruct now? And I really think we're too old to adopt current teen slang, by the way. Sounds way too desperate." Emma snorted. "Savage."

"Fine," Leslie huffed. "I'll do it my way. 'O, she will sing the savageness out of a bear!' *Othello.* Happy?" They continued across the commons back to Emma's room. "I don't know where we should go from here."

"If Alexa is the only non-cheerleader who got a note, I think we should look into that. Especially since Alexa and Kisten seemed to have more personalized notes."

"We're non-cheerleaders," Leslie reminded her, "and we got notes."

"Okay, sure. Who's queen of semantics again? Ours were more personalized, too, but I meant to look at Alexa as a *suspect*. We know she was mad at Kisten, and she could've written a note to herself to throw off suspicion, right? Do you think I'm a suspect? I don't think *you're* a suspect."

Leslie laughed. "No, I don't think you're a suspect."

The fourth-period bell rang. "Now, if it had been Charlie Foreman's body we found," Emma said, "you'd be the first on my list."

Chapter 12

Alexa Champlain was in a study-hall class fourth hour, which was run by Rhiannon Pressman, the new teacher of muumuu fame. Emma knew she'd proclaimed study hall as an important way to assist in building study skills, but in reality, Rhiannon was mostly relegated to babysitting note-passers.

Her muumuu today was solid pink instead of the floral motif one usually saw in muumuus, which succeeded in giving her the appearance of cotton candy. She was young, maybe Emma's age, and Emma could see in her full lips and blue eyes a much prettier picture than her muumuu suggested. She bent over a big textbook.

Leslie gave Emma a gentle shove and a nod toward Rhiannon's desk, with an unspoken decision Emma should use her charm again. *Not that it worked so well the first time, but...* She came forward and stood next to Rhiannon's shoulder to whisper, "Excuse me. Hey there, Ms. Pressman? We just need to see Alexa Champlain for just a quick second, pretty please? Thank you so kindly, ma'am."

Rhiannon tilted her head sideways at Emma. "Alexa," she called. "Come up here."

Alexa slumped in the back of the room with her head down. She shot a poisonous glare toward Emma as she skulked up the aisle then planted her hands on the desk. "I told you, I already did my homework. Why do you keep crawling up my butt?"

Rhiannon's head dropped.

"Alexa!" Emma reproached. "That's uncalled for. Ms. Pressman is calling you up here for me. I need you to come with me, please."

"Why? I already talked to the principal and some jerk from the police department. I. Don't. Know. Anything." She threw her shoulders back in defiance, and Emma could see other students' heads come up to check out the disturbance. Some regarded Alexa with interest, but Emma could have sworn the girl in the front row looked scared.

"You need to go with Ms. Lovett now," Rhiannon said. "Don't act like this."

"Act like what? What?" She threw her hands up. "Everyone around here acts like everything they do matters so stinkin' much, but it doesn't. This stupid school doesn't matter. You all don't mean squat. I'm so glad this is my last year. I'll be eighteen in two months, and then I'm so, so outta here." Alexa glared at Rhiannon like she was a bug on the floor. "This stupid class is the worst, most useless waste of time in my whole life. You just sit here like a fat lump, reading your book, doing nothing. It's all just... just... ugh!" She suddenly swept a hand over the top of the desk, sending its contents tumbling to the floor.

"Alexa!" Emma put a hand on Rhiannon's shoulder. "That is enough. You can now add Saturday school to your list of detentions this week. Ms. Parker is there in the back of the classroom. Join her now before you get in any more trouble." *Oh my word. This girl is in such a state, and our poor new teachers are going to quit before we even get to Christmas.* She scuttled around the desk, picking up papers and the book Rhiannon was reading. "I am so sorry, Ms. Pressman. This shameful behavior is unacceptable. We don't tolerate it here at Thomas Jefferson. Everybody is so upset, it's just... Alexa, go. Ms. Parker is waiting."

All the students in the class had abandoned their studies to watch Alexa storming through the room and Emma babbling away as she tried to clean up the mess. Rhiannon stayed seated.

"I'm so sorry about Alexa, Ms. Pressman. She's had a bad week. Here." She gave the heavy book to Rhiannon. "Ooh, the Smithsonian. I got to go there on a field trip when I was in high school. Have you seen it?"

Rhiannon snatched the book from Emma. "I've never been. Just get that girl out of my sight."

"Of course, of course. Class, y'all go back to work now, okay? I apologize for the disturbance." She joined Leslie and a fuming Alexa at the back of the class.

Alexa tromped out of the room in platform sandals with Emma and Leslie following. She'd teased her highlighted hair into a wild pouf, and she had not-so-girlish cleavage wrapped tightly in a red V-neck tee.

Don't these kids have mothers? She's only seventeen, and she's trying to look twenty-five. Emma internally shushed herself. She sounded like someone's grandmother at the tender age of twenty-seven.

"Didja find out who sent me that note? That bitch, I'll kill her. Was it Caitlin? What's the frickin' holdup?" Alexa wrapped her arms around her chest, pushing the cleavage almost out of its boundaries.

Leslie stood eyeball to eyeball with Alexa. Leslie was tall, but the platform sandals made Alexa almost measure up. Almost. "Now you listen here, Alexa. If you don't watch your mouth, the only holdup is going to be you holed up in detention for the rest of your natural-born life, not just for the two weeks of Saturday school you earned right there. Got it?"

Alexa stared defiantly at Leslie, chin tilted up. Caitlin had raised her chin in a posture of courage, but when Alexa did it, Emma understood the whole SSP reference.

"Got. It?"

Alexa dropped her pose. "What can I help you with, Miz Parker?" She oozed barely disguised smarminess, but it sounded better than the gutter talk.

Emma said, "We'd like to hear more about the note. Are you sure you didn't see anyone in the library at the time you came in from the restroom?"

"Well, yeah. There were a lotta people in the library. Two classes came in and out while I was there—Mr. Lambert's class and that new guy who always wears overalls. He's like the farm teacher? Teaches all the ag kids. He was there with his class for like five minutes is all. The only one who looked suspicious to me was that bit—that witch Kisten."

"Are you sure she didn't look suspicious because of the way she ended up with your homecoming date?" Leslie asked.

A pained look crossed Alexa's face. For a moment, she almost seemed like the little girl she really was—really should have been, anyway. Whatever had happened in her life so far made her grow up fast. "He wasn't actually my homecoming date," she confessed. "I just thought he would be. Then he asked that anorexic cheerleader, Kisten, and I felt, you know, betrayed. Like, why would he flirt with me and then not ask me?"

"Why does the chicken cross the road?" asked Leslie. "What is the meaning of life? Why do you drive on a parkway and park on a driveway? The reasons for the behavior of men are just more of those unanswerable questions we all have to live with. 'They say men are moulded out of faults and, for the most, become much more the better for being a little bad.'"

Alexa stared. "Huh?"

"It's from a play," Emma said. "Shakespeare. *Measure for Measure*, right?"

Leslie nodded and smiled.

"She likes to quote from Shakespeare. Can I offer you some advice, though? In plain English?"

Alexa tilted her head toward Emma in what she assumed was an affirmative.

"You're such a beautiful girl. You really are. But you get so aggressive and angry that people won't look at you in that way. And your language—that's definitely a message you don't want to send."

"Yeah," said Leslie. "You want a nice boy to ask you to a dance, right? Your attitude and your potty mouth—"

"Not to mention those horrible things you just said to your teacher—"

"Not to mention those things, Alexa. Name-calling is *tres* unattractive."

"That's bullying, Alexa," Emma added. "What are you hoping to accomplish by calling her names?"

Alexa's face fell. "I dunno. She's fat and doesn't do anything but read her book and complain about other people. She said my clothes are show-offy. Maybe I called her a name because she called me one. I work hard to stay in shape. Why shouldn't I show it off?"

"What's sauce for the goose does not have to be sauce for the gander," Emma said. She continued right on as she saw Alexa's confused face. "What I mean is, if you let every little frustration turn into a war, nothing good will ever happen. Same with the language. Don't let every emotion show every time you have one."

Leslie nudged her.

"Yes, yes. I know, I know. It's a lesson I could use myself."

Alexa's face fell. She crossed her arms over the top of her cleavage, this time hiding it. "Can I go now?"

I wonder if anyone else knows there were other classes there. "Did you tell the policeman about those two other classes you saw in the library?"

"Nuh-uh. I just thought of it 'cause you were being so bossy with the questions. That cop barely asked me anything. Seriously, can I go?" Alexa asked.

"Go back to class, Alexa," Leslie said quietly. "We'll let you know if we find out anything more about those notes. Think about your detention and Saturday school this week and how you might prevent a repeat."

AS THEY RETURNED TO the English hallway for their fifth-period classes, Emma asked, "Do you think that did any good? Do you think she'll make a change?"

"Sure. She'd change," Leslie said, "if we were living in an after-school special, circa 1985."

"Really? But if we can't ever teach them life lessons like that, why do we do it? Certainly not just for the lasting importance of clauses and phrases." Emma picked up her Shakespeare bust and balanced it on top of her head.

"It's not all sudden, miraculous presto-change-o like that," Leslie said. "We just keep offering our wisdom and being there when we can. Eventually, some of them make life-altering decisions based on their experience here. Some of them don't." She shrugged. "But ten years down the road, when you meet a kid you helped, and they tell you they're going to be a doctor or a firefighter or, hey, even a teacher because of your influence, it's worth it. Or maybe you're the only one in their lives who was supportive and encouraging. They remember. Just one makes it worth it."

"Have you ever had one of those? Ten years later?"

Leslie smiled. "I've had a couple, actually. Amazing stuff. I'll tell you all about it sometime. Meanwhile, what are you thinking regarding Alexa?"

Emma put the statuette back on her desk. "I don't think she had anything to do with the notes. I think she's just an insecure girl who doesn't handle rejection well. What teenage girl does? But she doesn't seem cunning enough to send notes to all those girls and us, too, including herself in the mix just to throw us off the track. Plus, she was in the library that whole time with us. She wouldn't have had an opportunity leave notes in our rooms before we got back." She shrugged. "I guess all we can do is watch her. Did you catch what she said about the two classes that came in? Mark Lambert, the science teacher, and Otto Henry of our new-teacher group. We know so little about them. I think I'll stop by Otto's class after school and feel the situation out. Maybe I can ask about what sort of research projects they're doing. You know, make it into 'Hey, how can we transform this into a cross-curricular activity?' and see if I can find out more about the goings-on in the library. Maybe his reaction to my questions will give me a clue."

"That's a great idea. Do you want me to come too?"

"Nah, I think you freaked all the new people out a little. You're a little scary, Les."

"Okay, Pollyanna Pureheart. We'll just call on my fear-inducing mojo if we need it later. Go work your magic after school. Be careful, though. Go right after the bell so there are still lotsa people on campus."

"Okay, Mommy." Emma laughed. "I'll be careful."

"Are you going to Kisten Hollis's service tomorrow?"

"Of course."

"Meet me there? It's at the Marston Funeral Home on Crandall."

"Yes. See you then. Stay savage." Emma smiled.

Leslie clicked on down the hall. Emma steeled herself for another overly quiet and tense class period.

She should have died hereafter.
There would have been time for such a word.

—*Macbeth*, 5.5.17–18

Chapter 13
Saturday, September 19

Emma arrived at the Marston Funeral Home at ten o'clock Saturday morning. The low-slung brick building had vibrant ivy crawling up its walls and flowers lining its walks, but Emma still hesitated to enter. Her experience with these types of places did not stand out as positive events in her past. The neckline of her short-sleeved black dress constricted, so she opened the top button.

She'd slept fitfully the night before. In her dreams, she'd been lost at sea on a dilapidated dinghy with nothing but never-ending ocean surrounding her. She recognized it as a metaphor, like Kisten's murder and the threats were the never-ending ocean, while she stayed stranded without any good clues about where to land.

The main thing Emma had found out after school on Friday was that Otto Henry had a fifth-period planning hour and had already gone for the day. When she'd called Leslie to tell her, neither one of them knew where he lived and so couldn't go ask him at home. *Plus, that'd be weird, right? We knock on a man's door to ask him about his trip to the library? Not very subtle, anyway.* They hadn't seen Detective Niome since the day they'd found the body, and so far, they didn't even know what killed her.

Poison. Emma had googled it, and there were thousands. Millions, even. And many poisons were things anyone could get ahold of, from rat poison to common household cleansers. Leslie and Emma's discussion had touched on the poisonous frog they'd seen at the science fair, which they planned to investigate after the funeral. Maybe that would be an opportune reason to find the science teacher, Mark

Lambert, too. She could ask him to share his scientific expertise on poisons and sneak in a question about the reason his class went to the library yesterday.

But at the moment, here she was at her least favorite place to do the most distressing thing she could think of. *Who would want to snuff out a life that had barely even begun?*

SHE OPENED THE HUGE walnut door at the front of the building. The sweet, musky scent of flowers assaulted her nostrils. There must have been dozens of arrangements sitting in the foyer. She smelled roses and lilies and even spied a pot of jasmine in one corner that smelled to Emma like South Carolina.

She took a deep breath. In any other setting, the flowers would breathe life into her. But here, the smell was cloying, almost overpowering, and as it mixed with furniture polish and the perfume of little old ladies, it almost made her nauseous.

Leslie, looking stylish and serious in a deep-gray fitted suit, waited for Emma at the entrance to the nave. "Come on," she said quietly. "Abigail saved us a seat." They proceeded to the far side of a pew over to the left. Abigail patted the space next to her, eyes red rimmed under Aunt Bea bifocals.

Emma went in first, checking out the other mourners. The seats were full, but she only saw Nathan Farrar with a few other teachers and the cheerleading coach at the end of the second row on the far right. No Hunter, because he had a freshman football game to coach. She could see Caitlin Bauer in the front with three other cheerleaders and recognized some faces she'd seen at the demonstration the other day, including the siblings Sarah and Joseph. Otherwise, no one else from TJ High had shown up. *I guess we're not the only ones who hate funerals.*

She sat down. Abigail squeezed her hand. Emma had no problem hearing her thin voice in the ghostly silence of the nave. "Do you remember that reverend who spoke to a group in the courtyard the other day?"

Emma nodded. "Yes. The Pentecostal preacher."

Abigail consulted the program. "His name is Billy Barrows. That was Kisten's church. I guess he will be speaking."

Leslie leaned over. "In tongues? How will we understand what he's saying?"

Emma elbowed her hard. Humor didn't work in *every* situation.

"Sorry. Really," Leslie said contritely. "Abigail, I'm sorry."

"Remember when Kisten talked about that horrible note she received?" Emma asked. "She said something about it sounding like something she'd hear at church with Pastor Barrows." Abigail nodded then patted Emma on the knee as music began to play.

The organist played a slow rendition of the hymn "In the Garden." Emma knew it because of her father. "The only song I want at my funeral, Em," he'd said, "is 'In the Garden.' That's such a nice one. Can you remember that? 'In the Garden.'" She'd hugged him and promised his funeral wouldn't be for a long time. But it wasn't such a long time—only two years later, his lungs choked with emphysema, his heart giving out. And she'd remembered.

The casket in the front, made from a rich mahogany and surrounded by flowers, was closed, thank goodness. A picture of Kisten Hollis sat on an easel next to it. In life, Kisten had been pretty in an ethereal, waiflike way. Her long blond hair fell around a heart-shaped face and elfin grin. In the picture, she wore a TJ High School cheerleading uniform.

The music slowed to a stop as the man they'd seen at the school approached the podium and cleared his throat. His wild white hair had been tamed somewhat, although combing it down from the top of his head succeeded only in directing it to the back. He wore a brown polyester suit with a white shirt and no tie. When he stood behind the podium, he seemed bigger than Emma remembered. That size increase was reinforced when he spoke.

"Brethren and sistren, we are here to remember the life of our sister Kisten Hollis. Kisten was involved in many activities in her school, in her family, and in her life, but what she was most involved in was God." His voice cracked. "All things are controlled by the power of God, and we may ask ourselves, why would God use his power to take Kisten from us?" His voice rose. "We believe our prayers will be answered, and I say to you, who would pray for the death of this beloved child? By his power, God raised the Lord from the dead, and He will raise us also!" He raised his hand to the air, and many people in the pews did so as well. "For as in Adam all die, so in Christ all will be made alive!"

During this last statement, he slanted his face to the sky and raised the other hand so that both palms faced up. Many people in the nave murmured, "Amen," and Emma heard a strangled sobbing from the front row. She glanced over at Leslie, who looked ready to launch from her seat. Emma placed a hand on Leslie's arm, willing her friend to calmness.

The reverend's voice slowed and softened. "Our prayers will be answered. But we know that God's ways are not man's ways. All things work together for good to them that love God. Kisten is in a better place. God's will be done." He squeezed his eyes shut, pressing two fingers against the bridge of his nose, as if trying to lock something in his head.

Murmurs of "God's will be done" echoed throughout the room as Reverend Barrows left the pulpit. He stopped at the casket on his way and placed both hands on it. He bowed his head. The sobbing from the front row got louder. Emma didn't know how long she could stay there, marinating in the sadness. It didn't help that funerals reminded her of her friend George and the recurring nightmare of his revisit.

She also didn't know how long she could restrain Leslie, whose arm strained against Emma's hand like a horse chomping at the bit.

Thankfully, the organist played one more hymn, and people started filing out. Emma pulled Leslie out a side door. "Sorry," she said. "I can't deal with the receiving line. I felt the same way 'bout the one at my wedding. I wasn't comfortable getting congratulated by all those people, and I don't think it would be comforting in this situation either."

They sauntered toward the parking lot. "Can you believe that guy?" asked Leslie. "Don't you think that's giving the parents false hope, all that talk about raising people from the dead? And why didn't anyone get up and talk about Kisten? Oh, sure, we got a brief 'She was involved in school and family, God be with her, yada yada yada,' but what about Kisten the person? That funeral wasn't about Kisten. It was about the ways in which we should all convert. It's complete and utter BS, I say. Capital Bull, capital—"

"Shh! Say it a little louder, and everyone will hear you. It's metaphorical, anyway, Leslie. We live forever in the afterlife, if you believe that. It gives comfort, that's all. And if the death of a child doesn't require some comfort, I don't know what does."

Leslie shrugged. "Whatever. I'm comforted by knowing that when I die, I won't have to deal with the memories of my bastard ex anymore. The worms crawl in, circle of life, it's all good."

"Cynic."

"Yeah. Are you going to the graveside service? I'll drive."

Emma shuddered. "I'll go. But just for a bit. I have a thing about cemeteries."

THE PINEWOOD CEMETERY sprawled on the east end of town. They had to drive past Emma's neighborhood to get there, and Emma waved ruefully toward the house and wished she could be with Trinculo and Sir Toby instead of on her way to a cemetery. She hated cemeteries.

She didn't use to feel one way or another about them. She'd visited some of the oldest graveyards in the South as a child, sometimes on school history field trips, sometimes to visit her grandparents on both sides, and once to see the grave of her great-great-great-great-grandfather Abney Lovett. Well, she wasn't sure how many greats. A lot. Multi-great-grandfather Abney had fought for the Confederacy in the Civil War, and although her parents maintained that they personally would've fought for the Union, her father still said Abney Lovett was a great man.

When she was twenty-two, they'd gone to visit her father's grave. They drove up and down the rows of headstones until her mother had found the courage to go to his. They stopped under a copse of trees, and as soon as Emma got out, a sense of urgent dread had spread right down to the pit of her stomach. She'd tried to move forward, but the feeling was so strong it doubled her over. She'd had to get back in the car, and they left without ever seeing his grave.

She'd had that same feeling since then, sometimes when she was in antique stores, or sometimes in very old houses. Her mother said womanhood had brought her "the sight," just like her mother had, but Emma thought it just brought her the crazies. Tears welled up as they pulled through the gates. She'd never seen her father's grave.

Leslie parked her red convertible next to the hearse that had brought Kisten, or maybe some other poor soul, to be laid to rest here. The cemetery was beautiful, with new and very old headstones arranged next to massive trees and around rolling hills, surrounded by pine forest. The two women approached the back of a long line of newer stones, where they could see people gathered around Kisten's coffin.

When they reached one of the giant pines, Emma stopped and grabbed Leslie's arm. "Here," she said. "Let's just stop here."

Leslie looked at her strangely.

"I'll explain later." *I'm just going to breathe now, in and out. If I don't get any closer, it'll be okay.*

Leslie stopped.

They watched in silence as the coffin was lowered into the ground. A woman Emma assumed was Kisten's mother had to be restrained from throwing herself in after it, and then she fell limply into the arms of a tall, balding blond man who must be Kisten's father. Her heart ached for these people, and as she watched, her resolve grew. She and Leslie would find the person responsible for bringing such tragedy to parents. *No parents should have to outlive their children.*

As people started leaving the graveside service, Emma saw Will Capshaw coming up the hill. He wore a dark suit in which he looked very uncomfortable but which looked *very* comfortable on him. Emma had to do that mental slap again. *Stop it. Hunter. Hunter!*

"I'm glad you're here," he said. "I wanted to tell you something interesting I've found in the lab."

He walked toward the parking lot with the two women, and Emma was shocked to see him heading toward a gleaming black Harley. Leslie pinched the soft skin under Emma's arm and mouthed, "Dangerous." Emma yanked her arm away.

"So, Dr. Will," said Leslie. "What'd you find out?"

Will pulled a helmet from the built-in case on the back of the hog. Emma never understood why they were called that.

"I don't know why I'm telling you this." His eyes met Emma's. "I guess I've developed an opinion about our chief detective and how much good he can do, or should I say, can't do. And I heard all about what you did last year for that custodian."

"We don't want to get you into trouble, Dr. Capshaw," Emma said. "Even if Carl Niome is... less than effective."

"Well." Will smiled. "I am the medical examiner. I have some discretion as to who can assist me in my examination. Would you like to assist me?"

Emma and Leslie nodded. *Just don't flirt with him, you idiot. This is about solving Kisten's murder, nothing else.*

"I thought you might," he said. "The poison comes from a natural source, not a man-made one. Not plants, either. Could be an insect or a black widow or brown recluse spider. Possibly it comes from an animal. Amphibian? Reptile? Something like that. I'll keep testing."

"But she didn't have any bites on her or anything like that, did she?" asked Emma.

"No. We found trace amounts of the poison in her insulin vial. Somebody would have had to extract the poison from the animal and inject it into the vial."

Leslie's eyes grew bigger. "Did you say the poison could have come from an amphibian?" He nodded.

Emma's eyes grew to match. "I told you!" she cried. "Frog poison!" She grabbed the ME's hand and joggled it, ignoring his confused expression. "Thanks for the heads-up, Will. We have to go back to school. Now. I don't want to get you involved until we know for sure it's a lead because it involves another student. But if what we're thinking pans out, we'll have a substance for you to test."

Will's face fell. "I thought maybe you ladies would like to meet me for lunch."

"Sorry, Will. Back to school. We'll be in touch!" They were already halfway to the red convertible.

Chapter 14

The banner posted above the doors of the old gym read "TJHS Science Fair: Experiment, Fail, Learn, Repeat." Inside, the gym was an echo of Emma's and Leslie's visit from the other day, except this time there were other adults strolling around the tables, and the students who stood behind their projects were in jackets, skirts, and ties.

Emma saw Blake Candelar in the corner with his terrariums. "How do we approach this?" she murmured. "I mean, if this kid is poisoning people, couldn't it be dangerous? I know Detective Niome's been ultra-not-helpful in the past, but he at least has a gun."

Leslie waved her off with characteristic nonchalance. *She* hadn't been attacked in the dark of night the previous year by an unseen assailant in a poncho. Well, only once. Emma had been attacked twice.

"Dangerous, schmangerous. What's he gonna do? Throw a frog at us in the middle of the fair? Somehow, I don't think that equals instant convulsions. Everything that happened last year happened when no one else was there. Look at all the people here. It's fine."

"Still, I think we need backup. At least let's get his teacher. I wanted to talk to him anyway about being in the library where the notes were found." Before Leslie could say "backup, schmackup," Emma walked over to Mark Lambert, the science teacher in charge of the fair. He was sauntering up and down the aisles, checking on various student projects. "Mark? Sorry to interrupt. Could we borrow you and Blake Candelar out here in the commons? Please? Thank you so very much."

Mark Lambert was a tall, skinny guy with curly dark hair and serious glasses. He appeared more the science type. More than Blake Candelar did, anyway. *No judging the book by its cover, Emma. Remember?*

"Sure, we'll come out," he said and gestured Blake over. "Blake, c'mere for a second."

Blake Candelar seemed more like a skater, although in deference to the fair, he wore a bright-blue tie over his T-shirt. The shirt said "Scientists do it experimentally," and he had blue tips on the spikes in his hair. *Must be a spirit thing, for Homecoming. Or maybe he just wanted to.* He seemed the type to do whatever he felt like, which was sort of what worried Emma. The three teachers and the student went back through the gym doors and stood closer to the entrance to the main office.

"Did you know Kisten Hollis?" asked Emma.

Blake shrugged. "Yeah, I knew who she was. She was pretty quiet. Didn't talk much. I think she was in one of those holy-roller churches, you know, the kind even the churchy kids make fun of? People rolling around on the floor, speaking in tongues—"

"Yes, yes, we know," said Leslie. "We met her pastor. Did you ever, say, go out with her? Get rejected by her, perhaps?"

Mark interjected. "No offense, ladies, but what's this all about? You interrupted me trying to judge these terrific science projects to query a student on his love life?"

"No, I never went out with her," Blake said. "Like I said, I didn't really know her. And yeah, what's this all about?"

Emma couldn't tell if he was telling the truth. He didn't seem nervous about being questioned by two teachers, didn't act defensive or upset at all. But Mark Lambert's class had been in the library when the notes were left for Alexa, Kisten, and the other cheerleaders. *Maybe he's Kisten's killer.*

Emma tried a different tack. "We are so impressed with your science fair project. The one about frogs?"

Mark put his arm on Blake's shoulders—the mentor and his protégé. "Wasn't that an amazing experiment? We're sending the results to Washington to correspond with another study. There might even be national recognition if it pans out."

Blake scuffed his feet on the floor like he had the last time he was soaked in a compliment shower. "Yeah, thanks. But I told you all about that before."

"The poisons you talked about," Emma asked. "The ones from the alkaloids on their skin? Could those really... hurt someone?"

Blake and Mark were both shaking their heads.

"Like I told you," Blake said, "we're just finding out the potential qualities of the alkaloids. Although alkaloids can be poisonous, like strychnine or nicotine, the amounts of frog poison you'd need to extract to hurt someone would be monster. We don't have those resources here. Or the resources to make it into medicine, which, like I said before, is the reason for my experiment."

"Do you need anything else from Blake?" asked Mark. "He needs to return to his project to answer questions from the attendees."

Emma and Leslie shook their heads, and Blake shuffled back into the gym. *It just seems so strange that we're talking about poisons from natural sources and here's this kid studying poisonous frogs. This detective work is so frustrating.*

Mark stayed. "Besides, Blake hasn't gotten to the point where he can actually extract the alkaloids. He's just studying their makeup to apply to certain medicinal developments. The large-scale extraction would have to happen in a huge research lab and with many frogs, which presents the whole other issue of animal testing. That's way down the road."

"Are you sure there's no way for him to get the poison out, Mark?" Emma asked. "Was Blake in the class you took to the library yesterday?"

Mark looked nonplussed at the change of subject but recovered quickly. "No, only my geology class was at the library. And yes, I'm sure. Blake is a really smart kid, but I know there isn't anybody in this area with the resources and the... ability to pull off something like that. His experiment is entirely theoretical."

"What grade are the students in your geology class?" Leslie asked.

Mark's eyebrows scrunched together in a question. "Freshmen?"

"Do you know if any of them might have a reason to be angry with other students at the school?" Emma asked. "Cheerleaders, for example?"

"Again, why are you asking all these questions? Did someone get hurt? Is someone...?" He drew a breath. "You asked about Kisten Hollis. I thought she died of an insulin overdose. She was poisoned?"

Leslie pulled them all over to a more secluded corner. "Shh. Yes, it looks like she was poisoned. No one is to know, Mark. We don't want to throw the students into a panic."

"But what if it's dangerous?" he asked. "What if other kids are at risk?"

"Well," Emma said, "they found the poison in her insulin vial, so it went straight into her body. The nurse said there are no more diabetics on campus this year. And if it's a natural poison, like an amphibian one, it won't kill you to ingest it. Those acids in peoples' stomachs would kill it before it could get into the system."

Mark smiled. "Thank you for the explanation, Ms. Lovett. I *am* a science teacher."

Emma flushed. "Sorry. I just thought..."

"No, really. It's refreshing to talk to an English teacher about something other than Shakespeare."

"Hey!" Leslie said, but Emma was already pulling her the other way.

"Thanks, Mark," she said. "Remember, mum's the word."

"Let me know if I can help," he called to their retreating figures.

"'It's nice to talk to an English teacher about something other than Shakespeare,'" Leslie mimicked in a high, whiny tone. "It's nice that science types can do anything that isn't boiled on a Bunsen burner. I'd like to boil *his* burner..." She trailed off into a grumble and a growl.

"Come on. Variety is the spice and all that. You can't help it if most people don't appreciate your literary knowledge." Emma giggled. "That sounds kinda nasty, you know. Boil his burner."

Leslie glared her way then joined in the laughter. "I'd like to research *his* chemicals."

"I'd like to hydrochloric *his* acid."

Their giggles stopped abruptly.

"Okay," Emma said. "That's just stupid. So what do we do now? If Blake Candelar is no longer a suspect? Do we completely trust he isn't one? Do you think Mark will really be able to keep the secret? Between him and Caitlin Bauer, that's already two people too many."

"I hate how we keep dismissing suspects as fast as we find them," Leslie complained. "Why is this happening? As far as complete trust that Blake didn't do it—I've known Mark for ten years, and he's the nerdiest of all the science geeks. He might not appreciate fine literature, but if there was a way to extract the poison from that dart frog, he'd know it."

"Why isn't Mark a suspect?" Emma asked. "He knows about the poison in the dart frog."

"Sure, but he doesn't know Kisten. You saw her class schedule—she had Mike Williams for science. Mark has no real connection to her at all. Plus, he's tall. He'd have had to kneel in a squat position, practically, to vandalize the gym."

Emma thought. "I think we're still missing a motive. I mean, I understood the whole SSP rivalry as a motive, but it doesn't look like Alexa could kill anyone. Blake didn't know Kisten, and even if he did, we agree that the poison didn't come from him, right? And we still have to look at the fact that we got the notes too. I don't even know Blake. Who hates all the cheerleaders and the SSP and us? What's the connection?"

"I don't know. Maybe there's no connection, and that's why we're so stuck."

"What, just some random crazy person stalkin' Pinewood, knocking off teen girls? And teachers such as us—as young and vibrant as teen girls?" Emma asked. "I mean, even last year's crazy killer had a motive, as whacked as it was."

Leslie snorted. "Yeah, most reasons for killing another person are pretty whacked." She adopted a crossed-arm, splay-legged stance and flashed a few gang signs. "That's wack, G. We don' need no more killing in da *hood*." She made another sign that Emma was pretty sure translated to "I love you" in sign language then some more that looked like she was calling a really complicated play on the baseball field.

Emma stared. "What in the Sam Hill do you think you're doin'?"

Leslie came out of a sort of pretzel pose. "Jus' chillin' like a villain, bro. Keepin' up wit' the lingo."

"The lingo from where? South Compton?"

"Come on. You know these kids try to make like they're anything but boring suburbanites. You've seen the baggy pants. You've heard the music. They all like to play gangster wannabe. The thing they don't seem to realize is they wouldn't last five minutes in a *real* inner city."

"Would any of us? I mean, you grew up here, for Pete's sake. You've gotta cross the entire Continental Divide to get close to an inner city, Gangsta Girl." Emma sighed and faced back toward her classroom. "Speaking of our own precious suburbanites and their lack of cultural diversity, I should probably run into my room and attack some freshman essays. *To Kill a Mockingbird* is the subject, and race relations then and now. I always wonder what they really understand, bein' in this sheltered environment. I mean, my town and school were small, but we did have some variety as far as skin color. Here, it seems like all we have is just a lighter shade of pale."

"You might be surprised," Leslie said. "I think a lot of them are trying to pay attention to what's going on in this crazy world. Are you really gonna grade papers right now? How long did it take them to write? You know the rule..." Leslie wiggled her eyebrows.

"I know, I know. If they have two weeks to write one, I should have at least that amount to grade everybody's. I'm already here, anyway." Emma pulled out her keys and wiggled them.

Leslie shook her head. "Have it your way, Angel May. I'm going home for a nap."

"Hey, I'll see you at the dance tonight. You and *Edward*." Emma pursed her lips and made kissing noises.

"Yeah, just you wait." Leslie posed again, farther down the hall. "Eddie and me be *tearin' up* the floor. Jus' you wait."

Emma tried to picture Edward purposely tearing up anything. "You bet. See you then." She opened the door and went in to attack the pile of freshman essays. And when she finished the last one, even though they hadn't caught any murderers today, Emma still considered it a victory.

"And never since the middle summer's spring
Met we on hill, in dale, forest or mead,
By paved fountain or by rushy brook,
Or in the beached margent of the sea
To dance our ringlets to the whistling wind,
But with thy brawls thou hast disturbed our sport."

—*A Midsummer Night's Dream,* 2.1.21–26

Chapter 15

Emma was excited about the dance but also a little worried. The situation at the school seemed volatile, despite what she'd told the science teacher. And dances—well, they were volatile without potential murderers lurking about. At the prom the previous year, Leslie had broken up two fights, and Emma had spent the majority of her chaperoning time in the bathroom with a tearful and hysterical girl who was sure she'd seen her boyfriend kissing someone else. Emma had tried to persuade her that all boys looked alike in the penguin suit, but to no avail.

After exercising Sir Toby and feeding her and Trinky, Emma spent a little over an hour getting ready, pausing to munch on carrots and an apple she'd sliced and perched on the bathroom counter next to her toothbrush.

All through her preparation, she thought about what she would do if they found Kisten's killer. *What if that person really does have something planned for tonight?* Emma recalled the killings at Columbine High, right here in Colorado, and shivered. She had to squelch the picture of a random intruder, or worse yet, a student, spraying bullets all through the dancing crowds.

But poison seemed like a totally different MO. A poisoner would be a person who killed quietly, avoiding notice or fanfare, which seemed the opposite of the Columbine killers. Although, there were the notes and graffiti. That was a "please notice me" thing.

Emma didn't think running around and getting in people's faces would be an effective way to investigate right now. The more she thought about it, the more Emma knew that quietly observing the situation would be most effective in catching *this* murderer. He or she would be sneaky and unobtrusive, not announcing their presence like the Fourth of July. Emma could work with that. She could be watchful. *I'm gonna be on the sly, checking for anyone who isn't where they should be, or maybe someone who is there and should not be, if that makes sense.*

She was just smoothing on lipstick and zipping her dress—she'd chosen a sleeveless, almost-floor-length red tank dress, fitted at the waist and flared at the bottom, bordered at the hem with a riot of flowers—when the phone rang. Enjoying the swishing floral pattern as it tapped at her ankles, she left the bathroom and picked up her cell phone from its place on the living room coffee table.

"Hello, lovely. It's me."

"Hi, Hunter." Emma heard the smile in her voice, and it stretched her lips. "Are you ready to tear up the dance floor with me?"

"I don't know. I thought Nate said we had to spend the whole time jamming balloons in between couples so they can't dance too close."

She laughed. "I think Nate's going to have to jam a balloon in between us. I plan on dancin' *real* close."

"I don't know who Nate's kidding," Hunter said. "He'll be smooching up to Delilah Thornberry before it gets to the second song. You know it."

Delilah Thornberry was Emma's neighbor and the mother of Rainshadow, Leslie's lost-to-the-Peace-Corps love. Delilah and the principal had gotten together during the murder investigation the previous year. *Hmm. Maybe that adorable hippie-meets-skateboarder couple'll get engaged during this investigation. Something good oughta come out of all this craziness.*

"I'd like to watch people at the dance tonight, see if we can get any ideas about who might've left those horrible notes for us and maybe who killed Kisten."

"Em, I don't think you guys should be playing detective again. I just don't want you to get hurt."

"Hunter, my love, I love that you're concerned. But we talked about this, remember? Whoever killed Kisten used a poison made from a natural substance that was put in her syringe or vial. That kind of poison wouldn't affect people not taking injections."

Hunter's voice sounded hollow. "What if this killer uses another kind of poison? Or brings a gun?"

"Hunter Wells. We are *not* going to be those people who hide away in a box because there are terrible people in the world. Do you want to be those people?"

"No." He sighed, an explosive whoosh through the line.

"I just want us to all be aware of our surroundings. Don't be a worrywart."

"Okay, I won't worry. Just don't do anything crazy, please. Leslie too."

Emma bent to rub Sir Toby's head, careful to avoid flying dog fur. "I am all gussied up. Of course I'll be careful. What time are you picking me up, kind sir?"

"Um. Do you want to go to dinner first?"

"I know this sounds over-girlish, even for me, but a big dinner will make me too bloated for my dress. I'd just thought to have a salad here."

"Hmm. Does that mean it's a *tight* dress?"

"Well." Emma chuckled. "It is a little form-fitting."

"Can't wait. Are you sure you don't want me there now? I could come over, and you could model it for me. I'm just saying..."

Emma could almost hear his lecherous grin. "Oh, I think you're going to have to wait. You're just lucky my momma's not forcing you to come to the door and meet her before you take me out."

Now it was his turn to laugh. "Come to the door in Mississippi? Isn't that where she's living now? That would be quite the introduction."

"No, she's back in Holly Hills. Speaking of which, when are you coming down South with me to meet her? I've been after you about that for more than a month of Sundays."

Hunter coughed. "We'll talk about that some other time, honey. How about I pick you up at eight?"

Emma glanced down at the red flats she'd chosen to wear just in case she had to run after a killer. She scuffed them across the floor in annoyance. Parent introductions were becoming a real point of contention between them.

"Emma? Eight o'clock?"

"Yes, that's fine. I'll see you then."

"Can't wait to see you."

She clicked the phone off. *Why is he so skittish about meeting my momma?* They'd been dating for almost a year. Another mystery she was going to have to get to the bottom of. Of which she had to get to the bottom. *Whatever.*

EMMA AND HUNTER ARRIVED at the school at about eight fifteen. Hunter put the *s* in spiffy, in his suit and tie, and Emma had twisted her long brown hair into a sophisticated chignon, anchored by strategically placed rhinestone pins. Hunter had actually gasped when she opened the door.

They stood near the wall next to the new gym door to get a feel for the layout. Since Emma told Hunter of her quiet, watchful plan to find Kisten's killer, he wanted to know what they were looking for. Emma said anyone that shouldn't be there, if that made any sense, which made Hunter laugh and laugh.

The floor was covered in a protective tarp, and small, round tables were placed at intervals along the wall, ending with a long table at the east end covered in bowls of different colors of punch and plates of cookies. The DJ and his requisite disco lights were in the far west corner, and the whole place sparkled in white fairy lights and shiny silver tinsel.

Emma had always thought high school dance decorations were somewhat chintzy, but she appreciated the effort that went into creating the ambience. This year's homecoming theme was "Xanadu." Assumedly, this was what they saw when picturing that mythical place. Or maybe they'd never read any Samuel Taylor Coleridge poetry but had seen the roller-skating Olivia Newton-John musical from the '80s. That was probably it.

A large majority of the students attended Homecoming, since there were no age requirements as one might see at a junior or senior prom, so there must also be a good number of chaperones. Charlie Foreman and some other coaches sat at the front, taking tickets, and Emma received a big hug from social studies teacher Martha Bonaventure. She had been one of the suspects from the previous year's murder, but like Edward, she'd ended up simply misunderstood and underappreciated. Three of the other English teachers—Mrs. Miller, Mr. Palmer, and Mr. Wuster—stood behind the snack table, and Emma waved to her colleagues. The three newbies, Otto, Diane, and Rhiannon, sat at a table in the east corner, and when she waved to them, only Otto waved back.

The students appeared to be having fun. The boys got sweaty fast in their ties and suit coats, so most of them were down to their shirtsleeves by now. The girls all wore obvious salon hairstyles. That was another thing that mystified Emma—all those ringlets, elaborate stacks of ringlets that fell out and got plastered to their faces as soon as the dancing began. *What's the point?* She reached up to poke at her own little upsweep and felt satisfied with the zillion-pin wall.

My hair's goin' nowhere. Emma spotted a large group, Blake Candelar among them, who didn't look like couples at all—just a large group of pals, all dancing together.

Leslie approached Emma and Hunter with Edward in tow. "Emma Jean Louise Marie Lovett, don't you look elegant." Leslie was also elegant, as usual, wearing a sleeveless emerald sheath that clung in all the right places and sporting impossibly high-heeled strappy sandals. She towered over Edward, who looked inordinately pleased to be here and had even put on a real tie instead of the usual goofy bow tie.

Poor Edward. He is so out of his league. Leslie is sweet to bring him, though, and however abrupt she might be, I know she'll never hurt him or lead him on.

Edward reached over and kissed Emma's hand. "You look so lovely, my dear."

Hunter took her other hand and squeezed it then leaned over to stage-whisper in her ear. "Is that really your middle name? Jean Louise Marie?"

She giggled. "No. It's Rose. Leslie makes stuff up whenever she feels the need. You know that."

Leslie stood on Emma's other side and leaned in. "What are we going to do to keep an eye out for trouble? You know the kind I mean—SSP trouble, cheerleader trouble, killer trouble." Her eyebrows waggled up and down.

"We are being quiet and watchful," Emma said firmly. "Subtle, even."

Leslie snickered. "Forget quiet and watchful. I wanna daaaance!" She cavorted out to the floor.

Edward followed. Emma and Hunter watched for a few minutes as Edward tried to lead Leslie in some sort of foxtrot, but they then had to move on out of sheer embarrassment for poor Edward. They strolled about the floor and complimented some girls on their dresses. Even Alexa Champlain wore a semi-demure black gown. She wasn't falling out of it, at least.

Otto, Diane, and Rhiannon had moved to the corner of the gym. As Emma watched, Diane and Rhiannon's heads bent toward each other in discussion while Otto snapped his fingers and hip-bumped an invisible partner. Finally, it was like he couldn't take it anymore, so he grabbed Diane's hand and pulled her out of the conversation and in for a dance. Rhiannon stopped talking abruptly and stared sadly at the two as they navigated a two-step to the strident beat of the techno music.

Why do the DJs at high school dances play music like they're headlining at a New York nightclub?

Leslie strode over to the duo and whispered something to Otto. He shook his head. As Emma watched, she leaned in one more time. Otto shrugged and shook his head again. Nathan Farrar, the principal, waved to Hunter and Emma from the floor, where he and Delilah had joined a conga line.

When Edward finally gave up trying to rein Leslie in and just started jiggling in place, Emma and Hunter joined them on the floor, jiggling with him. As Emma did her required walkabouts to monitor the floor, she watched everyone carefully, but she didn't see anything out of the ordinary. It was just like all the dances she'd been to as a student and now as a chaperone. After a while, they all forgot about everything but the jiggling.

"WHOOO-EE!" LESLIE TRILLED. "I'm thirsty." She and Emma went to the punch bowl. "You know, I've been over here three times already, and I'm still thirsty. Plus, if this stuff is spiked, it's weak. I don't even have a buzz."

"You know there's no such thing as spiked punch anymore. Are you forgetting the breathalyzing flashlight thingie the kids have to breathe on to get in and outta this dance? We are smack dab in the middle of the twenty-first century, lady, and don't you forget it!" She crooked her finger at Leslie, who leaned in. "What'd you say to Otto?"

"I asked him if he knew Kisten Hollis!" she yelled over the music.

Emma gasped and socked her in the shoulder. "I said quiet and watchful!" she shouted back. "That's loud and obnoxious!"

"I'm only kidding!" she yelled. "I only asked if he was having fun and if he'd tried the punch. He said no!"

"Jeez, Leslie. You like to give me a heart attack with those jokes. Well, good. Maybe at least he doesn't hate us as much as the other two. You just keep on with your goodwill-ambassador stuff and maybe someday..." She checked out Leslie's strappy sandals. *How on earth?* "Well, it's no wonder you're thirsty. Talk about tearing up the floor! That little pivot thing you do is very cool," Emma said, pulling her along as she headed for the long table, "and I will never understand how you do it so well in those stilettos." She poured a cup for each of them.

A student who'd been sitting at one of the round tables jumped up and ran past the punch bowl. Emma recognized him as the kid from the science fair who'd created those cool sign-language-translator gloves. She was pretty sure he was crying.

"Hey, that's—" Leslie started.

"I know, I know. You embarrassed him at the science fair, if you recall," Emma said.

"I wasn't trying to embarrass him," Leslie whined, "but you're right. He was much more comfortable around you."

"I will go talk to him. You enjoy the punch and cookies. I'll be right back. Remember—quiet and watchful!"

Leslie saluted her and jammed a cookie in her mouth as Emma hurried off.

SHE FOUND THE BOY FROM the science fair in the alcove between the concession-stand window and the coaches' office. He'd scrunched up in the corner, sweaty blond head between his hands.

"Hey." Emma knelt down, even though she worried a little about splitting her dress. "I don't think you ever told me your name when we were gazin' with astonishment at your awesome science fair project."

He spoke from under his folded hands. "My name is Sam. Sam Wheatley."

"Well, Sam," Emma said, "I'm real concerned about you. Do you want to tell me what's wrong?"

"It's so embarrassing. I don't know if I can," he said, rubbing his hair with his knuckles.

"I am completely certain I could beat you, hands down, with the most embarrassing story ever. Would you care to wager?" The pulsing beat of the music in the gym was muffled in the hallway, but whenever the door opened, it swelled briefly like a wave coming onto a beach.

He waited for the girls who'd come out to pass. "I dunno. Maybe. Is yours about really crappy people doing horrible things? It's my date. Apparently, she's not really my date."

It was getting hard to squat like that, so Emma just sat down sideways so the skirt remained stitched together. "What do you mean?"

"I mean it was all a joke. She just told me. She and her friend like these two jocks, Sawyer Hammond and Gino Ramirez, but they both brought senior girls to the dance. So my date—Yvette Rogers, and her friend is Sally Dorn—said they just asked us as a joke. Yvette thought it'd be just, like, hysterical to get me all dressed up and parade me in front of all her friends and tell me what a sucker I am. She said I was lucky to get her to come in with me, but no way was she my date, and she and all her friends laughed like they just told the best joke." Sam's head sank farther into his knees. "I'm the joke."

"Sam, you are not a joke. That Yvette doesn't know what she's saying or what she's doing. Girls can be horribly mean, and you don't deserve that." She patted his shoulder. "Nobody does."

He nodded like what Emma was saying made sense. "What's yours? Your embarrassing moment, I mean. I could use some comic relief right now."

Emma shifted her position on the floor. "I'm happy to oblige you there, Mr. Wheatley. And this is really embarrassing because I wasn't even a kid. I was a full-grown adult." She smiled widely at Sam, trying to will him to feel better. "When I was in teacher school in Mississippi, I liked this man—a classmate. He worked at a Neilson's Department Store, and I went to see him there once. I found him on the sales floor, and as soon as I reached him, I bumped into a store mannequin. I said, 'Oh, I'm so sorry,' to the mannequin. And to make matters worse, I kept talking to the mannequin. 'I thought you were a person!' I said. To the mannequin. All the while, this man I was interested in watched me hold this awkward, one-sided conversation with the store dummy. I felt like the only dummy in the store, that's for sure."

Sam shifted from his scrunched position and straightened his shoulders. "What did the guy do?"

Emma stood and helped Sam to his feet. "Oh, he laughed. We both did. But it wasn't like he was laughing *at* me, more like *with* me. It was embarrassing, but one nice thing y'all have to look forward to as you get older is being an adult around other adults who know we're all in the same boat. We all get embarrassed together."

Sam wiped his hands down his nice pants, like he was wiping away the bad experience. "I guess I'm better off just heading home now. I'm in the middle of the fifth season of *Game of Thrones*. Thanks for checking up on me, Ms. Lovett."

"Oh, Sam, don't go home. It's your homecoming dance." She thought for a minute. "I've got an idea. Come with me."

The large group of non-coupled students still danced and bounced around in the west corner of the gym. Emma hurried over to Blake Candelar and leaned in to speak to him. He nodded and gestured Sam into the middle of the crowd, where they all started to jiggle together.

She slid back to Leslie at the snack table. "We need to find Nate and explain why he needs to suspend a girl called Yvette," Emma said. "Her friend too."

"You got it." Leslie gestured toward Sam and Blake as they jumped and bounced. "You did a good thing there." She downed what Emma knew would have to be her fourth cup of punch, at least, in one giant swallow. "Not only do I not have a buzz, but my stomach hurts. Let's go to the restroom."

Hunter patrolled the floor as the two women passed by. "Leslie feels sick," Emma yelled. "We're going to the restroom."

"Okay! What about you?" he yelled back. "You feeling okay?"

"Perfect! We have to send a message to Nate, but then I'm back to shake my groove thing!" Emma did a hop-skip to catch up with Leslie.

Leslie's dress was askew, so she shimmied her shoulders as she walked, trying to straighten out the straps. Then Emma watched her friend speed up, clutching her middle. The music faded as they moved farther from the gym.

"Do you think *looking* at your stomach in the washroom mirror might help it feel better?" asked Emma as she ran after Leslie down the hallway outside the gym. "I don't think that will help." *Why are you making a joke now? Maybe she really feels sick.*

"No, I have Advil in my purse. Plus, I need to powder my nose." She stopped for a moment, hand on her abdomen. "Ugh. I almost feel like throwing up." She ran and pushed the bathroom door open.

The music still thumped but sounded like it was coming through cotton as the door closed. There were five girls already in there, all in various stages of plastered hair and sweat—a normal scene for a dance, although usually at least one of the girls would be crying over a boy, and one would be swearing over another. These five all stood against the back wall, hands to their stomachs. Leslie ran into one of the stalls. Emma could hear retching.

"Ms. Lovett," one girl wailed. "We don't feel so good. We think we may have food poisoning."

Look at all these sick girls. What if they've been poisoned—the same poison that Kisten got? Maybe a large ingested dose could make people sick like food poisoning. Emma ran to the one who'd called her name—a former student named Allie—and smoothed her hair back. "Did y'all eat at the same restaurant?"

"We ate at Rephele's," Allie said. "I don't know where the others ate." Two girls said Rephele's, one said Pantuso's, and the other said Olive Garden.

Emma asked Leslie through the stall door she had entered, "Did you and Edward eat at Rephele's? I know only three of these—"

A long string of curse words spilled from behind the door of the stall, a famous Leslie string she never used in front of students. *What on earth?* "Leslie, I know you saw all these little pitchers and their big ears when we came in here. What's going—" Emma stopped talking when Leslie came out of the stall.

Her face was deathly pale, and she swayed like a flower in the wind.

"Oh God. Leslie, are you all right?" Emma stepped forward and caught her just as she sagged to the floor. She started convulsing, her eyes rolling back in her head, arms flailing. Emma could barely keep hold of her.

"Oh God. Leslie!" She grabbed the girl who appeared the least sick. "She's having a seizure. Call an ambulance. Go! Quick!"

The girl hopped over Leslie and Emma and ran out. Emma dimly registered her screaming for help all the way into the gym, like hearing it under water. Leslie's thrashing seemed to go into slow motion, and tears sprang from Emma's eyes like fountains as she tried to hold on to her friend.

It barely registered when Hunter, Nathan Farrar, and Edward piled into the bathroom with Emma. She couldn't respond when the EMTs came with a stretcher. They had to pry her away to load Leslie on. She didn't understand when they wheeled Leslie out the door. Mindlessly, Emma held fast to Hunter's arm, but her grip fell away when she, too, lost consciousness.

Chapter 16

Emma opened her eyes to the gentle stroking of her forehead. She looked up into Hunter's soft blue eyes, realizing she was still lying on the hall floor. She saw no one else there. "Leslie?" she asked.

"They took her to the hospital. I told them we'd be along. They wanted to take you with them, but you kept slapping everybody's hands away even before you opened your eyes. So I told them it was just stress and sent them on their way. It is just stress, isn't it? Do you feel okay? Edward and Nate took the girls with the stomachaches to the hospital too. Does your stomach hurt? We really need to go to the hospital."

Emma reached down and touched her middle, just to confirm. "No, it feels fine. I'm just..." Her voice broke. "Did you see her? She was all thrashin' and gaspin'. Did you tell them she was throwing up before the seizure?" Her sob turned into a hiccup. *How could this be happening?* "It must be the punch." Emma tried to stand up. "Get everyone away from the punch!" She launched herself from her prone position in the hallway, ran over, and threw open the double doors to the gym.

The gym was empty.

"We sent everyone home," Hunter said quietly, coming up behind her in the doorway. "It wasn't hard to get them to go. I think the whole crowd cleared out in less than ten minutes, while you were still a little loopy. The police are on their way. Nathan and Delilah collected all the cookies and punch bowls." He gestured to a corner table. "They're over there, waiting for crabby Carl and his crew."

"I drank the punch," Emma said. "You drank it. Lots of kids drank it, and they seemed fine. She stopped and thought. "Leslie asked Otto if he wanted punch at the dance, and he said no. Do you think he could've...?" Silence pervaded the gym. It seemed eerie now that the music was gone. "I didn't see him at the refreshment table, though. And I was being watchful." Shrugging, Emma dropped her head into her hands. "Maybe I'm not at all watchful because I don't remember seeing *anyone* we've been wondering about at the refreshment table. Maybe it was something else. I am the single worst detective in the history of detectives."

Hunter squeezed her tight, and that helped. A little.

"Come on." She stood. "We have to get to the hospital."

HUNTER AND EMMA RAN through the sliding doors of the Pinewood Hospital emergency room and up to the desk. She remembered this place from the previous year—a hospital made to look like a ski lodge. The chairs in the waiting room had embroidered bears and deer, and a fireplace to the right of the front desk burned cheerfully, even though fall had yet to make an appearance, weather-wise. The room was empty.

Emma and Hunter stood in front of the desk. "Leslie Parker?"

"They're still working," said the desk attendant, a youngish man in blue scrubs. "Are you the people who were with her at the time she got sick?"

They nodded.

"I think the doctor has some questions for you. Wait right here." He left.

Emma paced back and forth in front of the desk. "Oh God, oh God, why is this happening?" she moaned. "No one else got sick like this." She grabbed Hunter's arm. "I wonder if the amount has something to do with it. I only had one cup of punch, and I know she had at least four. But that's not it—you had three, and you didn't get sick. Oh, I am as worthless as a steering wheel on a mule."

All Hunter could do was pat her back and murmur soothing words.

"Excuse me," Emma said to the desk attendant, "how are the other students? Weren't there some others who came in the same time as Leslie?"

"They are in other rooms in the ER," he said. "I'm not allowed to release specifics to you because you aren't family members." He leaned forward and whispered, "But they all seem to be doing fine."

The sliding doors at the back of the ER whooshed open. A small, rotund woman in scrubs and a lab coat approached them. She took down her mask, her face expressionless. *That's so they can deliver bad news in a calm manner. Oh, please don't let it be bad news.*

"I'm Dr. Belsing. I need to ask you some questions about Leslie."

"Is she going to be all right?" asked Hunter.

Dr. Belsing held her gloved hands to the sky in a shrug that only raised her palms and not her shoulders. "We just don't know at this point. We're not really sure what's wrong with her, and she doesn't seem to be improving. She had a CAT scan, and we're in the process of some bloodwork. We also gave her an endoscopy to check her stomach. Did she have anything strange to eat?"

"I don't think so," said Emma. "We had a murder at the school earlier this week. The girl was poisoned. But Dr. Capshaw, the ME, said it was some sort of living-creature poison—insect or animal or the like—and ingestion wouldn't harm anyone. I know Leslie wasn't on anything injectable. I was with her the whole time"—she turned toward Hunter—"except for when I went to see Sam Wheatley, so it's not like she'd ever have been alone for someone to inject her with something."

Hunter nodded. "Plus, Edward stuck to her kinda like glue any time she wasn't with you."

Dr. Belsing's penciled eyebrows rose. "What sort of living creature?"

"Dr. Capshaw doesn't know yet. What does it matter if ingestion wouldn't kill you? It would have to be another poison this time."

"Well," said Dr. Belsing, "in Leslie's case, it—"

Dr. Belsing was interrupted by the whoosh of the sliding doors at the front. Will Capshaw burst through, holding a printout and a syringe. He shouted, "Rattlesnake!" and breezed past Emma and Hunter, grabbing Dr. Belsing and rushing her through the back doors.

"What th—" asked Hunter. "Who's *that*?"

"That's the ME working on Kisten's case. It must have been rattlesnake poison in her insulin vial. But again, how would that apply to Leslie? I know she isn't shooting up." She gazed at the doors, willing them to whoosh open again with some good news, that Leslie would be fine now that the poison was identified. "What do you think Dr. Belsing meant by 'in Leslie's case'? Leslie's not allergic to anything." She paced back and forth in front of the front desk. The desk attendant was starting to look annoyed.

"Sweetie, let's sit down. All we can do now is wait."

"I'm no good at that. I'm worried." But she allowed Hunter to lead her to one of the couches. The fabric showed alternating deer and evergreen-tree shapes. Emma traced them with her fingers because if she didn't do something, she'd go crazy. Hunter's strong hand on her back just lay there like a weight instead of delivering the intended comfort.

THEY WERE SITTING IN the lobby two hours later, watching a rerun of *Friends*, when Dr. Belsing came out with Will Capshaw behind her. Emma and Hunter both stood up.

"Well? What happened? What's goin' on? Is she okay?" Emma would have continued asking panicked questions if Dr. Will and Hunter hadn't reached forward at the same time to place a hand on her arm. She stopped talking. Will immediately withdrew his hand. Hunter held on tighter.

"She's going to be fine," Dr. Belsing said.

Emma breathed a sigh of relief.

Hunter didn't let go of her arm. He stared at Dr. Will.

"Dr. Capshaw figured out it was rattlesnake venom this evening. I guess he's been trying to identify it because of a student's death?"

"I went to the police to tell them I'd figured out what killed Kisten, but Niome was at the school because of what happened at the dance. So I went there, and he told me you were all here."

"Thank God he came here," said Dr. Belsing, "because I wouldn't have known to administer an antivenin. You have to travel much farther west to naturally encounter rattlesnakes. She'll probably feel nauseated and sore, but she should be fine."

Will's big brown eyes searched Emma's. "Are you okay?"

"I'm fine, Dr. Capshaw. Thanks so much for asking. We've just been so worried about Leslie." Emma detached her arm from Hunter's grip, but when she saw the stricken look on his face, she reached for his hand. That seemed to help for the moment. "And thank *you*, Dr. Belsing. But... I thought this type of poison wouldn't kill you if it was ingested." She questioned Dr. Will, aware of Hunter's hand squeezing hers tightly.

"Usually, it won't," Dr. Capshaw confirmed. "But Dr. Belsing figured out Leslie has an ulcer. The hole in her stomach allowed the poison access to the bloodstream. The other people who got stomachaches must have drunk a lot of punch to feel any effects. They've been given the antivenin, too, just to be safe."

"Leslie has an ulcer?" asked Emma. "How'd she get one of those?"

"Usually a combination of high stress and diet," replied Dr. Belsing. "She should have been diagnosed and on treatment a long time ago, judging by the damage I saw when I did the endoscopy."

"That makes no sense at all," said Emma. "Leslie is the most cool and collected person I know. As for her diet, I get that. She doesn't cook at all, really, so she compensates by eating out a lot, or making pounds and pounds of hors d'oeuvres and snack foods."

"Well, that certainly could contribute." Dr. Belsing nodded. "And as for the high stress, sometimes the way a person appears has nothing to do with who they actually are."

"I guess if we've learned anything by now, that should be it." She turned to Will. "Thank you, so much, Doctor. I-I thank you, really."

"No problem." He bored into her with those brown eyes.

Emma tried not to squirm. She was ultra-aware of Hunter's grip on her hand.

"I gave the information to Detective Niome, so maybe that will help find your killer. Whoever it is doesn't know that much about the effects of the poison, or he wouldn't have put it in the punch. He has to know something about milking snakes, though. It would take some work to extract the amount of venom needed, probably from more than one snake. You're looking for a collector."

Hunter broke in. "Can we see her now?"

"Go ahead," said Dr. Belsing. "She's probably tired. And just to let you know, her voice will be hoarse from the endoscopy tube."

"Tube?" asked Emma.

"Yes. An endoscope is a tube with a camera attached. We insert it into the stomach through the mouth, and it tells us what her stomach looks like. That's how I found the ulcer."

Emma's face squinched up. "Oh God. Did you tell her you put a tube in her throat? Holy catfish! Does she know you saw inside her stomach?"

Dr. Belsing shook her head. "She's been sort of out of it."

"Don't tell her. Really." She pulled Hunter toward the beds in the ER. "Thanks again, Doctor. 's'. Doctorsss."

Hunter and Emma whooshed through the doors and approached the one bed with the circular curtain pulled all the way around. Emma's shoes clicked on the linoleum floor and echoed through the nearly empty space.

"I don't like that ME," grumbled Hunter. "He looks dangerous."

Emma covered a smile. *He's cute when he's jealous.*

"Why can't Dr. Belsing tell Leslie about the endoscopy?"

"Oh, I just can't imagine she'd deal well with that. Last year, when she fell on her rear end, she pitched a huge hissy fit just about sitting on one of those donut thingies. I can't imagine she'd welcome a tube down her throat and people lookin' at her insides. Does not compute."

The quiet ER and the empty beds were testament to the general good health of Pinewood. The students must've all received their antivenin and gone home. Emma peeked around the circular curtain surrounding the only occupied bed. Leslie had her head propped up on two big pillows, blond bob sticking out in five different directions, the flimsy hospital gown making her look scarecrow thin.

"Hey, you," said Emma.

"Hi," Leslie croaked. Her eyebrows rose. "Hi," she tried again. Still croaky. "What is up with my voice? I sound like Milton Berle."

Emma came to her side. "Oh, no problems, girly. I'm sure it's just the strain, you being poisoned and all."

Leslie nodded then stopped with a hand to her throat. "Ow. Meh. Hell of a strain, being poisoned. Dr. Will told me he saved my life."

Hunter interjected from the other side of the bed. "He *told* you that? Of all the arrogant, self-aggrandizing—"

"No, no. He didn't say, 'Hey, Leslie, I saved your life. Worship me.'" She smiled at Emma. "Though I've gotta admit," she rasped, "I kinda do. He just told me he found out about the poison, and they used an antivenin, and—poof!—all better."

Emma took her hand. "Did Dr. Belsing tell you why you got so sick when no one else did? Did she tell you—"

"About the ulcer?" Leslie nodded from her prone position, pillow sliding up and down under the crazy hair. "Yeah, she told me just now as I woke up. Though I guess the screaming meemies that have been living in my stomach for the past six months should have told me sooner."

"Leslie! You've been feeling sick and haven't been to a doctor? Why didn't you tell me? I found this great doctor down on Eleventh Street. He—"

"Yeah, yeah, yeah." Leslie made the shushing motion with one hand. "Whatever. I'll be fine."

Edward poked his head around the curtain. "Leslie? Are you all right?" He came to her bedside, although he seemed flustered by her state of undress, wrapping his arms across his chest. "Oh my. This is awful. I'm so sorry. What a terrible homecoming date I've been."

Leslie laughed, or tried to laugh. It transformed into a sort of choke, and she put her hand to her throat again. "Edward," she squawked, "Homecoming was fine, except for the bastard who poisoned me. *You* didn't poison me, did you?"

He huffed and puffed and stuttered.

"No, I didn't think you did. I'll be fine, Eddie. No worries."

"Do you think... do you think we might do it again sometime? Sans poison, of course."

Leslie raised her eyebrows Emma's way in a "please save me" look.

"Edward, Hunter," said Emma. "Could you two excuse us? We need a little recovery time. Girls only, you know."

"Of course," said Edward. "Hunter, coffee? I think there is a machine down in the pediatrics wing."

Hunter reached across the bed to Emma. "Call me when you're ready to go? We'll come back and get you both home and safe."

She nodded. The two men left, and the circular curtain closed to envelop Emma and Leslie in a protective cocoon.

Emma took her friend's hand. "Les. You need to take better care of yourself. Ulcers are very treatable with some medication and a change of diet."

"Right," she grumbled. "I don't have a man anymore. Might as well take away *everything* I enjoy."

"Leslie. There are many enjoyable foods that are also good for you."

"Name one."

"And what's this I hear about high stress? Why didn't you talk to me if you are feelin' stressed? Or to a counselor? Someone?

Leslie raised her chin defiantly. "I am not feeling stressed. Stress is for wussies."

"Come on," Emma admonished. "I know you've been sad since Rain left. You went all ballistic on the religion thing, and you never talk about your ex-husband. That whole being-left-for-another-man thing is very stressful. I'm ashamed I couldn't see it before."

"I'm very smooth, don't'cha know? Thanks for the reminder of Tim the Bastard. I'm fine. It's fine." Her hands rested on her thighs, and she picked one up to start pushing cuticles down.

She really does look thin in that gown. Her elbows seem sharp enough to rip the sheets. "I'm sorry, Les. It's just that you can't hold all of that inside. Just talk to me about one thing. Baby steps, you know. How about the religion thing? You were very upset with me the other day when I was talkin' about God."

"I don't mind if you talk about God," Leslie said. "I'm okay with not believing the same things everybody else does. It's fine. Never mind."

"What do you believe in, Leslie? Maybe since this has been in the center of this... this new mystery that we don't want and shouldn't have to solve, it'd be a good topic to start with. Maybe we can figure out if religion is important to the investigation if we talk it through."

Leslie turned her face away from Emma. The right side of her hair had matted to her cheek. "That's just it, I guess. I'm not sure if I believe in anything. I mean, I'd like to know there's something more out there, but all the evidence I've seen points to the contrary. I'd like to feel so strongly about something that I wouldn't need concrete proof. But I just don't. Then I think, what if God is punishing me for my disbelief? What if Timothy turned to men and Rain turned to the Peace Corps because of something I've done?" Her eyes filled with tears. "What if I'm thirty-eight, single, and childless because I *deserve* to be?"

Emma put her arms around Leslie, careful to avoid her neck. "Don't be silly. You are wonderful, strong, and caring. You deserve everything you want, and you know that. You do believe strongly in some things without proof. You believe in friendship. You believe in teaching. You believe in Shakespeare, and you've never seen *him*."

Leslie gave a wan smile. "And what about my general intolerance? Like those Pentecostals. You were so admiring of them just because of their blind faith, and all I could do was watch them with my mouth open. The rolling on the floor, the speaking in tongues—I just think that stuff's crazy. I think they're all bonkers. How do I get over being that judgmental? I think if I just—"

Emma straightened herself from the hug, eyes growing bigger.

"What? See, you think I'm judgmental too."

She shook her head slowly. "No, no, it's not that. I was just remembering. The Pentecostals. The Holiness churches back home. They did all that tremblin' on the floor, speaking in tongues, and..."

"And what?"

Emma took a deep breath, held it, and blew it out. "They also handled snakes."

"'Tis a strange serpent."

—*Antony and Cleopatra* 2.7.48

Chapter 17
Sunday, September 20

Emma stood outside the doors of the Pinewood Holiness Pentecostal church at nine o'clock Sunday morning. She wasn't sure why she'd come by herself, but Leslie was still in the hospital, and Hunter was being smotheringly solicitous. She was afraid she'd snap at him in the middle of the service. She'd thought about calling Will Capshaw then chased the thought away. She needed to figure out if Pastor Barrows or maybe another member of Holiness Pentecostal Church had killed Kisten. She wanted to do it alone because her partner-in-detecting was Leslie, and that was that. Plus, her partner-in-love was Hunter, and distractions were unwelcome. *Distractions bad. Church good.* She felt safe going here, planted in the middle of a public place, and she had no intentions of eating or drinking *anything* she hadn't made herself. Maybe ever. Except if Mrs. Albert made it.

The church was a simple, square building whose log exterior fit nicely with its mountain surroundings. It sat right up against a large patch of pine trees Emma assumed was national forestland. Pinewood was strange in that there were sections full of business and industry broken up by these huge expanses of forestry owned by the government. Emma wondered how they decided where to commercialize and what to keep natural. *Very cool to see the occasional deer in the grocery store parking lot, though.*

She remembered church as a pretty formal affair, with women in dresses, hymnals on pews, and the organist and choir on risers in the corner. Her entrance into the Holiness church defied those expectations. There were metal folding chairs set in rows across the floor and a podium next to a long rectangular table that had two large boxes on it. People wore jeans and button-up shirts, with a few dresses here and there—a scene reminiscent of a family reunion or casual picnic. Emma wore a simple forest-green skirt with a blouse, so she didn't feel too conspicuous. Sort of blending in with the scenery.

She sat on a chair in the back row, smiling at the few parishioners who caught her eye. Nobody seemed upset to see her, or really even noticed her at all. *Could one of these people have killed Kisten? And why would they? Because she wasn't religious enough?* The only thing Emma knew for sure about Kisten's lifestyle was that she'd been a cheerleader, and cheerleaders wore short skirts. *Maybe that'd be a reason to ground her or... keep her off the team, I guess. But kill her? It doesn't make sense.*

She saw the pastor, Billy Barrows, waiting in the corner with his head bowed. He had an object in his hand, which Emma couldn't see. *Do Pentecostals use rosary beads? I don't think so...* He was probably preparing for his sermon.

"Ahem." She heard a deep voice. "Is this seat taken?"

She startled. "Will! I mean, um, Dr. Capshaw. What are you doin' here? Do you go to this church? You don't seem like... surely you aren't... I mean... hi. How are you?"

He wore baggy jeans and a short-sleeved sweater. She could see the edges of a tattoo on a bicep peeking out from under one of the sleeves. He held on to a leather bike jacket.

Wow. Maybe dangerous is good. Sure is sexy. Stop it, stop it! You. Love. Hunter. "Do you go to this church? How are you?" *Points for witty conversation, Emma.* She sounded like Repeato-Girl.

"Hi, Emma. Call me Will, really. No, I don't go to this church, but one of my nurses does. She mentioned something about snake handling, so I thought..."

"Me too. I remember these churches from where I grew up, and the snake-handling thing occurred to me when you told us about the rattlesnake, so *I* thought..."

He swiveled to face her. "Looks like we're both thinking the same thing."

Emma flushed. "So, what? You were just planning on going up to Billy Barrows after the service and asking if he's trying to poison and terrorize the high school, including one of his own parishioners?"

"No. I thought some quiet observation might tell me something. What were *you* planning on?"

She shrugged. "Beyond what you just said, I'm not sure, now that I think about it. I figured I needed to do *something*, and with Leslie still in the hospital, I might go crazy sittin' at home all day, wondering who wants to kill us."

"What? No plans with the history teacher?" He smirked. "You guys could... I don't know... play miniature golf? Go bowling? That would take your mind off things."

"Hey, I like miniature golf. And I can't bowl, but I'm sure it's a fun distraction. Why, what would you—"

She was interrupted by hands all around her shooting up into the air. Reverend Billy Barrows stood at the pulpit.

Another man got up from his chair and started to play the guitar.

The reverend started to sing, "What would you give in exchange for your soul?" He sang loudly, and others joined in, repeating the phrase over and over, voices swelling in volume until, on what seemed to be an invisible signal, the singing stopped and quieted to a consistent hum. Emma just watched, because she didn't know the words. She tried a little humming to look more like a parishioner.

The hum continued until Billy Barrows spoke. "Brethren and sistren, we come today to raise up hands in the name of the Lord. We come today to pray for the soul of Kisten Hollis, who had fallen from the faith. She needed the power of the Holy Ghost." His voice rose.

"Have you got the Holy Ghost, huh? Yeah. You got the greatest power in you that's in the whole world."

Reverend Barrows stared at an invisible point on the back wall and whooshed his hands, like he was flinging something distasteful from his fingertips. "Right inside that body is the greatest power ever been known to man and ever will be known to man, is God Himself," he called. "You that has the Holy Ghost has got it in you. It's *your fault* for not using it. It's not God's fault. God gave it to you to use, and if you don't want to get in shape to use it—hey, listen, hold it, hold, let me tell your mind, listen to me. Kisten had the Holy Ghost, she just didn't use it. Kisten, Kisten, you couldn't know, you couldn't've known, I kept it from you..." His voice cracked, and he stopped his litany abruptly.

As Emma watched, his hands came up the sides of his face like spiders crawling, and when they landed in his standup tufts of gray, he started hitting himself in the head, smacking himself in the temples like the spiders had burrowed into his brain. She glanced over at Will, horrified, but he just stared ahead.

After what seemed like forever but was, in reality, only a couple of seconds, the preacher stopped and shook himself. "Do you want to use it? Do you?"

More hands were raised to the sky, and sporadic amens peppered the air.

"Children!" He almost yelled now, and the voice Emma had thought of as reedy took on a dramatic lower tone. He cleared his throat. "Now we need to learn how to worship God worse than anything in the world. We learn how to repent a little bit, but some of us ain't learned how to fully repent! Repentance is to quit doing anything and not go back to it. Change your walk of life!" he bellowed. "Change your walk of life, change your way of thinkin', change your way of talkin'." At this, a woman in the front row fell to her knees, sobbing.

Will and Emma stared at each other. *I don't know. It does seem like this level of emotion could sure drive someone to murder. It's powerful feelings, for sure.*

"Change everything in you." He put his hand on the sobbing woman's head and said softly, "Jesus can make a new creature in God out of you."

At this, a large man in denim overalls arched his balding head backward and started muttering. The sounds he made were not any language Emma knew. He had been doing that for about thirty seconds when a man to the left of Emma and Will joined in. Will gripped Emma's hand, and she didn't even have the presence of mind to pull away. By the time the reverend spoke again, maybe ten people were taking part in this alternative form of communicating. *Oh, lordy lordy. We sure are conspicuous now. But what should I do? I'm no actor, and I'm not feeling the spirit like these people.* She held tight to Will's hand.

"And these signs shall follow them that believe!" Billy Barrows boomed. He stood behind the two boxes sitting on the table. "In my name shall they cast out devils; they shall speak with new tongues; they shall take up serpents; it shall not hurt them." He opened one of the boxes and thrust his hands in. To a chorus of *ahhhs* and small screams, he brought out a massive, curling snake.

It undulated as Billy Barrows held it aloft by its middle. Emma knew snakes were supposed to be held by the head to keep them from biting, but this man cradled the snake's stomach with eerie calm. He reached in with his other hand and brought out two more writhing reptiles. Only about ten feet away, Emma could see the rattle on one. She watched, transfixed. Will looked disgusted, like he was watching poorly practiced circus theatrics.

"Are you in the spirit?" the Reverend shouted. "If you got the spirit, join me in followin' the signs. Join me!"

Emma was astonished when three men and one woman got up. They went to the box, and each retrieved a snake. The woman, one of the few she'd seen in a skirt, took her smaller snake and placed it on top of her head, drawing its head and tail over her ears, framing her face with the snake. Emma held her breath, but the look on the woman's face could only be described as beatific. She held on to the snake frame and smiled.

Will's voice came into her ear. "I guess I don't have the faith because this scares the shit out of me. Can we go?"

Emma couldn't believe the scene in front of her. People were either down on their knees with heads in hands or swaying like reeds in the wind, eyes closed, muttering in the language nobody knew. She nodded, and they ducked out a side door. The Sunday-morning air flowed crisp and clean, and they both breathed it in.

Emma released Will's hand, flushing again. "Whoo-ee! That was the wildest scene I've been in for a long time. You?"

"I've seen some things," said Will, "but that was right up there. Do you want to get coffee? We could discuss what we learned and how it might apply to Kisten and what happened at the homecoming dance."

"You said whomever we're looking for would have to be a collector, right?" Emma asked, leaning against the side of the church.

"Yes, that's right."

"I wonder..." She tilted her head toward one of the side windows. "Yes, coffee, but we have to wait until the service is over. I saw two Pinewood students in there, and I think we should ask them one question." Sarah and Joseph, the brother and sister who'd been knocked over at the vigil at the school, were at the service. Emma hadn't seen them until after Reverend Barrows started preaching.

"Let me guess. The question is whether or not that box of snakes belongs to Barrows."

"Yes. That's a collection if I've ever seen one." Emma shivered at the memory of the snake cradling the woman's face.

EMMA AND WILL EACH drove their respective modes of transport to a coffee shop in the middle of town, Emma having politely refused a ride on Will's motorcycle. As much as the thrill of the open road sounded exhilarating, ever since Emma had seen a man on a motorcycle die at the hands—at the wheels—of a Mack truck, "hawgs" had terrified her.

The man hadn't been killed by the truck, but the impact had sent him skidding across the road and the motorcycle arcing through the sky to land on top of him. All the leather and the strongest helmet in the world couldn't have saved him. Plus, Emma remembered the hand-holding happening at the service. *No flirting. Just investigate.*

Will waited for her at a table in the back of the shop. She ordered a bagel and coffee and sat down with him.

His eyes blazed. "Wow" was all he said.

"You know, I've heard about those churches my whole life, but I'd never actually been in one of them," Emma said. "Don't you think they're amazing?"

"I'm torn between amazing and completely wacko," Will said. "The jury's still out."

She nodded. "No, I know. Most people would be right there with you on the wacko. But I just mean... it's amazing to have such a powerful belief in something, such an all-fired *trust* that you'll be protected from harm. Don't you ever wish for that? I sure do."

Will sipped his coffee. "I believe in lots of things. I have trust that I will be protected from harm, to an extent, just by being aware of my surroundings and considered in my choices. But I don't *seek out* the harm to prove my trust. I don't believe that God, the universe, whatever, gets its jollies out of tests."

"What about that Harley out there?" Emma teased him. "Aren't you seeking out a little harm there?"

"Well, I didn't say I hide out in a box, either." He grinned. "Aren't you seeking out a little harm here with me? What if the history teacher sees us?"

"His name is Hunter, and it's not like I'm sitting on your lap." She changed the subject, knowing that Hunter would not be happy if he knew she was here. "So what do you think? Do you think that pastor killed Kisten Hollis? Or someone else within the church? Sarah said the snakes belonged to Barrows, and he brought them with him every time."

"I don't know. It certainly seems possible, doesn't it? Especially with all that 'Kisten had the Holy Ghost, but she didn't use it. She'd fallen from the faith' nonsense. And what about that weird pause when he was smacking himself in the head? What's up with *that*? Definite weird behavior. As if the rest of it wasn't."

Emma thought. "But why would he hide the venom in her insulin vial? That doesn't fit with what we saw in there. Those people face the harm by choice. They take up those snakes with both eyes open. Kisten had faith that the insulin would lower her blood sugar, not that it would kill her."

"I don't know. That pastor doing it still seems pretty likely to me."

Emma considered. *I know I didn't see Pastor Billy Barrows anywhere near the punch bowl last night, or at the dance at all—I was more watchful than all that, I think.* "What about the notes? Kisten's sounded religious. It said something about her going to hell, if I remember, but that could be a general threat that has nothing to do with religion. But wait! She even said the note sounded like something the pastor said at her church. I think she even mentioned Barrows by name."

She stirred another cream into her coffee, noting that her mug was more like cream with a little bit of coffee rather than the other way around. "Plus, same thing with putting the poison in the punch bowl at the dance. Only a few of the kids at TJ even go to the Holiness church. So we're going to have a big secret snake venom poisoning to weed out all the kids who are faith-free? I just don't buy it."

"What notes?" Will asked.

"Oh, you didn't know about that? Girls from two popular groups at the school got threatening notes. So did Leslie and I. Plus, there was some vandalism on the gym wall that said about the same thing as the notes. They seem related, especially since Kisten was one of the girls who got a note." She munched on her bagel, sipping her cream-with-coffee. *Good.*

"Hmm. No, I can't see that as a churchy-type thing either. 'Course, I don't really see torturing 'heretics' as a churchy thing either, but I guess tell it to the Crusaders. Should I worry about you? Now that two people who've been singled out—all got these notes, I mean—have been poisoned."

Emma got up to put her bagel basket in the tray above the trash can. "No, don't worry about me or the others. We've now been exposed to the snake venom, and that seems to be the killer's only means of destruction. I can't think about it anymore right now. I have to go home. Thanks. Thank you for sitting through church with me."

He smiled. "I will get you on the back of that motorcycle one day."

She pictured motorcycles past, arcing over the street to land smack dab on top of past drivers. And she pictured Hunter, her handsome philosopher. *I can't. I won't.* "Um. Don't spend a lotta time holdin' your breath."

EMMA PULLED INTO HER driveway and smiled at the twitching tail-wagger whose face was pressed up against the window. Sir Toby greeted her at the door, and Emma talked to her and Trinky while cleaning off the smudgy tongue marks left on the window. "Hi, babies! My, did we have an adventure today. Some really brave, possibly crazy, people pulled snakes out of a box and played with them. Kinda like this." She perched the cat's body on the top of her head and dangled her paws on either side of her ears. Trinky just sat on the top of her head, purring. "Well, it was a lot scarier than that," she said. "Trust me."

Emma sat on the couch to watch TV. She flipped through numerous religious programs and finally found a *Law & Order* rerun she could try to solve as she watched. Maybe she could call Detective Niome tomorrow, now that everybody knew the type of poison that had killed Kisten, to tell him Pastor Barrows had a collection of snakes. But she knew he was less than helpful as a rule. Maybe she could find Allie, the student in the bathroom who'd had a stomachache the night of the dance, and ask her if she'd seen anyone who didn't belong at the punchbowl. She took her phone out and pulled up the photos of the notes, but the Scribble font was so common. Knowing the name of the font didn't seem helpful. *Sheesh.* The television murders were a lot easier to solve than this one was turning out to be.

"I have been studying how I may compare
This prison where I live unto the world;
And for because the world is populous,
And here is not a creature but myself,
I cannot do it."

—*Richard II*, 5.5.1–5

Chapter 18
Monday, September 21

Emma checked Leslie's room first thing when she arrived at school Monday morning. The same grizzled substitute she'd had for the in-service was perched on a stool at the front of the room. No Leslie. Emma knew she'd been released from the hospital on Sunday, but phone calls to her house went unanswered. *I hope she's okay. I'll try her again at lunch.*

Detective Niome wasn't at the station yet when she called him, either. This annoyed Emma, although she knew most jobs didn't require people to start by seven a.m. For some reason, she had a need for everyone to be on call and ready to do anything possible to catch Kisten's killer. *A child's killer, for Pete's sake! Is that too much to ask?* So she left a message about Pastor Barrow's box of snakes with Officer Ted, the monosyllabic sidekick with the Incredible Hulk shoulders.

When she got back to her room, Hunter was sitting at her desk. He was twirling her Shakespeare paperweight from the top of William's somewhat conical head. "Hey, lovely," he said.

"Hunter. Hi." She flushed, feeling a little guilty about her meeting with Will yesterday. *But why should I feel guilty?* She hadn't done anything. Fleeting impure thoughts did not an infidelity make. "Happy Monday."

He flashed a dimple. "Happy start-of-the-week to you too. How's Leslie?"

"I don't know. She's not here today, and she didn't answer her phone yesterday."

"Probably just taking a little extra recovery time. I'm sure she's fine. The question is, how are *you*?"

Emma started. "I'm fine. I didn't get poisoned, you know. Just had a little... fainting spell, that's all."

He placed the bust gently back on the corner of the desk. "No, that's not what I mean. You've been a little... distant. I was wondering if something's wrong."

"N-No, of course not. I'm just preoccupied, you know, with Leslie getting sick and the whole snake-venom poisoner. Leaves not much room in the brain." She bent down and hugged him. "I'm fine." *I'd be finer if I wasn't so all-fired distracted by Dr. Will Capshaw. Why is he in my head? Hunter is wonderful. Just because he doesn't have tattoos or drive a motorcycle doesn't mean he's boring. Maybe he's just smart.* Emma hoped she wasn't backsliding into one of those girls who wanted the bad boys, because she didn't think her heart could take it.

He hugged back, hard. "Good. I thought it might be the whole meeting-your-mom thing."

"No, that's not it. But since you brought it up, why have you been so freaked out about my momma? She's as harmless as a firefly, I promise."

"Does she glow in the dark too?" He sighed. "I want to meet her. Really. And I want you to meet my parents too. I've been dying for a trip to the beach. It's just—"

"What?" Emma brought her stool over and sat next to Hunter. "It's just what? It bothers me that we've been together a year, and this connection hasn't happened. My family is really important to me."

"I know. I know it is. Family matters to me too."

"Then why?" She squeezed his hands.

"It's just that I had this girlfriend in college. Melissa. We'd been going out for about six months when her parents came into town to visit. We all went to dinner, and they were really nice and all, but then she started hounding me to meet *my* parents. So I drove her up to Stockton from LA one long weekend. And that was nice too. But from then on, she had this... oh, I don't know... this drive. She started dropping little hints about marriage and babies, even brought one of those bride magazines into my apartment. We were barely twenty. She went completely bonkers."

"Did you break up with her?"

"No, I didn't. Not 'til about five months later. I told myself it was a common phenomenon for girls and that patience would help her realize we were too young, and I held on. Until—" Hunter cracked his knuckles, the loud pop echoing in the small room.

"Until?"

"Until she came to my place one day with her little twin nieces. She was babysitting, and she brought them in and painted this whole picture for me that had apparently been in her head. She told me what our babies would be named, and where we would live, and what jobs would be best for us. I couldn't handle it. Anyway, that's why I haven't done the parent intro. Call it the fear factor."

"Did you ever tell her you felt this way? I know that list she made for you sounds aggressive and pushy, but maybe she didn't know how she was coming across. She was blinded by her wants for the two of you." *Or maybe she didn't even know what she wanted. Do I even know what I want? Sometimes I'm not sure.*

"No, she and I never talked like this, about our feelings and fears."

Kids were starting to come in for first hour. Emma stood and then squatted down next to Hunter. "I promise," she whispered. "I promise to keep my biological clock out of things. My momma won't affect that, anyway. *She* thought I was way too young to get married the first time, and she doesn't want me to make that same mistake all over again. I promise, okay?"

He stood up. "I know. I know you're not like Melissa, all girls aren't crazy, etcetera, etcetera. My brain knows it. Just gotta teach my reflexes. I'll see you at lunch?"

She nodded and waved to him as he strolled out the door, watching him go despite a couple of catcalls from her students. *Hmmm. Maybe we both need some more self-exploration on the concept of long-term commitment. I don't know. I just know I want to be happy. I* think *I can be happy with him.* Emma took her place at the front of the room. "Now, class, how about we write some memoirs?"

HUNTER WASN'T IN THE small lounge off the library when Emma got there at lunch, but Leslie was. Her pale face was expressionless as she shoved food around on her lunch tray, and her usually flawless razor-cut bob was less than pristine. It unnerved Emma to see this break from perfection.

"Hi," Emma said. "How are you feelin'? I saw a sub this morning. Thought you were taking a recovery day."

"Yeah, well, I needed to sleep in. But I didn't want to waste a whole sick day on being sick." Leslie patted her cheeks, obviously trying to bring some color to her wan complexion.

Emma laughed. "Isn't that the point of sick days?"

"Maybe for some people. I usually call mine 'well days,' and when I can't deal with this place or waking up early one more time, or even if I just want to take the day and drive to Denver to shop, that's when I use them. Keeps me from being sick, I swear."

"You're not eating," Emma said. "That's a new one."

"Mrs. Albert found out about the ulcer," Leslie said glumly. "She's making me—ack!—healthy food. No spices, nothing fried or too rich or too good. Please don't make me say any more. It's too depressing."

"Well, you oughta be happy she's concerned about your health. We all are. Did you try it? The... what is it, anyway?"

She squinched her face. "It's some sort of a salad. I'm afraid to try it. I know what it's going to taste like, and I think I might lose the will to go on."

"Come on. Try it. Besides, you've gotta have the will to go on. We still don't know who killed Kisten or who tried to kill you and possibly everyone at the dance. Plus, we have to find that Shawn guy over at the junior high so you can start schooling him in the lessons of love."

Leslie took a bite, shrugged, and took another. "Not totally indigestible, I guess."

"You know Mrs. Albert's a genius." Emma took a bite. "C'mon. I think it's fantastic! She'll get that ulcer fixed faster'n green grass through a goose, just you wait."

Leslie tried some more salad and nodded. "What's been happening since I've been out? Not the Shawn thing, the killer thing. Fill me in."

"Well, I went to see Reverend Billy Barrows preach at the Holiness church yesterday. He handled some purty big snakes, as did some of his congregants."

"You went to that church by yourself? Are you crazy?"

"I wasn't by myself. Dr. Capshaw was there too."

Leslie smirked. "Hmmm. Playing detective with Dr. Will? How is he? As a detective, I mean."

"Shut. Up." Emma dipped her fork into more of Leslie's healthy salad. It was good, with walnuts and apples and a flavor Emma didn't recognize. A healthy, non-ulcer-aggravating spice, she was sure. "I didn't go to the church with him. He came all on his own. He had the same idea I had as far as the pastor killing Kisten."

Leslie moved the tray back to her. "And how did it go? Did you confront that Barrows guy? What about the other people handling snakes?"

"I did see those students, Sarah and Joseph, who were at the demonstration here at the school. They confirmed the snakes belonged to the pastor. But no confrontations from me or Dr. Will at the service. It was way too uncomfortable, what with the people muttering in strange languages and a woman making a snake frame around her face."

Leslie's eyes widened. "A woman making a what?"

Emma sighed. "Never mind. You had to be there. Anyway, I don't think he did it. I called Niome this morning to let him know about his collection, but I just don't buy it, Les. I know he said things at the funeral that may have sounded like he blamed Kisten for being faithless, or whatever, but what about the notes and the graffiti? In this day and age, we are much too aware of interlopers on campus for somebody not to have seen him and reported it." With her animated hands, she almost knocked her brown-bag lunch clean off the table. "And what about the poison put in the punch bowl that almost killed you? I'd never seen him here at the school before that demonstration, and I am ninety-nine-point-nine percent sure he wasn't anywhere near the dance."

Leslie took another bite. "Maybe he's blaming the whole school for being faith free. Dances, people making out on the dance floor, spiking the punch. A haven of sin and all that."

"Maybe. But I just don't see it. Again, I didn't see the Reverend at the dance. I didn't see anyone who didn't belong."

"Who made the punch for the dance?" Leslie asked. "Couldn't he have done it before it came out to the table?"

"I thought of that already." Emma tapped the empty salad tray. "See? Genius, I say. Speaking of whom, Mrs. Albert made the punch as a favor for the homecoming committee. I checked. Whoever's doing this feels personally wronged by those girls, by us. I just—"

"Hello, ladies. How's your lunch today?" Edward stood in the doorway, back to the original bow tie and high-water pants. "Any ideas on the killer? I meant to tell you—I saw Alexa Champlain next to the refreshment table at the dance. I think her purse was sitting on the round table next to it. I only saw her there briefly, though. I think she was just powdering her nose. I never saw her with the punch." He smoothed his hair. "Detective Niome came here earlier, looking for Blake Candelar."

"Gah! We've already covered that," Leslie said. "He needs to catch up. Did he say anything to you? Emma called him this morning about snakes."

"Just that he 'had it covered.'" Edward made air quotes with his fingers. "But he warned me not to eat or drink anything, just in case."

"That figures," said Emma. "Just in case he's totally incompetent, like we always thought. Leslie, why don't you go ahead and get him back? Then tie 'im up and leave 'im in your house, so we can continue—"

Leslie's eyes popped right out of her face, and she vibrated her head furiously.

Oh, yeah, shoot. Not everybody knows about that. Emma blushed and covered her mouth with her hands then made a hole and spoke through it. "I mean, get him back into your good graces so we can continue our own investigation." She removed her hands and mouthed, "Sorry." *Of course that football-star-meets-homecoming-queen-and-someone-ends-up-deflowered story is not the kind of story Leslie wants advertised.* Emma barreled through Edward's briefly alarmed expression at the "tie him up" sentence. "Niome's such a dolt," she finished lamely.

Leslie tapped Emma's shoulder. "I'm going to keep looking into the Reverend Barrows angle. I need something to do after school that'll keep me away from Pizza Hut."

"Can I do anything?" asked Edward.

"Sure, Eddie. Why don't you come with me? Watch my back. Unlike Emma, who flits around unprotected, I am careful with this temple that is my bod."

Emma snickered. "Sure. Careful. Tell that to your friends at Pizza Hut. Tell it to the giant hole in your gut. Hey! It's a poem." She smiled, pleased. "I'll run in to Alexa's fourth-hour study hall and see if she had any punch. Maybe if we treat her like she is someone who can help us, she'll adjust her attitude accordingly. I really don't think she has the sophistication to plan Kisten's murder. Plus, can you see her milking a *snake*?"

Everyone shook their heads.

"Nope, me neither. Edward, since you saw her sitting near the punch bowl, I'll make sure to find out if she saw anything."

The door to the library burst open, and Hunter tore past the front desk and into the lounge. "There's another message," he wheezed. "It's on the wall in Leslie's room."

Emma, Hunter, Leslie, and Edward pounded through the halls to Leslie's room. Fourth period had just started for everybody, so students were already in class. Thank goodness, because if they saw the message, there was bound to be panic.

Leslie's back wall usually held black-and-white Ansel Adams and Scott Mutter posters set off by bold red and purple backgrounds. Now, the framed posters were scattered on the floor. On the wall, the red and purple construction paper had been shredded away to leave a big space in the center. In crimson spray paint, dripping down like a hideous wound, was written "Why don't you die already?"

Some of the red construction paper patches left on the wall stood out like more splashes of blood, so after taking a picture of the dangling shreds to give to the police, Emma started taking those off.

Leslie simply sat down at one of the students' desks and stared. "Who is it that hates me so much?" she whispered. "'Do all men kill the things they do not love? Hates any man the things they would not kill?'" She put her head down on the desk. "Ohhh, this really bites for my ulcer. I bet Bassanio didn't have an ulcer." Her voice floated up. "Shylock? No way. His gut was as strong as steel."

Edward patted her back awkwardly.

Emma questioned Hunter, who stood on the other side of the bloody message, taking down paper remnants. "Did you see anyone around? What were you doing here anyway?"

"I was looking for you. I always go from your room to Leslie's room to the lounge. You're usually in one of those places. Anyway, lunch wasn't over yet, so there were a couple of kids in the hall. No one I knew."

"Well, I hope it won't be someone I recognize. This is horrible and scary," said Emma. "Did someone call the police?"

"Yes. I ran to Nate's office before I found you. He said he'd have Detective Niome come right away. Nate actually skateboarded back here with me to look at the message. But all he could say was 'No way, man.' This is for sure something he's not prepared to handle."

"I don't know if any one of us is prepared to handle this," replied Emma. "It's so awful. I mean, think about it. It really has to be someone here, a student or staff member, doesn't it? No way could a stranger come in, what, like four times now to do damage and no one sees anything? Even Reverend Barrows."

"*Especially* Reverend Barrows, what with the Don King hairstyle and early-seventies wardrobe." Leslie's voice wafted up from under the hair falling forward on her cheeks. She still had her face on the desk.

Emma noticed the door in the back corner of the room. It did open to the parking lot. "Hey, look. I bet somebody could get in this way without being seen. Even Billy Barrows." She glanced at her phone. "It's almost time for fifth period. Leslie, why don't you bring your class to my room? I'm sure we could take our minds off this killer with a rousin' game of... something. Literary Jeopardy? Seniors vs. freshmen."

Emma glanced once more at the corner door before heading out. *I need more time to think. Why would someone focus on Leslie and me and cheerleaders and maybe SSP? We don't even have anything in common beyond the fact that we're all here. Could it be just because we're all women? Fairly visible women here at the school, I guess, but is that enough to kill for? Maybe someone thinks everyone is bullied by cheerleaders and SSP, and that Leslie and I aren't doing enough to stop it. But why would it be just my and Leslie's responsibility to stop it all? Ugh, it's all too much.* "C'mon, Les. Let's go teach."

Leslie lifted her head from the desk like it was heavy, averted her face from the ruined wall, and followed the other three out.

"Life is as tedious as a twice-told tale,
Vexing the dull ear of a drowsy man,
And bitter shame hath spoiled the sweet world's taste,
That it yields naught but shame and bitterness."

—*King John,* 3.4.108–11

Chapter 19
Tuesday, September 22

Emma spent Monday evening with Leslie, going over all the clues they had so far. A big fat zero. Blake Candelar and his poisonous frogs had been ruled out. Alexa Champlain was a long topic of conversation. Emma had found her after school to ask if she'd seen anything suspicious next to the punch bowl, to which she'd received a haughty list of all of her non-detention-worthy activities at the dance, including a fairly comprehensive list of who she'd seen there and how no one unusual had approached her. The possibility of Alexa learning about snakes and then handling them to extract their venom strained even Hollywood-movie credibility. Her MO was unsophisticated and in-your-face, and snakes were... sneaky. Subversive. Behind the scenes. It just did not compute in Emma's book. The paint on Leslie's wall, now, she could see Alexa doing something like that, but not the snakes.

They'd spent most of their time sitting on Emma's little striped couch, gleaning comfort from Trinky and Sir Toby on their laps. Emma's lips had tightened as she remembered. Those crimson messages on the walls shouted, "I'm frustrated! I'm confused! I don't understand something, so I'm lashing out! People disappoint me!" And Emma could see why it would happen to Leslie. Anyone who didn't know the real Leslie and only saw the façade of perfection might see her as the perfect target. This killer really couldn't see the forest for the trees.

They figured it had to be a student or staff member because they'd had to rule out Pastor Barrows and most of his flock. Leslie had called the church and discovered that the congregation was on a retreat for four days prior to Kisten's death and had only returned after they got the news.

Emma reminded Leslie of her thoughts about the doors in the backs of their classrooms leading to the parking lot, and they decided it could be a way for people to get in and out—if they had a key, which went right back to student or staffer. Charlie Foreman was the only staffer Emma thought poorly of, really, but being a chauvinist didn't automatically translate to killing women. The only thing they knew about the three new staff members came from the conversation Emma had overheard in the bathroom, and that had been about *men*—a stepfather, a stepbrother, and Charlie, the overexcited lister of insults. Emma had asked some more questions about 4-H and the ag program run by Otto Henry, as in, were snakes ever a type of animal taught in 4-H? Leslie said no, it was all farm animals like sheep, pigs, and cows. Or chickens. But they did some internet research on the subject, just in case.

Emma remembered something they hadn't followed up on—Otto's class being in the library the day of the notes. They'd been so distracted by all the goings-on at the homecoming dance, and then Leslie's ulcer, and—*excuses! These are all excuses. Good grief, Charlie Brown.* She made a mental note to follow through on that angle ASAP.

The whole investigation had ground to a stupefying halt, and Emma running around all nervous and twitchy wasn't helping matters. *I feel like an anti-detective, a sleuth who's been turned inside out and spit back out onto the floor to emerge as an empty-headed toddler.* She remembered a quote from Hamlet about the great baby trapped in its swaddling clothes, or clouts. *Look at me, remembering and associating some Shakespeare. At least there's that.*

THEY MET OUTSIDE LESLIE'S room before first period. Leslie squared her shoulders and took a deep breath before they entered. Emma gasped. The back wall was clean.

Paint. The janitors must've stayed to paint over the graffiti. Oh, the unsung heroes, she thought for the hundredth time since she'd started this job. All the paper scraps were gone, but Leslie's prints were laid gently atop her black lacquered desk, ready for repositioning.

"Oh, bless our custodial staff," said Leslie. "I was so not looking forward to seeing pale bloody paint-shadows of death threats on my wall." She picked up one of the prints and handed it to Emma. "Wanna help?"

"Oh, I can never get it all crooked and artsy like you do it. Mine just look crooked like I can't see so well. I especially couldn't do justice to your cool new feet picture. But I'll—"

"Look at this." Leslie had picked up the other two by their frames and spied something on the desk underneath. "Wow. Look at this." She picked up a small gold-plated pin, the kind that poked through shirts and letter jackets and was connected to an earring-post back on the other side. The pin had three letters—FFA.

"What is that? What does it stand for?"

Leslie's eyes gleamed. "It's our first real clue. Vandal-slash-killer must have dropped it during his reign of terror through my room. Custodians are always picking up things that end up on the floor in my room to keep them from getting vacuumed up. They leave them on my desk. His pin must have been on the floor, maybe under Ansel Adams."

Emma's eyes went wide. "His?"

Leslie slapped the pin into Emma's palm. "FFA stands for Future Farmers of America. As in, Thomas Jefferson High wins 4-H awards all the time. As in, we have this really great agriculture program and a studly, overall-wearing new teacher. As in—"

"As in Otto Henry? I was *just* thinking about him this morning because we never followed up on questioning him about his class being in the library on the day the notes showed up." Emma clapped her hands together, shifted the pin to her fingertips, and lifted it up, examining it in the fluorescent classroom lights. The pin was in the shape of a little metal owl grasping some sort of a crest.

"As in Otto Henry."

"You think, really?" Emma said. "I mean, I know we didn't come off so great with that group of new teachers, but really? Couldn't this be a kid's FFA pin?"

Leslie pointed. "No. Pay attention to the fine print at the bottom of the owl's butt. It's a supervisor's pin, and he is the only FFA teacher at TJ High."

"Ooh, finally. Yay! That is a genuine clue, then." Her face fell. "But Otto's really nice. He doesn't seem like a killer or sneaky or subversive—nothing like that."

"I was just remembering something," mused Leslie. "A whole lot of people came to see me when I was in the hospital, including most of the teachers and a lot of students. But I had to have a shot, Demerol or something with an equally high street value, and I was pretty out of it for a while. Edward told me those three came to see me—Otto, Diane, and Rhiannon. He told me I stared at them like they were aliens from outer space. I don't remember, but they were there. Maybe he's pissed because I wasn't falling all over myself in gratitude about their visit." She took the pin from Emma's hand and sat at her desk, rotating it over and over.

"We got our first threatening notes before you ever went to the hospital, though. And that still doesn't give us a reason why he'd try to kill all those people. I mean, even if he felt slighted by you, he'd—shouldn't we take that to the police? We shouldn't have touched it. What if there were fingerprints? Oh my gosh, I'll never,

never get this detectin' thing right." Emma dropped her head in her hands.

Leslie patted her head. "Naw. Look how small it is. Plus, the janitor picked it up too. There's no way there'd be usable fingerprints." She got up from the desk and patted Emma on the back. "Besides, we don't need to worry about police procedure when our chief of detectives is so useless. We just need to catch us a killer."

Emma stared. "Maybe we should. Worry, I mean. This is really exciting, a real clue, but if I'm reading people so wrong that I can't even comprehend Otto as our killer, then maybe I'm missing the danger level too. Should we leave it to Carl?"

"I think if we had a detective who followed some discernible procedure, maybe. But with Niome... not so much. What are we going to do about Otto?"

"I don't know. The direct-confrontation method worked last year, but only with the suspects who turned out not to be suspects. And if it's Otto, hasn't he proved himself to be not only violent, but premeditatively violent? To figure out about Kisten's insulin and be able to inject the venom into it? That's possibly not a word, I know. *Premeditatively.* I'm all twitterpated, but this killer doesn't seem to be. This... this campaign of terror was planned. He's out to punish someone."

Leslie held her head in her hands. "I just don't get it. Why would he be concentrating on girls? Why would he want to punish girls? He seemed nice, all shucks and Barney Fife, with the overalls and the blue-jeaned pigs. And he was dancing away at the homecoming dance. He said he didn't have any punch, but... " She pursed her lips. "I mean, sure, he might not be all that comfortable around us, but still, everything about him feels... nice."

"I think it was blue-belted pigs." Emma thought some more. "Maybe it's something with his mother. Doesn't it always have something to do with the mother? Maybe she locked him in a closet when he was little so she could go carousin' with men. She didn't want Otto cramping her style."

Kids were starting to come in for Leslie's first-hour class. "I've got an idea," Emma said. "Can you tell them to wait?" She pulled Leslie out of the classroom and over three doors to her room, where her Creative Writing class meandered in.

Leslie sat down in a student desk to wait for the plan.

As soon as the whole group arrived, including a boy with purple hair who kicked Leslie out of his seat, Emma began.

"Hey, students." She smiled. "Today we're going to do a writing sketch on character motivation. Your character's name is..."

She glanced at Leslie, who mouthed, "Otis."

"Whose name is Otis. Otis hates women. Hates them so much that he wants to hurt them indiscriminately. I want you to write a character sketch on Otis and why he hates them so much."

A redhead in the back row raised her hand. "What does *indiscriminately* mean?"

Emma laughed. "Can anyone help Mary out on that one?"

Purple hair raised his hand. "It means without boundaries. He hates all women regardless of race, creed, religion, size of their boobs, size of their—"

"Ahem," said Emma. "We get the idea, Matt. Thank you very much. And now that the definition has been phrased so eloquently..."

The redhead raised her hand.

"Look it up, Mary. Now that the idea's been clarified, I'd like to change the requirement a little. Otis doesn't hate *all* women, he..." Again, she deferred to Leslie.

"He hates women he perceives as social," Leslie offered. "Maybe the popular type or ones who are in the public eye, who know a lot of people, who can talk to anyone."

Mary raised her hand. "Why would he hate women like that?"

Emma grinned. "That's what you're going to have to figure out using your super-creative brains and extensive knowledge of cop shows. Go to it."

They fell to the task, and Emma went into the hall with Leslie.

"I'm surprised nobody asked if this assignment had anything to do with Kisten or the poisoned punch bowl. You do realize someone will write about how Otis got kidnapped by well-socialized female aliens and probed in all the wrong places," said Leslie.

They both laughed. "Oh, I'm sure," Emma said." But maybe we'll get some inadvertent help on how to proceed from *someone* less *X-Files* and more... case files. Perhaps someone already knows who poisoned Kisten and the punch bowl and will let it slip in the guise of this fictional character. I think it's a good assignment, anyway."

Leslie raised her hand. "What does *inadvertent* mean?"

"Get to class, you. I'm sure your kids are ready to invoke the five-minute rule. Think about 'Otis,' and we'll talk more about it at lunch." Emma went back to her students, all of whom had started talking the second she left the room. But after she listened for a bit, she smiled. They were all talking about Otis.

LESLIE BROUGHT FOOD into Emma's room at lunch. "Mrs. Albert made health food again. I'm afraid this one may have bran or tofu or something equally frightening." Leslie placed the two trays on Emma's desk and shuddered.

"Come on, Les. Doesn't your stomach feel better?" Emma sat down and tasted it. Some sort of casserole, and healthy or not, Mrs. Albert was a miracle worker.

Leslie shrugged. "Sure, it feels a little better. But I think that's more because of the little purple pills I'm swallowing than from depriving myself of all that is good and holy." She spooned up some casserole and tasted it. "Well, I guess this is okay. Did you get any good Otis sketches?"

"I think you'll survive." Emma took another bite. "Yes, there were some good ones. Including the alien one you predicted, although she got way more into the explanation of the probing than I really cared to read." She grimaced. "The one that made the most sense to me, as far as this case is concerned, came from a kid named Grey. His Otis hates people because he feels like they all have it better than him. Otis only recognizes the slights against him from other people and can't see that everyone has their own trials and tribulations. It made sense to me."

"So where do we go from here?"

"I don't know. Maybe we should go talk to Otto. See if we can get a feel for the situation or his outlook on it. I doubt he has a rattlesnake in his desk he could throw at us."

Leslie spooned up some more casserole. "Okay. But if he does throw a rattlesnake our way, I'm using you as a human shield. I've had enough venom in me to last a lifetime."

Emma picked up their trays. "Fair enough, I guess."

To get to the agriculture building, the two women had to go outside. They went through the library lunchroom and opened a door at the end of the hallway that separated the library from the English classrooms. The ag shop was a long, low-slung building east of the parking lot and football field.

Emma had never been there before, but for some reason, she expected pens and cattle. Maybe smells. Instead, they found two large classrooms and a huge, open warehouse. The corner of the warehouse had a transplanted garden, but there were no farm animals in sight.

They went into one of the classrooms. There were only about ten students, none she knew, writing diligently. Emma glanced at one of the papers. It seemed to be full of word problems. Well, she guessed there must be math involved in farming. A woman Emma didn't recognize stood in the front of the room, wearing cowboy boots and Rockies jeans.

Emma mouthed at Leslie, "Where's Otto?"

She shrugged and proceeded to the front of the room. "Hi there. I'm Leslie Parker, and this is Emma. We're looking for Mr. Henry."

The woman patted her frizzy hair. "You and everyone else. He didn't show up for work today. The secretary said she hasn't been able to reach him, and his friend Diane came in earlier all worried. I'm just subbing, but I know Otto from 4-H competitions. I hope he's all right."

"We do too," said Emma. "We'll let you know if we hear anything." They nodded at the substitute and left the room.

"He's escaped," whispered Leslie as they traveled back toward their classrooms. "He must know we're on to him."

Emma stopped. "How would he know that? We're only just now askin' questions. No one else besides the custodians knows we found the pin. No one else knows anything. Maybe he's just sick."

"Well, he has a lot to learn about this profession if he's just sick," Leslie said. "It's not like a regular job where you might be able to get away with not showing up. Thirty kids are in your room, waiting for you, every seventy-two minutes, and when you're not there and there's no plan, administrators and parents tend to get upset."

"You make it sound like glorified babysitting."

"Some days it feels that way. Only sometimes, mind you."

"I like it," said Emma. "The kids are the best part. But what about Otto? What do we do now?"

"I don't have any idea. We could find out where he lives. Go visit him there?"

Emma put a hand up. "Oh no. He could have a *den* of rattlesnakes at his house. No way are we going over there."

"Chicken. I guess we could call Detective Niome and send him over. I wouldn't mind sending *him* into a den of rattlesnakes."

They'd reached Emma's room. "I doubt he'd be able to just barge into Otto's house. Don't they need a warrant? Somehow, I don't think finding his FFA pin in your room would qualify as probable cause."

Leslie walked backward toward her room, something she did often despite a tendency to back into lockers or students. "Warrant, shmarrant. I say we go for it."

"No way. I say we go to fifth hour then meet up after school to figure out more about Otto and how we can find him." She peeked inside her room.

One of her ninth-grade-composition girls, a timid loner named Ali, stood in front of the Wondrous Wendy poster from the in-service—Emma had hung it in the corner over the reading chair—scanning all the positive affirmations she and Leslie had written. Ali nodded and smiled at Emma. *That's right, Ali. I'm trying to teach you the important stuff.*

On the other side of the door, Leslie shook her head and made a tsk-tsk motion with her hands, which she continued until she backed into a water fountain. Then she shrugged and pivoted, gliding the last few steps to her own room. Emma closed her door and smiled back at Ali. *I'm ready to abandon thoughts of serpents and venom and concentrate on students and victory!*

Chapter 20

Emma was halfheartedly trying to grade papers in her living room, but a *Buffy the Vampire Slayer* rerun was on TV, so mostly, she was watching that. She loved Buffy, not only because the supernatural world of vampires and demons fascinated her, but because Buffy was so fabulous. She put the *grrr* in "girl." Some people might call Emma's love of this campy comic-horror series very un-literary. But those people had never seen Buffy kick butt.

Sir Toby and Trinculo were nestled next to her on the couch but leaped off and raced to the door at the sound of the doorbell. She wanted to watch Buffy throw a vampire across the room, but instead, she groaned and grunted herself out of her seat to go answer it.

It was Leslie bearing pizza. She wore one of her signature rock-concert T-shirts, this one with a long tongue lolling out of a huge mouth. The Rolling Stones, Emotional Rescue tour, 1980.

"Hey," said Emma. "You're not supposed to eat that."

Leslie breezed past. "You're not going to believe this. I found this little place on the very, very east end of town. This isn't pizza. It's health food."

"Sure. And this isn't my house. It's the Waldorf Astoria. Welcome to the dog-hair penthouse."

"No, really. Look." She went into the kitchen and put the box on Emma's breakfast-nook table. "The crust is made outta cauliflower—can you imagine? Low-fat feta cheese. The marinara sauce has no fat, of course. And look at all these vegetables. It's a veritable homage to the four food groups, and it only cost, like, three times as much as a regular pizza because it's so healthy."

Emma crossed her arms and leaned back in a pose she hoped conveyed suspicion and discontent.

Leslie pointed. "See, it's even got turkey pepperoni. 'What, old acquaintance? Could not all this flesh keep in a little life?'"

"I get that you love all those King Henry plays. But those guys are all dead, you know. What would your doctor say?"

Leslie flashed an impish grin. "I don't know. Maybe we should ask a doctor."

"What does that mean?"

"Oh, don't you worry your pretty little debutante head over it. Now eat." Leslie took out one of the larger pieces and stuffed almost half of it into her mouth.

Emma got a couple of plates and napkins, and they sat down at Emma's small breakfast nook, which sat off the back end of the kitchen. Trinky and Sir Toby were lurking around, sniffing for scraps Leslie was only too happy to provide.

"Stop that." said Emma, stepping over to mute the TV. "They're not supposed to beg. So what's up? You just got bored? I told you after school that my attempt to hack into the computer to find out more about Otto didn't work. I'm not nearly as computer savvy as I think I am."

Leslie dropped a piece of pepperoni. "Oops. No, I didn't get bored. I got inspired." Leslie reached into the pocket of her shorts and dropped a piece of paper on the table. "Otto Henry's address. Abigail Patterson gave it to me, although I told her I was taking it to the police."

Emma grabbed the paper and crumpled it in frustration. "I told you, no way. That guy is probably dangerous. Possibly a killer. We can't waltz into his house alone like every stupid girl on every horror movie we've ever seen. We need backup."

Leslie's eyes grew wide. "Who said anything about alone?" As if on cue, the doorbell rang. "And didn't you say I should be consulting a doctor?" She hopped up and sprinted to the door.

"What th—" Emma shoved the last of her pizza into her mouth and walked to the front room.

Dr. Will Capshaw was leaning in the entry. *Oh no. I can't deal with danger of this type either. Double danger and distraction and just—my heart can't handle it.*

"Emma," said Leslie. "Meet Dr. Backup."

He smiled lazily. He wore faded jeans and a white T-shirt stretched tight across his biceps, liquid brown eyes roving over Emma's face. She couldn't maintain the eye contact, instead, flushing and looking down at the floor.

"Leslie filled me in. I'm sure the three of us could handle him and his snakes."

Emma threw her hands up in the air. "Doesn't anybody here read any books? Watch any movies? How about the news? Does anyone watch that? This is a matter for the police. Leslie's almost been killed already, we've all had threatening letters, and this is just too dangerous. I swear, y'all only have one oar in the water right now." She glanced at Will, who seemed to be holding in a laugh, then swiveled her gaze to Leslie. "And if you say 'dangerous, shmangerous,' I'm gonna beat the tar outta you."

Leslie collapsed on the couch. "You sure sound cute when you're mad, Em, but we're stuck. You know the police can't go into Otto's house without a warrant, and this investigation is going nowhere fast. Come on. It's still daylight. We'll just knock on the door and ask some polite questions. Then we'll be out. Pleeeez?"

"Do either of you have any weapons, at least? Butter knife, letter opener, something? Where's my pink stun gun when I need it?" Her face fell, because she thought her pink stun gun was at Hunter's house. *Ugh. I really should invite him too. But the thought of these two together and the smart-alecky comments they'll probably make toward each other, on top of all this stress we're already dealing with... nope.*

Will came in and closed the door. "Those types of weapons don't do any good. Too easily reversed and used back on you. I am pretty adept at martial arts, though."

Emma rolled her eyes. "Your body is the weapon, right?"

Will grinned. "So says my sensei." He sat next to Leslie and ground his hands into his knees. "I had to cut that young girl open, Emma," he said, and he closed his eyes like he was seeing it again. "I had to look at the insides of a seventeen-year-old, and no one should have a reason to do that. I think we should do what we can to find out who killed her."

Emma sighed. "Okay. But we have to leave now during daylight. And if it looks like it could get too hairy, we abort the mission. Got it?"

Leslie saluted. "Got it. Hairiness equals skedaddle." She patted Will's shoulder. "My, my, some people are such worrywarts, *n'est ce pas*?"

"So where does Otto live?" asked Emma.

"You're never going to believe this," Leslie said. "It's synchronicity, serendipity, and fortuity all rolled into one. He lives in Melvin's old house."

"You're kidding," said Emma.

"Who is Melvin?" asked Will.

Emma sat on the couch arm, picking a dog hair from the couch back behind Leslie. "Melvin McManus is that custodian who was murdered last year at the high school."

"Oh yeah." Will nodded. "Heard about that."

"He happened to be in the wrong place at the wrong time and got the wrong end of a big pewter paperweight smashed into his skull for his troubles. He lived in this cute little house right over by the school." Emma frowned. "How awful to think a murderer might have taken up residence in the home of the murdered."

"Yeah, well, at least we know Melvin wasn't murdered by Otto," said Leslie. She leaned over to Will and spoke in a stage whisper. "Emma caught the murderer. She eavesdropped on some shenanigans, made some connections, and—bam!—we set a trap, and the mouse crept right in."

The "Well, well, well, what do we have here?" look Will gave Emma made her shiver.

Maybe he thinks I'm *the dangerous one.* "I could absolutely use that pink stun gun right now. And some more connections. *Any* connections would be helpful." She groaned in despair. "I still can't believe it's happened again."

"Somehow, your high school is starting to sound more like Hellmouth High of Sunnydale, California." He gestured to the television, where Buffy was drop-kicking a demon. "Only without the vampires. Two murders in two years? I'm glad there are seasoned investigators such as you two working the case." He stood up. "Should we go interrogate?"

Emma led them to the door. "No interrogation. Just polite questions."

This time, Leslie and Will both saluted. "Got it."

THEY TOOK EMMA'S LITTLE green Honda to Otto's house, since Leslie's red convertible was conspicuous and since Emma refused to get on Will's motorcycle—never mind the fact that it couldn't fit three. They pulled into the modest subdivision with small box houses. Melvin's old house stood exactly as Emma remembered, small and square and white with blue shutters, right down to the mailbox shaped like a one-room schoolhouse. She felt a twinge of sadness, remembering the nice man she'd only met twice but learned so much about during the course of their investigation.

Noting the empty driveway and general stillness in the air, the three of them marched up the path and rang the doorbell. No answer. They tried to peek through the windows on either side of the door, but the shades were closed.

Leslie said, "I think we should go in. We know the layout. We know how to break and enter without breaking."

Emma shook her head. "We had an excuse last time we were here. How are we gonna explain it this time? We want to invest in property close to the school? And what if Otto comes home?"

Will was already at the back gate. "I really am house-hunting. Sounds like a great excuse. Come on. I'll keep watch." He whistled for a dog, which demonstrated quicker thinking than they'd had last time they were here. No dog, so he creaked the gate open. "I'll stay back here."

"What if Otto's inside?" asked Emma. "We may need that martial arts thing."

"Good point. Leslie, you keep watch. Emma and I will go in."

And I will keep any and all lascivious thoughts at bay. I think.

Leslie pouted. "How come you get to have all the B and E fun? It was my idea."

"Come on," said Emma. "You can practice your whip-poor-will whistle. Use it as an early warning signal."

"Oooh. Okay." Leslie perched on the gate post and pursed her lips to start practicing bird calls.

Easily entertained, Emma thought to herself, observing her friend. *Always helpful on a stakeout.*

The back door was, predictably in a small town, unlocked. Emma and Will entered, calling out for Otto. No answer. The back door opened to a small, linoleum-tiled kitchen. There were pictures of students holding ribbons over the heads of cows and goats hanging on the refrigerator door. No pictures of snakes.

"I guess we should split up," said Emma. "You go left, and I'll go right."

"What are we looking for?"

"I guess snakes, snake paraphernalia. Maybe a brown bottle with skull and crossbones. Clues, you know."

"Sure," he said. "Clues."

Emma went into the small bedroom to the right of the kitchen. It was undecorated, with a plain green comforter on the bed and a bookshelf filled with books and magazines on agriculture. *What is it about bachelors and the lack of any homey touches whatsoever?* Emma didn't know how anyone could stand to spend time in such sterile, boring places.

There were no clues in Otto's bedroom. Besides the magazines and books, which were all farming and no reptiles, she found nothing. Clean under the bed, closet with lots of button-up shirts and six identical sets of overalls. *Six? Maybe he wears sweats on Sundays. Or a suit for church. But I don't see a suit.* She also didn't see boxes or cages or anything suspicious. No sign of Otto.

She came back out to the living room, where Will was lifting cushions off the couch. "Find anything?"

He showed his empty hands. "There's no sign of any animals, no pieces of paper that might be used to type threatening notes." He held up some envelopes. "Even his bills are boring. Phone bill, utility bill, rent. No personal letters, no pet-store flyers, nothing. If he's our guy, he's hiding his stuff somewhere else."

"Well, I know there's no basement or attic. Did you check the pantry?"

"Lots of cans of sloppy joe sandwich meat. Some chips. That's all."

The couch was boring, too, a plain brown with no pillows or accents. Since Will had searched under the cushions, Emma knelt down and peered under the couch. "What's this?" She pulled out an envelope. Her face fell. "It's empty." The envelope had Otto's name and address typed on the front, with a return address out of San Francisco. "Heritage Harbor," she said. "Do you think that's a business? Sounds like a hotel. I bet he'll never miss an empty envelope that was headed for the trash. I'm gonna take it." Emma pulled open the back door, still holding the folded envelope. "I'll google it."

At the gate, Leslie still practiced her bird calls. "Find anything?"

Will gestured to the envelope Emma held in her hand. "Not much. Empty envelope with alliterative address." He smiled. "See me use English-teacher words? Alliteratively?" He flexed a tattooed bicep. "Me speak gooood."

Leslie took the envelope from Emma and put it in the pocket of her shorts. "I guess we can't expect all investigations to spell themselves out, alliteratively or any other way," she said. "Maybe we can—"

"Excuse me!" The door to the box house across the street popped open, and a woman came out and stood on her front porch. "Can I help you?" The woman had walked straight out of a 1950s movie, with pink curlers wound all over her head and a shapeless green housedress covering ponderous breasts and thick arms. She crossed those arms over her chest and glared. "I don't know you! Who are you? I just saw you comin' out of Otto's house, but I don't see Otto with you. Did you just enter my neighbor's house without his permission?"

"Hi there!" Emma called across the street. "We were just looking for Otto. Can you—"

"Oh no. I saw you three sneaking in and out and all around and up to no good, I can tell." The woman raised a *tsk-tsk* finger and pointed it at Will. "You all look suspicious, but you are definitely a thug, I can tell. Painting all over your body. I bet you drive one-a those Hell's Angels motorcycles, don't'cha?" she asked, completely ignoring the little green Honda in the driveway.

"Ma'am," Will said. "Have you seen Otto Henry? There's a really good reason we—"

"We teach with Otto, and we're worried about him," Leslie said, starting toward the woman. She was stopped by the finger.

"Stop right there!" hissed the woman. "You teach with him? You with the tattoos and the rock and roll T-shirts and the breaking and entering? I don't believe that for one second. You're all mighty suspicious. Wait right there. I'm calling the police." And with that, the woman turned tail and ran back in, slamming the front door of her little box house, which differed from Melvin's—Otto's—house only because the shutters were red.

"Holy cow," said Emma. "What should we—"

"We should run!" Leslie shouted, pushing Emma toward the Honda. Will had already opened the back passenger-side door and hopped in. Emma peeled out, as fast as four cylinders would take them.

EMMA, LESLIE, AND WILL drove into the driveway, laughing over their close call with Otto's neighbor and a joke Will told about dead bodies and a silo. They'd discussed, for a moment, what might happen if the neighbor with the curlers had actually called the police, but none of them believed she actually would, or if she did, they were certain her description of a Hell's Angel with a rock 'n' roll tart alongside him would not result in recognition of two teachers and the medical examiner. They piled out of the car and stopped when they saw Hunter sitting on the front porch. With flowers.

Oh no, ohnoohnoohno. "H-Hi, Hunter," said Emma. "You remember Dr. Capshaw, don't you? From the hospital?"

Hunter stared at Will. "I remember. So I take it you forgot about our date, Emma? It's Tuesday."

Emma's hands flew to her mouth. "Oh shoot. I'm sorry." She stared at Leslie and Will, nodding like a bobblehead doll. "Tuesday night's game night. I've finally started beatin' him at Risk, and..." She hugged herself at the elbows, squeezing hard like she could force a good explanation to appear. "I'm sorry. I forgot."

Will watched the exchange between Hunter and Emma but showed no inclination to jump in and explain.

Leslie grabbed him by the arm and started dragging him away. "Hunter. Emma. Have a great game night. We'll see you tomorrow." She got into her red convertible and sped away, with Will close behind on his Harley.

Hunter watched them go. His face was unreadable and expressionless. "I can't believe you forgot about game night. Where were you?"

"We went to Otto Henry's house."

"The new ag teacher?"

"Yes. See, we found his FFA pin in Leslie's room after her wall was vandalized. We think he could be the one who killed Kisten Hollis."

He crossed his arms over his chest. "So you went off half-cocked to his house? What were you going to do? Hog-tie him to the bed? What if he was there with his snakes and an accomplice or something?"

"We weren't alone. Dr. Capshaw was our backup." *Oh no oh no oh no. That is the wrong thing to say.*

His face fell. "I thought I was your backup."

"You are my backup, Hunter. It's just... Leslie brought him along because of his medical experience, you know. And then there's the whole martial arts thing—"

"Martial arts thing? What, he's some sort of black belt?" Hunter's face screwed up like he'd tasted something awful.

Emma shook her head miserably. "Some sort of something. I don't know. I'm sorry. He was just along for the ride, really. We're so lost with all the stuff happening at school, and I know you're busy helping Charlie Foreman and the football team, and it's... let's play Risk, okay? I'm all ready to beat you again." She hugged him and kissed him on the lips, both cheeks, and his nose.

He grabbed her by the shoulders and just studied her, searching her face like he could find answers there, like he could jump into her mind and swim around. Then he stood and went to get the game.

They played for about three hours, and not much more was said. Emma didn't know what to say.

Are all thy conquests, glories, triumphs, spoils
Shrunk to this little measure?

—*Julius Caesar,* 3.1.149–50

Chapter 21
Wednesday, September 23

Emma was writing lesson plans for the day on the whiteboard, but her mind was elsewhere. It started on the whodunit rollercoaster she'd found herself embroiled in, then jumped to the guilt-o-whirl concerning her repressed interest in Will Capshaw. She loved Hunter, she really did. The part where he wasn't so dangerous or mysterious, well, she loved that too. The thrill of the chase and obsessions with bad boys only sparked briefly, and she'd gone as far as she wanted down that road when she'd been married. She and Will did have a little chemistry, that was true, but when she thought about exploring that and then followed that vision through to the part about not being with Hunter, the thought made her feel icky. *Maybe I should buy Hunter some flowers to make up for forgetting our Tuesday date night.*

She shrugged at the empty room. It was more important to keep herself and the people around her safe. The paltry clue-maybe-not-a-clue they'd encountered at Otto's house had been discouraging, but a deranged rattlesnake owner couldn't be kept a secret forever. Emma was angry with herself for not getting the envelope back from Leslie the previous night because she'd forgotten the name on the front. She knew it started with an *H*, which was that infuriating thing her brain did when a memory escaped her. Happiness Harbor? Honorable Harbor? Some sort of Harbor whose name never came to her, and Leslie never answered her phone. *Ugh.*

Motive was still an issue. She went back to the papers her creative writing class had submitted, explaining the behavior of "Otis," and flipped through them again. A highly creative bunch of people, her students, but not ranking so high on the reality scale. Mary, the hand-raiser, had written that Otis was raised by wolves, and a woman had tried to take him from his pack, which was why he hated them all. Then there was the whole alien-kidnap theory. Emma was pretty sure none of these could apply to Otto.

Of course, she didn't really know that much about Otto. Maybe there were wolves somewhere in his past along with those blue-belted pigs.

As the students started coming in, Leslie followed behind Sophia Bracken, a tiny, elfin-featured girl who sat in the front row. Sophia had written a pretty typical paper on Otis's motive—he was abused by his mother.

"How was game night last night?" asked Leslie. Her tone seemed slightly mocking.

"It was fine. A little strained."

"Why? Did he conquer your favorite country?"

Emma threw her hands up, exasperated. "Look, Les. I know you think Hunter is boring. But you don't really know him all that well, do you?

Leslie leaned her hand against Emma's desk. "No, I really don't. You're right. I'm sorry. It's just that I find Dr. Will *so* intriguing, and you know he's way interested in you too. I think you're too young to be tied down to one person, that's all."

"Maybe so. We'll talk more about it later. About not knowing someone so well, though. That sure does apply to Otto Henry. We know literally nothing about him besides his job title."

"And? Dr. C. and I googled Heritage Harbor after we left you and Hunter to your Risk-y night."

"Heritage Harbor. That's it. I could only remember it started with an *H*."

"It's some sort of genealogy place. Maybe he was trying to figure out his ethnic background, although to me, the red hair and freckles seem like clue number one."

"Hmm..." Emma pulled out Mary the hand-raiser's essay to show to Leslie. "Maybe he has a stranger heritage than we know." She passed the wolf paper for Leslie to chortle over. The bell rang. "Class! Class, I believe you know the drill. The first five minutes is brain barf in your journals. Your pen shouldn't stop moving 'til I say stop. Go, go, go now. Don't move too slowly now."

The students got right to work, and Emma was very pleased at feeling like she was getting the hang of this teaching thing.

She motioned Leslie out the door, since she didn't seem in too much of a hurry to get to her first-period speech class. "Well, we're still stuck on finding a reason why Otto might want to kill people, and I seriously doubt he was raised by wolves. I think we should talk to some people who know him. Maybe we could go at lunchtime and talk to those two new teachers he eats with."

Leslie nodded. "Diane and... who's the other one again?"

"Rhiannon. But neither one of them is very predisposed to talk to us, as we've seen. Any ideas?"

"Oh, come on," said Leslie. "*Everyone* is predisposed to you, Pollyanna, in case you hadn't noticed, and remember Edward said those three were among my hospital visitors. It was during my oh-so-out-of-it time period, but we must assume some concern was shown for them to show up."

"Maybe one of them is the poisoner," Emma said, "and they're sorry because they poisoned you by accident."

"Ha. Or maybe they came to the hospital to finish the job."

"Yes, well, that's why we need to be careful. See if you can work words like *genealogy* or *ethnic background* into the conversation without sounding threatening. We can express our own concern about

Otto and his whereabouts, for sure. That'd be a good way to start the conversation. Meet me back here before lunch?"

Leslie tapped her long fingernails on the doorframe. "No, sounds like too much time spent detecting, leaving less time for lunch. I need lunch. All this healthy food makes me constantly hungry instead of just hungry all the time. 'O, Banquo, fail not our feast!' Let's divide and conquer and save a few precious munching minutes. You go see Diane, and I'll stop by Rhiannon's."

"All right, Macbeth. Don't think I don't know Macbeth is planning to kill Banquo right there. Your new diet is not gonna kill either one of us, I promise. See you afterward, then." Emma smoothed her long floral sundress and fluffed her hair, clearing her brain in preparation for a discussion. "All righty, y'all can stop with the brain barfing and put your pens down to listen," she said as she re-entered the room. "Now, who can tell me about exploded time?"

HER SECOND-PERIOD AMERICAN Literature class was very exciting because of the students' discussion about Kurt Vonnegut's *Cat's Cradle*. Emma had been very concerned about her ability to navigate the religious themes present in the book, especially now that she'd had some conflict in her own social circle, for Pete's sake! She was treading on little cat feet, to be sure.

When the class had started talking about the child's game Cat's Cradle and what it might symbolize, she couldn't help but smile when Cathy Upton said she thought it was as if Vonnegut knew everything about life could be seen as questionable, like the fact that there's no cat and no cradle anywhere in that yarn game.

And then.

And then Aaron Stites, a student she'd had her first year in Sophomore Composition and now in American Literature, raised his hand. He said, "I like books like this. I've been reading it at home, and maybe like every few pages, I just have to stop. I have to stop and sit down and just *think* for a while. I like that."

Well, if that*'s not reason enough to be a teacher, I don't know what is.*

SHE CARRIED HER "I'M changing the world" sensation on through third-period Advanced Composition and research paper fun. Then she followed the wave of students as they flowed out of the classrooms, headed for lunch, and broke right, ready to question Diane Seymour about Otto. *I'm not sure how to work a genealogy question in, exactly, but it's easy for me to express concern about Otto. I* am *concerned. Unless he's a killer, and then I'm just angry.*

Emma skimmed over the shiny brown brick tiles of the commons and out into the courtyard. The September air had just begun to cool after a hot summer, and a light breeze vibrated the leaves of the grand old tree in the center. Down the left side wall, three doors led into classrooms. The art-room door was wide open, and some students sat on concrete benches, enjoying the air and drawing portraits of each other. Emma continued past to the second door, which held the remedial studies room. Diane had to travel there from the business wing every day to administer her A-plus Program, which Emma thought would be such a drag. She knew lots of teachers had to travel, though, because the school was bursting at the seams and there was never enough space.

Diane Seymour sat at the back at the teacher's desk. She was practically drowning in a gray suit with shoulder pads that made her look like a miniature linebacker, and which Emma was pretty sure hadn't been in a clothing designer's studio since the late 1980s. The walls of the room were lined with computer stations, presumably set for the A-plus Program. The center of the room was arranged with tables for study-hall students, although Emma thought tables were more conducive to note-passing than studying. There were no students in the room yet.

Diane wrote furiously in a leather-bound journal, and her hands were shaking. Her face was pale, more so than the fluorescent lights and drab suit warranted.

"Diane, are you all right?" asked Emma.

Diane startled and almost dropped her pen. "You scared me."

"I'm sorry. I just wanted to talk to you."

Diane closed her journal. "Talk to me about what? What do you want?" Her face was defiant, sharp chin lifted. Her short, starting-to-go-gray hair was ruffled.

"I, um. I… I wanted to talk to you about the remedial program you're in charge of. The A-Plus Program? I thought maybe you could show me how it works. I, uh, have some kids that could really use help with their reading." *Now, I just have to figure out a segue to ask about Otto. Come on, Emma. Think!*

Diane continued with the suspicious stare. "I thought you only taught upperclassmen, motivated kids and all."

Emma came toward one of the computers. "Well, I don't know if you could call my Lit 9 bunch motivated. Motivated to hop on the bus, maybe. But even motivated kids have trouble reading sometimes. A little extra help can't hurt. Please?" she cajoled.

Diane harrumphed and pushed herself out of her chair. "I guess." She marched over to the computer and pushed some buttons. "See, this is the program. You can choose grammar, reading comprehension, speed reading, whatever. Then the computer"—she punched a few more keys—"plays a game with the student to help them learn. It's a real video-game type of thing with great graphics, but that teaches whichever concept they're struggling with. Then the computer shoots out a test. The student takes it, and once they pass it, they can move on to the next level."

Emma sat down at the computer. "Sounds great. Can I try it?"

"It's time for lunch. Can't you come back some other time? Here." She punched some more keys, and the printer next to the desk started whirring. "Take one of the tests. Then you can come back later and have it graded."

Time was passing, and Emma still hadn't found a way to delicately bring up Otto. "Diane, where's Otto?" *So much for delicate segues.*

Diane twitched like she'd been punched. Her back stiffened, her head came up, and she swiveled around to stare at Emma. "Otto? I'm sure he's over in the ag building." She switched off the computer and paced over to her desk, fists clenched.

Lie. She's lying. Maybe she knows he's the killer and she's covering for him. Maybe she helped.

"Please, Diane. You eat lunch with him every day. You know he hasn't been to school. Where is he?"

Diane put her journal in the desk and locked it with a small key she wore around her neck. *Ah. Maybe she talks about Otto in there.* "I don't know where he is. He was supposed to... never mind." She shook her head like she was dislodging something distasteful from her ear. "I think maybe he's... yes, that's right. He's at a 4-H convention in Denver."

"Then why didn't he tell Abigail? Get a substitute? Abigail says he just didn't show up for work." Emma watched Diane give her forehead a smack.

"I don't know! Maybe he's irresponsible," Diane snapped, "doesn't cross his t's, dot his i's, isn't always perfect like you." She pushed past Emma and went to the door. "I'm going to lunch. I'm sure you can find Otto all by yourself." Then she stomped out.

So much for the Pollyanna theory. I didn't even get to slip in a genealogy question, subtly or not. She hoped Leslie had done better or found out something. This was starting to look unsolvable. No motive, no note-writer, no Otto. No closure. Emma only hoped they could figure this mess out before someone else got hurt. At the printer, she grabbed the reading test. She glanced down at the questions, hoping the questions would be easy enough for her to justify her English teacher credentials. Then she stopped and checked again. Then she took off running toward the lounge.

Chapter 22

Emma sprinted into the small lounge off the library. Leslie sat at the table, sharing her health food with Edward and Hunter. She was laughing.

Emma collapsed into the chair. "Did you find out anything?"

"Only that Rhiannon Pressman can make anything she's wearing look like a muumuu. Today it was a green suit, but it still ended up looking like a muumuu. I think she could really get healthier if she tried some of Mrs. Albert's food."

"Did you ask her about Otto? What about the genealogy question? I didn't get that question in, and Diane left all mad at me. I do have something to show you, though." Emma raised her eyebrows up and down like Leslie always did, Groucho Marx style. "You first."

Leslie finished a forkful of Mrs. Albert's latest creation. "Rhiannon stammered a little about him visiting family somewhere, but she really didn't say anything more. I asked her if she knew anything about a place called Heritage Harbor, and she said no and got all businesslike about needing to go get toner for the printer—I guess since her study hall classes are in the business wing, one of her jobs is maintaining the equipment—and she left. It looks like she's totally recovered from yesterday's little snafu with you and Alexa Champlain, Queen of the SSP."

"Why?" asked Hunter. "If Diane didn't tell you anything, what's your news?"

Emma smiled. "Yes, Diane was as closemouthed as they come, after she got all flustered and made up some lie about Otto being at a 4-H convention in Denver. She was really upset, though, and

I think she knows something. She deflected all my questions with some comment about how she couldn't accomplish everything we accomplished because she wasn't perfect like us."

Leslie snorted. "Yes, we're so perfect. You with the cheating ex-husband and—oh joy!—me with the cheating *bisexual* ex-husband and the giant hole in my gut. The line of people wanting to be just like us starts to the left." She gestured to the empty corner.

Hunter laughed, and Edward's eyes bulged. *Maybe he doesn't know about Ronald and Timothy.*

"Anyway," Emma continued, "I feel like she knows something about Otto and where he is. I just couldn't get it out of her, just like all that businesslike blowing us off you saw in Rhiannon. They know something about Otto. Maybe they know he killed Kisten, or maybe they even helped him." She waved the paper in the air. "But at least Diane did show me her A-plus Program. She even gave me one of the tests to try for myself." She shoved the paper over to the other three. "Looky here."

Leslie took it. "It's a grammar test. I could do this in my sleep. Look at this question. How do you make the subject and verb agree in this sentence?"

Edward took the paper. "I know. You hold a gun to the verb's head until it says, 'No more! Yes, yes, I agree with the subject.'"

Leslie chuckled. "Edward, that was actually pretty funny. Nice, normal, unliterary wit. I'm impressed."

Edward blushed and looked like he might use the test paper to cover his face.

Emma grabbed it, exasperated. "No, noo-wuh. Look at the *font* the program uses."

They all three examined the font. "It's cute," Hunter said. "Looks like an elementary kid's writing."

Light dawned on Leslie's face. Simultaneously, the two women shouted, "Scribble!"

Hunter and Edward's eyes met.

"This font is called Scribble," said Emma. "It's the same font used in the threatening notes written to me and Leslie and to the other girls." Emma examined the font again, the word Scribble running through her brain like the stock market ticker that crossed the bottom of news broadcasts. Something tugged in the back of her mind, but she couldn't bring it to the front. *Scribble, scribble... why is that word bugging me?*

"So you think this makes Diane the killer?" asked Hunter. "Seems a little thin. I mean, can't you use this font in any word processing program? Couldn't a student be using the font here at school and printing those nasty notes on the computers in the business room?"

Leslie snatched the paper back. "Stop raining on our parade, Hunter. Sure, that's *possible*. But since she has classes in there, she is statistically more likely to be using those computers to print out nasty notes. She has more opportunity, see? And the computer is her means, although I guess rattlesnakes would be the means, also, and we haven't found our collector yet."

"Plus motive," Emma said. "The police look for means, motive, and opportunity." She sighed. "This is beyond frustrating."

Leslie shook the paper at Hunter. "It's better than bubkes, which is what we've got so far. What have *you* got?"

Hunter stood up. "Well, I don't have a black belt in the field of martial arts. Is that what you think I need?" He leaned over the table, nose to nose with Leslie, black hair falling onto his forehead. "Is it?"

Edward's body tensed, like maybe he was going to have to jump into the middle of a fight.

Emma threw her hands up. "Will you please can it? You two are about as useless as a screen door on a submarine. Now sit down."

They sat.

"Yes, you can find this font on most word processing programs. But I think we should follow it up. She was writin' in a journal when I came in, and she locked it in the desk in the remedial studies room. I think we should check it out."

Hunter stood up again. "You two need to take a break with the Nancy Drew thing. Edward and I can try to get ahold of the journal."

"Absolutely," Edward nodded. "You ladies need not endanger yourselves further. Leave the detecting to us."

Emma and Leslie watched as the men marched out.

Emma took a bite of today's healthy diet. "I guess we should let them go. Spend a little time soothing our frustrations with sustenance. Besides, this is yummy. I need fuel to chase down killers."

EMMA AND LESLIE TAUGHT their fifth-period classes, although the freshmen in Emma's class sensed her lack of focus and started throwing paper airplanes. Instead of verbally smashing heads, she absentmindedly picked the planes up off the floor and deposited them in the recycle box like nothing had happened.

As soon as the final bell rang, her freshmen fled like their hair was on fire. *Usually, they're not so excited to leave. I know I wasn't a very good teacher today.* She wandered over to the Wendy poster hanging over the chair and reached out to touch it. At least she hadn't called anyone a name.

She lifted the edge of the poster and saw a bit of Wrinkled Wendy—the back side of the shape that held all the bullying statements they'd crumpled up at the in-service—peeking out. She studied the harsh words and brutal insults before flipping it back around and rereading her and Leslie's idioms of strength and optimism. *Much better.* She left her room and headed toward the library, picking Leslie up on the way. When they got to the glass-walled library office, they found Edward and Hunter both sitting silent.

"Well, didja find it?" asked Leslie. "Didja find Diane's journal? What did it say, huh? What? What?"

Edward sat uncomfortably in his computer chair, hands twisting in his lap. "We went back to the remedial studies room because Diane has a business class fifth hour. There was no journal, ladies. Hunter even did some sort of smooth lock-picking on the desk so Diane wouldn't see the break-in. Nothing in the desk but a pocket-sized electronic checkers, a science textbook, and a candy bar. I'm so sorry. I very much wanted to find you the clues you needed. I feel like we let you down." His head fell.

"Candy bar?" asked Leslie. "What kind?"

Emma elbowed her in the ribs. "The word of the day is ulcer. Ulcer." She patted Edward on the arm. He seemed so dejected. "It's all right, Edward. She probably takes that journal with her everywhere. You just keep lookin'. We'll figure this thing out. Maybe tomorrow we can... create a distraction in her room or somethin' and sneak it out then."

"I've gotta go back to my room to tutor a student. Kevin Rafferty can't figure out the difference between theme and thesis," said Leslie. "Emma, I'll call you tonight? We can write our own 'create a distraction' plan."

"Yes. Just make sure you don't detour to the A-plus Program room for that candy bar." She stared disapprovingly at Leslie. "I mean it."

"Yeah, yeah. If I needed a mother, I'd call mine." Leslie waved at the group and click-clicked away.

"Hunter, will you call *me* later?" asked Emma. "I'd like us to, I don't know... plan another game night? Or maybe I could take you to dinner." *I just want us to be back to normal.*

"Of course." He smiled, a deep-dimple slide show.

"Ta-ta." Edward waved furiously. "Sorry we couldn't solve the case for you."

On her way through the courtyard, she took a detour into the remedial studies room. She went to the back, where the teacher's desk presided. The top of the desk was neat and clean, unlike her own frequently cluttered, constant-abyss-to-lost-stuff desk. Emma ran her fingers over the locked long drawer in the front. Hunter had done a good job. There were no telltale scratches and nicks to let Diane know there'd been a break-in. Maybe that little spy job he had before he started teaching gave him some special skills. *Take that, Miss Leslie. Nothing boring about that.*

But she discovered a gaping clue to the break-in when she opened the drawer. No way to relock it without the key, and it slid open smoothly. *Oops. Who's going to explain* that *to Diane?* Emma smiled to see the candy bar still intact but found nothing else of interest in the desk. She went to the bookshelf leaning on the left wall to see the books. Some young adult fiction and basic textbooks. She pulled the manual for the A-plus Program, curious to see if it was printed in the same font as the testing materials.

"What are you doing here?"

Emma jumped. Rhiannon Pressman stood in the doorway, and Emma noted that the green suit she was wearing did indeed look like a big, two-piece muumuu. Her face was as green as the suit.

"Oh, hi, Rhiannon," said Emma. "I was just—I told Diane I was interested in the A-plus Program for some of my kids, so I'm... I'm checkin' it out." She showed the manual to Rhiannon, even though it felt vaguely like the cookie she'd stolen from the cookie jar and been forced to reveal to her mother.

Rhiannon trudged into the room and leveled Emma with a suspicious stare. "Why can't you find out about the program when Diane is here? There's no reason to be sneaking around after school hours. Go home to you cute little house and your cute little boyfriend. I'm sure Diane will help you later."

"Oh, she did. She did help me," Emma said. She dug into the bag she was carrying on her shoulder and pulled out the grammar test. "See? She gave me this. I was goin' to go home and take the test, and..." She inched toward the door. "You're right. I shouldn't be here after school's out." She waved the paper at Rhiannon. "It's just that I've been busier than a moth in a mitten, and I got all the way to the end of the day without picking it up." She knew she was babbling, but for some reason, she kept right on. "Why, too much time here, and students will start thinking I really do sleep under my desk like we always thought our teachers did. Did you think that?" She ducked through the door. "See you later!" she shouted over her shoulder then ran to the parking lot to jump in her car and peel out.

Well, the Honda wasn't known for peeling. She rolled out as fast as four embarrassed cylinders would take her.

THE MOTORCYCLE SITTING in her driveway gave Emma's heart an involuntary flutter. Dr. Capshaw sat on her front stoop and caused another extra beat to escape, again, against her will. *So he's cute. So he's a little... unexpected. So what? Stop it, stupid.* She parked the Honda behind the Harley and stepped out. "What's up, Doc?" Emma said. She giggled. "I do love sayin' that. I say it to all my doctors. My daddy kept old VHS tapes in the back of his bookstore, and *Looney Tunes* and Bugs Bunny were the best." She stepped up and past his seated form to unlock her front door. *Now, you are in a committed and fantastic relationship, so behave that way.* "How can I help you today, Doc? Please come on in."

Dr. Capshaw followed her in and endured the animal attack that seemed to be the price of entry, calming the wiggles from Sir Toby with a strong hand stroking her fur, and allowing Trinky full access to slaloming in and around his legs. "I know I'm no detective," he said, "but I've come across something interesting, and I wanted to share. Can we set up your computer? I'll show you."

He strolled through to the kitchen and pulled Emma's laptop from the pocket shelf in the breakfast nook. "I know we figured out Billy Barrows and the Holiness Pentecostals were out of town when Kisten died and when everyone got sick at the homecoming dance. But watching that guy at his service—" Will shook his head. "There was just something about that guy that seemed... off, ya know?"

Emma shivered, remembering the woman with the snake framing her face. "A lot of that day seemed off, if you ask me. Are you thinking he killed Kisten from a distance or had someone else do it for him?"

"No idea." His fingers click-clicked on her laptop keyboard, then he swung it around. "But look at this."

She gazed at the screen. *William Barrows* was spelled out at the head, followed by numbers and records.

"You're not supposed to see this because you're not a nurse or doctor in this system," he said. "I don't want you to look at any of his records. I just want your opinion on this." He scrolled down.

At the bottom of the screen, it said, "No records available prior to 01-03-2000." This was what Will pointed at.

"So what?" asked Emma. "Maybe he's only been here since 2000. How long has the church been here? Maybe he's the one who opened the church."

Will's gaze trapped hers. His eyes looked like little drops of chocolate. She knew Leslie would encourage a correlation between this intriguing man and her favorite food of all time, but Emma ignored it. *I... love... Hunter.*

"Yeah, but here's the thing—patient medical records are cumulative," he said. "I should be able to see his whole medical history, at least the highlights. There's nothing prior to 2000. I think his real name isn't William Barrows."

"I hate to be all devil's advocate here, but again, so what? Lots of people change their name. It doesn't necessarily mean he's hiding. Maybe he just didn't like his real name." *This could be a clue, and surely, I don't need to give him such a hard time, but I don't need to feel this flustered either. I'm in a happy relationship, and I should* not *be droolin' over this doctor who also does martial arts and looks dangerous and hot in a white T-shirt and sitting on a Harley.*

He nodded. "Sure, lotsa people change their names, but that follows them, too, right? It's why you're always supposed to put aka this and aka that on all your forms. His original name should be a part of his records too." He brought the laptop over to the living room couch and plopped down with it. "I just feel like that guy's up to no good, and Kisten went to his church, and... and... I don't know."

After a moment's hesitation, Emma sat next to him. Not too close. "I remember. Since my divorce, I've had to put Emma Talicky as an aka on all of my college and teacher forms." She gestured to the computer screen. "But how could we find out more? Should we call Carl Niome?"

Will grinned. "That guy is a piece of work, isn't he? The other day he came into my office, wanting..." He leaned his face closer to Emma's. "You had the last name Talicky?"

She felt a blush creeping in. "Yes, well, I was young. There was the whole Talicky hickey thing, I... I..."

"Sure, sure," he nodded. "Hickeys can be dangerous. Dangerous and addictive." Will leaned his face even closer to Emma's, the computer sliding from his lap to rest on the couch cushion.

Emma locked onto his gaze as his lips moved in, closer, closer—

She jumped up. "Dangerous and addictive until they start showing up on other girls all over town," she said. "You really should, ah, um, should go... call Carl, I mean. You probably have a better... a more professional relationship with the detective than I do and could find out if Billy Barrows is really a wanted felon who kills young girls and threatens other ones."

Will's head followed her as she jumped up, and he smiled.

She got all the way to the door then stopped. She tripped back three quick steps to grab the laptop from where it had landed on the cushion. After snapping it shut, she practically hurdled the couch to get it back to its shelf in the breakfast nook. Sir Toby and Trinky, who'd both settled under the coffee table after Will arrived, now emerged and started sniffing and wandering around, sensing the change in atmosphere. "Please let me know what he says, and Leslie and I'll just keep looking for clues around the school."

Instead of a rejected or dejected look, Dr. Will Capshaw slapped his hands on both knees and stood up with a grin that Emma saw as mischievous. "Ms. Emma Lovett-formerly-known-as-Emma Talicky, I'll call that chief of detectives and see if I can pull him from his great clean-up-the-classroom crusade to follow up on Billy Barrows. Have no fear. I am on it." He jogged to the doorway and stopped. "I know you're involved with that other guy. But if you ever get un-involved, remember this. I would love to spend some time teaching you how to reassociate your bad memory of the hickey with something much, much better." He winked and turned away, closing the door behind him.

GREAT CAESAR'S GHOST on a cracker! What was that *all about? Am I losing my mind? I can't ever, ever go for a bad-boy type again.* Emma plopped down on the couch, staring at the door Will Capshaw had just closed. Emma felt like a completely helpless ninny, as Abigail Patterson might say, for salivating over someone she hardly knew when she had this wonderful man already in her life.

But she knew better, knew those roguish types couldn't stay put, lived too much for the chase. She thought about her ex-husband,

Ronald. He was so beautiful. It was almost like her brain flew right out her ear when she saw him. Even after he'd opened his mouth and proven that his brains had vacated the premises a while back, she'd been smitten.

And he'd loved her, too, she had no doubt. After he'd gone into taxidermy as a vocation, even after he'd cheated and ruined everything, he kept stuffing things and bringing them to her as love offerings. He'd behaved like Trinky, gifting mice on the porch, repeatedly expecting forgiveness for bad behavior. She knew she didn't want to go there again. *If Dr. Will flirts with me again, I will tell him, bluntly, that I love Hunter. I know I do.*

Oh, who was she kidding? She didn't know anything. A poor innocent girl had died, practically on her watch, and she still hadn't discovered anything helpful. She wanted, almost more than she wanted to be this amazing, Leslie-esque teacher, to find out who killed Kisten Hollis. *Time to get your mind off of big brown eyes with unfair eyelashes and get to work. What was the name again of that return address on the envelope we found at Otto's house?*

Emma scuttled into the kitchen to retrieve the laptop and brought it back to the couch, shooing Sir Toby and Trinky back to the floor. She opened the computer and typed in Heritage Harbor, even though Leslie had said it was a dead end, because maybe new eyes would bring new clues and ideas.

"Find the bearings of your life at Heritage Harbor," said the banner at the top of the web page. The home tab was just as Leslie said, a list of services relating to genealogy. "Find your great-great-great-grandparents. What percent Neanderthal are you? Meet your long-lost cousins from Africa." Emma giggled as she watched her very fair forearms and fingers typing on the computer keys. *You have no idea how much I'd love to meet my African cousins.*

Other tabs seemed to concentrate on selling products about ethnic heritage and family. She sighed. Unless she wanted to fork out two hundred dollars to find out what percentage of Neanderthal was in her DNA, or maybe forty-nine ninety-five plus shipping and handling for an Irish kilt made of her established family's tartan, it really was a dead end. She wasn't sure how to connect any of this to Otto Henry, and she couldn't see, at all, how it could relate to the violence at the school with the notes or the poisoned homecoming dance or Kisten Hollis.

She scrolled to the bottom of the page, just in case, skipped over the Contact Us button, and instead, clicked on the one that said More Safe Harbors.

New eyes, new clues, looky, lookie-loo. The More Safe Harbors button showed something totally different. "Heritage Harbor wants to do more than help you find your heritage. We want to help you find your family. Are you a black-market baby? Are you convinced you were switched at birth? Was your child stolen from right under your nose? We want to help. Contact Heritage Harbor at..."

And right there was the address Emma had seen on the top of the envelope they found at Otto's house. And now, Otto had gone missing. And Kisten was dead. But what was the connection? Was Otto a black-market baby who'd somehow found out, and the person who stole him was popular and extroverted, so now he was exacting revenge? That didn't make sense.

Emma clicked over to the message board. *Wow.* There were thousands of messages and a thread for each category the Heritage Harbor people were helping with—Switched at Birth, Black-Market Babies, Stolen Babies. She started scanning through the entries, searching for Otto's name or any story sounding like Otto, but before long, she was hooked and inhaling each tale. The stories ranged from unbelievable to heart-wrenching to both.

"I'm 25, and my mom just told me she bought me out of a hotel room in Alabama for $500. Can you help me find my real parents? M.P."

"I'm pretty sure the IVF Clinic in my town takes extra embryos from IVF procedures and uses them to make babies for sale. How can I expose them? T.F."

"I know my parents aren't my real parents because I found my mom's journal. How can I find my real parents? S.R."

She couldn't find any stories with the initials O.H. or B.B.—for Billy Barrows—anywhere. Just pages and pages of sadness and desperation. *Every time I think I have more of a handle on human nature, it throws me a curve.* Emma thought books and news and Shakespeare could prepare her, but really, people never ceased to go somewhere unexpected.

I have't. It is engendered. Hell and night
Must bring this monstrous birth to the world's light.

—*Othello,* 1.3.397–8

Chapter 23
Thursday, September 24

Emma awoke with a start and caught her laptop just as it started to slide across her lap. She'd been dreaming of babies. Everywhere she went, a baby was hiding. No, she decided in her dream. *Hidden.* Somebody had hidden all the babies, and it was Emma's job to find them and save them. Oh, babies. Emma loved them so. She loved people in general, but babies—those were some people she could get used to having around. In the dream, Emma lifted couch cushions and tabletops and flung them out of her way. She opened her dream refrigerator and swept the food from the shelves, searching, searching for every last one, or they'd all die. The babies would die, and Emma would die too. She had to find them.

She remembered the dreamscape changing to her classroom, and Wrinkled Wendy, as the keeper of the babies, yelling at Emma for her lack of understanding. All those babies wanted was someone to love them, someone to take care of them. Someone to keep them safe. The shouting Wendy had transformed from paper to lead and landed on Emma's lap, and the weight of the computer sliding from her legs was what spasmed her awake. Trinky and Sir Toby had apparently been sleeping on either side of her but had also awakened with her movement. *Holy cow.*

She couldn't believe she fell asleep reading that website. She picked up the phone from the coffee table. Five forty-five a.m. *Sheesh.* Maybe she should try some more lap swimming at the school. Or better yet, maybe she should grade the papers she hadn't gotten around to during the previous night's internet fest.

She thought maybe she'd get more done at school, though, so she jumped in the shower and contemplated her day. Maybe she could call Will—or have Leslie do it to avoid any more unwished-for awkwardness—to find out what Detective Niome knew about Billy Barrows. She might also figure out a way to steal Diane Seymour's journal. That thought made her uncomfortable, too, but she knew there was something going on with that woman, and Emma knew the journal might hold some answers. After feeding the animals and wolfing down a yogurt and an apple, she jumped into the little green Honda and took off. She couldn't stop thinking about all those babies.

AFTER GRADING PAPERS for an hour, Emma went to Leslie's room. She held the Wrinkled-slash-Wondrous Wendy paper in one hand and a laptop in the other. Leslie sat at her desk, also grading papers. *We all need to be doin' a better job of balancing teaching and detecting, that's for sure.*

"Who do you think this paper belongs to? Otto and Charlie? If this case boils down to someone feeling like an outcast, or not belongin' or being unwanted, maybe these words are a clue to their state of mind. And do you think Otto was a stolen baby?" She placed the doll shape on Leslie's desk.

Leslie was apparently deep in grading concentration. "Hmm? Do I think this whosit belongs to what?" She finished a comment on the essay in front of her and gave her attention to the paper doll. "Oh, look. It's poor little Wrinkled Wendy. Aw, these are so awful! Let's go to the other side with all of our positive affirmations." She flipped the paper shape over. "See? You are strong! You are smart! Why didn't we write something about ulcer-fighting willpower?" She trailed her finger down one of Wendy's legs. "You are—wait." She set the shape down. "Did you just say something about a stolen baby?"

"Yes, I did. You listen about as well as my grampa when he forgets his hearing aids." She sat the open laptop in front of her friend and curved around to Leslie's side of the desk. "Take a look at what I found here on the Heritage Harbor website."

THEY WERE STILL LOOKING at the sayings on Wrinkled Wendy when kids started drifting in for first period. Leslie's voice dropped to a whisper. "I can see what you mean about this line—'You never deserved to be a parent anyway'—maybe relating to all of the Heritage Harbor stuff we found, but that doesn't really make me think Otto was a stolen baby. Do you think *his* baby was stolen?" She smacked Emma's shoulder. "Shh. Hi, Carter." She smiled and waved to the student coming too close to her desk.

"We don't know for sure that this is Otto and Charlie's Wendy shape anyway, do we? I don't remember a lot of what Charlie said beyond 'fat' and 'loser.' He was getting so wound up I was afraid he was gonna have a stroke. And Otto never said his," Emma whispered, nodding her hello to a student she'd had the previous year. The five-minute warning bell sounded. "Maybe we should ask Charlie at lunch." She picked up the sign and the laptop.

Leslie made a face. "Lounge Lizards at lunchtime? Ugh." She stood. "Come on in. Gather 'round, everybody. It's your favorite activity—improvisational speeches!" She swept a cup of Popsicle sticks labeled with topics off the corner of her desk and headed for the front of the room. "Say toodles to Ms. Lovett. She and I are meeting for lunch to learn appetite-control techniques. Wish us luck!"

Emma left the room to a chorus of good-luck wishes from the speech class. *We're gonna need more than luck to figure this circus out.*

THEY MET IN THE MAIN office, Emma carrying two trays of Mrs. Albert's latest healthy, gourmet, ulcer-fighting fare, parmesan roasted chicken and broccoli. Leslie took her tray and set it in front of Abigail. "Abigail, will you watch all this for me? I have an errand to run in the teachers' lounge, and I don't want to waste this fabulous food by... oh, I don't know... throwing it at someone."

Abigail smiled like she understood perfectly. "Of course, dear," she whispered then turned to Emma. "Yours too?"

Emma nodded and set her tray next to Leslie's. "I doubt I am the tray-throwin' type, but it can't hurt. Any news about Otto?"

Abigail shook her head, the chains on her glasses wiggling. "I called the police to see if they knew anything, but that Detective Niome, he"—she moved Emma's tray so it lined up with Leslie's—"he said Otto was a grown adult man who had only been gone for forty-eight hours, and he knew a lot of things grown adult men might be doing for forty-eight hours, and then he wiggled his eyebrows like we were friends." She clenched her small fists, and her voice rose to a level that might be perceived at the next desk. "We are *not* friends. What if Otto's disappearance has something to do with poor Kisten Hollis? All the police give are insinuations and misinformation. That member of the police, anyway. Entirely too big for his britches, that man."

Emma and Leslie might have to struggle to hear Abigail in her normal conversation mode, but they heard her tsk-tsking all the way up the two small stairs and into the teachers' lounge. The clamor from the back table soon overwhelmed Abigail's disapproving noises, though, because Charlie Foreman was telling a joke.

"I dunno what you're talking about. That ain't my kayak, honey!" he quipped, slapping his meaty palms on his plaid golf shorts, and the other Lounge Lizards roared. They high-fived each other, and one coach even pounded the table.

Emma was glad not to see Hunter hanging out with this group and hoped he was waiting in their special library lounge. "I wonder if anyone's ever counted the number of penis jokes he knows," she whispered.

Leslie grinned. "Oh, I'm sure he's written Guinness for an application. 'Here are only numbers ratified, but, for the elegancy, facility, and golden cadence of poesy, *caret*.' That means *lacking*. I'll have to think some more for something Shakespearean that says something stronger than *lacking*. More like 'Your penis jokes suck.'" She marched across the lounge, Wrinkled Wendy in hand, with Emma following. "Oh Chuuuu-uck? I have a question for you." She unrolled the doll shape and set it down in front of Charlie. "Can you please take a break from your open-mic night and let me know which of these insults were yours and which were Otto's?" She pointed at the writing. "I remember 'fat' and 'reject' and 'ugly' from your overzealous performance at the in-service, but what else?"

Charlie stared at Leslie like she was stepping on his favorite toy, but still he looked down. "Parker, for a smart chick, you're pretty stupid. On what planet do you know guys who write like this?" He gestured to some of the sayings. "Sure, I said some of the same kinda things, but not in the same way, and looky here. 'Too fat to breathe?' I didn't say that. I just said 'fat.'"

He snorted and pointed to another note, one that had been erased and was barely visible. "Sinner reaping what you sow? Who talks like that? Not me, and not the ag teacher, for chrissake. This is totally chick writing, anyway."

I wonder how Charlie can see that and we missed it. That has religious overtones just like the note sent to Kisten.

He ran an indifferent paw over the Wendy shape and sat down to shove a handful of French fries in his mouth. "Go back to your health food, girls," he said, mush mouthed. "Leave the real insults to me."

"I DETEST THE FACT THAT he's right," Leslie whispered. They stood over by the mailboxes. "Guys are very unlikely to write about their sins reaping what they sow, or whatever. And I agree with you—makes us look pretty bad that we didn't read that note just because it'd been erased." She rolled the Wendy shape and stuck it under her arm.

"Except maybe Edward Dixon," Emma said. "He talks like that all the time." She stuck her hand in her mailbox and started riffling through the mail. "I don't feel like blaming us right now for missing that clue. We didn't know about the notes when we went to the in-service. And Edward wasn't at the in-service, anyway, so it couldn't have been him writing that way. And now that I think about it, there weren't any other girls in our group that day anyway, right? Except you, me, Diane, and Rhiannon Pressman. So this Wrinkled Wendy has to be theirs, right? How does that change our theory about Otto being the killer?"

"If Otto didn't write those notes or bleed paint all over my walls, what was his pin doing in my room, then?" Leslie asked. "These sayings could have been written by Diane and Rhiannon, I guess, but neither of them supervises the FFA, and we know that for sure. Maybe *all* the new teachers killed Kisten and developed this whole elaborate conspiracy of terror to make us all suffer because we couldn't recognize Otto for what he was—a poor, stolen baby."

Emma flipped through a calendar and dumped it into the garbage. "You are such a goon. I don't know either of those ladies to be married or to have children, but maybe one of them is. We know one of them hates her stepfather and stepbrother, but only because I was eavesdropping. It's sad, really. We should try harder."

She picked out a last mailer to throw away then peered into the back of the box. "What's this?" She reached in to pull out a piece of folded-up notebook paper. *Oh, please, please don't tell me it's another hateful note.* She unfolded it and scanned the contents. Her eyes grew big. "Holy cheese on a cracker!" she exclaimed, forgetting to whisper and causing the other teachers in the lounge to stare. "Look here. From Dr. Will."

Leslie read the note, and her pop-eyed look matched Emma's. "Come on!" she called, grabbing Emma by the arm and pulling her down the two small stairs and into the main office. She scooped up her tray from where it sat on Abigail's desk and started shoving food in her mouth as she traveled.

Emma followed suit. "Thank you, Abigail!" She dropped the note into the little silverware trench of the lunch tray, took a big bite, and swallowed. "We have one more thing to do before lunch is over." She started around the desk with the tray clutched in both hands in front of her.

"HOW DO YOU THINK WE should play this?" asked Leslie. "Good cop, bad cop? I wanna be the bad cop." They'd inhaled their lunches and dropped the empty trays back at the cafeteria and were now headed for the business department.

"Speakin' of cops, maybe we should get one," said Emma. "These confrontations tend to end badly." They crossed in front of the commons, Emma nodding to a couple of students who were eating their lunches right in the middle of the floor. "Remember? Do you recall the gun I had in my face last year, missy? Maybe we should grab Hunter to come with."

Leslie scoffed. "And do *you* remember the lovely love story we unearthed last year? Besides, you had that gun in your face at night. We got conked over the head at night. Listen to Macbeth—'Whiles *night's* black agents to their preys do rouse.' It's the middle of the day." She strode ahead of Emma to march left. "We're not rousing the night's prey, and we don't need anyone else to come along." Starting to back down the business hallway, she backed into a student coming out. “Oops,” she said, straightening her black pencil skirt and throwing her shoulders back. “Let’s do this.”

Emma sighed and straightened her own floral dress. “Fine. But let me talk. I’m the one with the sweet, swoonin’ Southern baloney, as you so eloquently put it.” She took one last look at the note that had been in her mailbox, then she marched into the business classroom.

“Howdy, Diane,” Emma cooed. “Can you tell us one thing? And it’s really important. Who is Simon Seymour?”

Chapter 24

Diane Seymour had been hunched over a book when Emma and Leslie burst into her business classroom, and in her shock, she almost flung it off the desk. "Wh-What? Did you find him?" She craned her neck, trying to look over Emma's shoulder. "Is Otto here? Did you find him?" Her short, going-gray hair listed up one side and flattened down the other, and her bloodshot eyes now tried to hold on to Emma's. Almost drowning in her suit and now gripping the book—Emma could see it was the journal everyone had been searching for—Diane looked like a small, deflated balloon.

"Did he find him?" she moaned. "Does he know what happened to the baby?" She collapsed onto the desk, pushing her face against the journal, rolling her forehead from side to side. "We've been looking for so long," she spoke into the desk. "Heritage Harbor... we thought they'd found the answer." She looked up. "Please. Where's Otto?"

Leslie stood behind Emma and stepped up so they were both facing Diane. "We haven't found Otto," she said.

Diane shrank farther into her shoulder pads.

"We've found Simon Seymour, though," Emma said. "He's going by the name Billy Barrows. Who is he, Diane?" She glanced over at Leslie, who nodded encouragingly. "We'd like to help. We're so sorry we haven't been more supportive of y'all as new teachers. We're caught up in the madness that's been going on here." *Not to mention, we think one of you could be the reason for the madness.* Emma reached over to pat Diane's elbow where it crooked around her head. "Is Simon Seymour related to you?"

Diane lifted her head and sat back in the chair, shoulders drooping against the seat back. “Simon Seymour is my father.” Her bloodshot gaze slid between Emma and Leslie. “I haven’t seen him in sixteen years. Otto and I have been looking for him for sixteen years, because the last time I saw him, he took my baby daughter, Eloise.”

Wait, what? Otto and Diane have both been looking for her daughter*? Oh my gosh. This is the stolen baby.* Emma squeezed her eyelids shut, afraid to learn anything more.

Diane sniffed, and two fat tears crawled from under her eyelids and tumbled over her cheeks. “He took our daughter because I wasn’t supposed to have her. I didn’t deserve her. We didn’t deserve her.” She started mumbling as the tears fell. “Weren’t perfect enough… too much mental malpractice… shouldn’t have been together… couldn’t…” She drew a sharp breath. “Do you know where Eloise is?” Her hands went to her mouth. “If you know where my father is, where’s my daughter? Oh God, where is she?” Her hands scrabbled over the desk to grab Emma’s. “Does he have Eloise?” she cried.

Emma clasped Diane’s hands and sat down next to her in a chair that, thanks to Leslie, had magically appeared. “Diane, we know less than you think we do,” she said. “I just now learned that Simon Seymour is here in Pinewood. Maybe you could start at the beginning, and we can all figure this out together.” She took a deep breath, willing Diane to do the same.

Diane breathed, too, with a hitch somewhere in the middle. “My father, Simon Seymour, was a pastor in our church in Texas. The Fifth Church of Christian Science, Abilene.” She ran a finger under her nostrils.

Emma and Leslie exchanged looks again, this time in confusion and surprise. *Christian Science? What?*

“He was very, very strict,” she continued. “And I was very sheltered by him. You may not have noticed, but I’m not very good around people. I get real nervous because I’m not used to them. I don't know how to behave." She sniffed again, and magical Leslie appeared with the Kleenex.

Emma glanced at Leslie, searching for a purse or a pocket. *Nope. How in the Sam Hill does she* do *that?*

"Anyway, I get nervous, but I had so many teachers that were so nice that I thought maybe I could be a teacher."

Emma glanced again at Leslie. *See? What'd I tell ya?*

Leslie's eyes said, *Two types of teachers. No, three.*

"When I was thirty-five," Diane went on, "I'd been teaching about five years, I guess, and I met Otto. He ran the 4-H program at our school in Abilene, and he was so nice. We got together." She sniffed with that hitch in the middle again. "I got pregnant with Eloise. Oh, my father went crazy. All those things he preached every day went down the drain in light of a baby out of wedlock. A baby with a heathen. He stopped speaking to me, except to scream scripture in my ear. He wouldn't sit at the table with me to eat, banished me from all parts of the house except my bedroom. I had to sit on my bed and eat meals off the nightstand."

Leslie, who at some point in the story had brought over her own chair to sit around the desk, now slapped her hand on the desk, making Emma and Diane jump. "Are you kidding? Why would he go crazy? You were thirty-five years old, a grown woman." Her fingers rat-a-tatted on the table. "'This is mere madness. And thus a while the fit will work on him.' *Hamlet,*" Leslie muttered. "Why, for Christ's sake?"

Diane sighed. "That's right. For Christ's sake. See, Otto was divorced. He drank whiskey and wasn't a Christian Scientist. Actually, he didn't even go to church. My father called on all his favorite buzzwords—he was always big on buzzwords—and said Otto was practicing malicious animal magnetism on me, and I, well, I knew very well that succumbing to Otto was the worst kind of mental malpractice. And I didn't—no, *we* didn't—deserve the benefit of a perfect child of God because we never found a spiritual sonship with God. So he took me away from Abilene.

"Otto never knew I was pregnant because my father—" Diane's voice cracked, and she corrected herself. "Because Simon took me away as soon as he found out I was pregnant. We moved to this teeny town in West Texas and just stayed there in some sort of weird cabin, in solitude, until the baby was born. It was my penance. I needed to heal myself and get right with God before the baby was born."

Leslie continued her rat-a-tat on the table, her eyes boring into the side of Emma's face.

I know what she's thinking—this is all so much malarkey and how can anyone believe in this crapola and look what happened. He stole her baby! Emma didn't know what to say to either one of them. "Did you have to go with him?" was what came out.

"I know it sounds so stupid to you," Diane said miserably. "You're both so strong and independent. All I can say is that's just the way things were for so long that I never even considered leaving. Not until Eloise came." She dragged her fingers along the entry she'd been reading in her journal. "Because the church believes we should heal ourselves, do everything through prayer," Diane continued, "he made me stay home when I went into labor. He locked me in the house and delivered the baby himself." She opened her mouth then closed it. The tears coursed down her cheeks. "It took so long and it hurt so much that, after Eloise came out, I fell asleep. It was only for a little while, but when I woke up and tried to get up to feed the baby, she was gone. Simon took her! He took her, and I didn't know what to do. I was such a fool, and I was so ashamed of my behavior that I really felt like I didn't deserve her. That's why I never called the police. Otto wanted to, but instead, we've just been trying find both of them again by ourselves. We go into schools together but not as a couple because people ask less sticky questions to single, unassociated colleagues. Heritage

Harbor had a real lead about Pinewood, I thought. But no. If I deserved her, I would've been able to keep her."

"No, Diane!" Emma cried, and this time, she was the one slapping the table for emphasis. "That is absolutely not true. Your father was the one in the wrong here. He was wrong to control you and criminally wrong to take your baby. Look, he did all these things to hide. He's been here, callin' himself Billy Barrows, runnin' the local Pentecostal church. Like I said before, one of my friends noticed something strange about him and just left me a note telling me Billy was really Simon. I'm so sorry to say that's all we know right now. We don't know where Eloise is, and we don't know where Otto is, either. That's why we came back to you, trying to find some answers."

Two students came in the door for fourth period, took one look at the disheveled Diane, and spun right back around.

Diane stood. "Did you say he was running a Pentecostal church? Why would he do that? He's not Pentecostal." She started around the edge of her desk. "I have to teach my fourth-period class right now. I have to find Otto. I have to..." Her eyes traveled around the room. "I don't know what I have to do." Her shoulders slumped, and the shoulder pads of her suit seemed to melt into her skeleton.

Leslie hopped up. "I know what you have to do," she said crisply and bustled over to Diane. "You have to go home."

"That's right, Diane. Go home and take a nap because you're going to need all your strength to find Otto and Eloise now that we know your father is here. I don't think he knows you are here. You weren't on campus the day he ran an impromptu service here. So that will be helpful. We have a planning period now, Leslie and I. Do you have a fifth period?"

Diane shook her head. "No, Otto and Rhiannon and I have fifth-period planning. That's when we've been doing all the research to try to find Eloise." Her hands went to her mouth. "Rhiannon!" she exclaimed. "Oh, Rhiannon's been helping us since I found her five years ago in Wichita. She's almost been like a daughter to us—so helpful and sweet. She had big father problems, too, only hers is a stepfather. I need to tell her about Simon."

"That's fine, Diane," Leslie said. "You stop and tell Rhiannon on your way home, and I'll cover your fourth hour." She patted Diane on the shoulder. "Emma, I assume you will go over to our library lounge and fill in our poor, intrepid librarian-slash-detective? And call Dr. Will back to find out whether that master criminologist, Carl Niome, has picked up Simon Seymour?" Without waiting for a response, she hustled over to the students who were coming in and began sending them to their seats.

The horrible knowledge that had been blooming in Emma's head as she listened to Diane's story was now in full flower, and she couldn't do anything about it but lead the shattered Diane past the incoming business students and out of the room.

Chapter 25

Emma had been so, so thankful to be at the end of the *To Kill a Mockingbird* unit in her freshman fifth period and thus able to start the Gregory Peck movie and melt behind the desk in the back of the room to perseverate about Kisten Hollis, aka, she was pretty sure, Eloise Seymour. It seemed that Simon Seymour was the logical killer of Kisten Hollis and maybe Otto Henry too.

The snakes that were part of the Pentecostal services had been the only snakes connected to anyone around here, and they had been easily controlled by Simon Seymour. It had to be him. She didn't care that they'd heard he was at a retreat. It'd only been a ski area forty-five minutes from Pinewood, and now that she knew how manipulative and twisted he'd been this whole time, Emma had no problem believing he could've figured out a way to sneak back and kill Kisten. *Eloise? Eloise Henry? Eloise Seymour-Henry?* Whatever. The beautiful little girl who'd been poisoned and now would never know her real parents, Diane and Otto. The girl who'd never be able to have babies of her own, if she wanted to, or be an astronaut or an engineer or run her own lunch truck.

It was so colossally unfair, and Emma couldn't wrap her mind around what had most likely happened. She'd had her life cut short by her own grandfather? It didn't compute for Emma. Even though he'd obviously committed another egregious crime in kidnapping her, it seemed he had done that out of a misguided sense of... saving her? *He thought taking her from Diane was saving her, so why would he kill her?* She glanced up at the video screen. Gregory Peck was just wrapping up his amazing closing statements to the jury, ruminating on time-honored codes of our society, and how we had to look beyond them for justice. She wondered what codes were being represented here and how to find justice for Kisten.

Maybe Simon had been trying to raise Kisten in the church, although which church and why he'd so bizarrely switched denominations, she could only speculate, and maybe Kisten had rejected the church, the same as Diane had done. Maybe her plans for Homecoming were against God, in Simon's eyes. Maybe that made him snap. She remembered the day she'd met Dr. Will at the Pentecostal service, and she remembered what Billy Barrows had said about Kisten. "Kisten, you couldn't know, you couldn't've known. I kept it from you..."

Maybe when he figured out so much had been kept from her, but she still didn't get right with God, in his eyes, he thought the only thing he could do was kill her? Emma pressed the heels of her hands against her temples as hard as she could, trying to understand. *No, no, that doesn't make sense. Who could do that? It's so hard, looking through so many different eyes.*

And maybe most importantly, she thought about Diane and her stolen baby, the baby she might've lost twice. She didn't see how someone for whom a relationship with God was so important could see taking a daughter from her mother as in keeping with that relationship. *That's not religious. Simon Seymour had it all wrong. I guess I can see why Leslie gets skeptical about the entire religion idea.* The bell rang, and her freshman students gathered up their things and glided through the aisles like seagulls on the waves, eager to head home.

EMMA'S ORIGINAL INTENT was to go straight home as well, but she didn't know what to do once she got there. So for a while, she simply drove. She thought about the disturbing events of the past few days, the threatening notes, the graffiti, the death of a student, and the near-death of her dear friend. Simon could have come through those corner doors into the classroom unseen, she decided, and could have snuck into the dance to poison the punch bowl. But Emma couldn't figure out any real reason why he would do that. He was short enough to write the messages on the gym wall, but then what about Otto's pin? Emma supposed Otto could have found Simon defacing Leslie's wall and then confronted him, but that explained even less and put more people in places they shouldn't be. Her thoughts were jumbled and discombobulated, and she smacked the steering wheel in frustration.

Emma was struck by a memory of Kisten Hollis. She was only in her speech class for a couple of weeks the previous year, and Emma had seen many speeches since the one Kisten had done before she transferred out, but suddenly, she remembered the speech topic. It was about perspective.

Kisten had alluded to some things her family did. Emma now assumed it was something to do with the Pentecostal church, which made other people look down on them. She talked about how lots of people assumed cheerleaders were stuck-up and snobby, but how she loved the idea of flying through the air and tumbling across the track at the football game, and how most of those girls were very nice and down-to-earth, which was why she wanted to try out.

She'd talked about many types of people, and how no one really knew anyone when they relied on stereotyping. She concluded with a fervent wish that people would reexamine their perceptions in light of real fact, would get to know other people beyond their assumptions, and would live life with less judgment and more compassion.

It had been her first and only speech, but it had been a good one.

Emma drove aimlessly through the main streets of Pinewood. Small stores, some of which were already sporting Halloween decorations, were still open—though hardly bustling—in the late-afternoon hour. She continued farther, where the shops became elegant early-1900s Victorians. Someday maybe she'd replace her dollhouse with one of these stately structures, which were as well-appointed as dignified old ladies. But probably not. She loved her dollhouse and could visualize small children running round and round her equally small living room. Plus, once the children got bigger, she couldn't take them to an old Victorian. They'd destroy it.

Emma curved off the main street toward the south edge of town. *What am I doing, contemplating children?* She couldn't even get over charming innuendo from dangerous doctors and back to full focus on her fabulous relationship with Hunter. *Plus, based on our conversation about his baby-marriage-crazy ex-girlfriend, Hunter's not ready for that anyway. She* still felt like too much of a child. Most likely, no one should be giving her more.

Parking by the beach on Pinewood Lake was easy. There were only one or two cars. *Maybe couples doing some off-season romancing?* She ambled through tall pines surrounding park benches and stone barbecues and continued through to the sandy beach.

The lake looked magnificent. Even after a dry summer, the waves lapped onto sand and rock. Emma could just see the small island, known to locals as Emerald Island, extending up in the middle. A small castle sat atop jutting peaks, rumored to have been built by pirates—but really, what pirates plundered a lake? Otherwise, the far shores were all but invisible.

The beach was deserted, romancing couples perhaps hiding in the woods. Emma took off her shoes and squished her toes in the sand, hoping the mixture of the roughness of the grains and the softness of their little dunes would help her think. These murders had to be about the topic of Kisten's speech. They had to be about perception. Whoever was causing this pain must think that the girls, the cheerleaders, the SSP, even Emma and Leslie, had something more than they did, or maybe that they weren't doing the right things, the spiritually right things, to deserve what they had. The killer couldn't perceive that all humans had pain, all humans had issues and problems, regardless of how it might seem on the surface.

Emma scooped some pebbles from the beach and sprinted toward the water then tossed them along with her frustrations out over the waves. She didn't have proof that Kisten was Eloise, that Billy Barrows aka Simon Seymour killed her, and that he maybe even killed Otto, but she had to take all the information she and Leslie knew to the proper authorities. Well, she had to take them to Detective Niome, regardless of how proper he was not.

Since Diane no longer appeared to be a suspect, Emma also thought about those notes, probably printed in the Scribble font on the computers in the business department. All those *S*'s bothered her again. Emma kept feeling like there was an important letter *S* she kept missing, an important topic she'd seen or heard that she couldn't put her finger on, that might give some answers. *S*—SSP? No. Spirituality? Scribble? No, no, no. Science?

Science? Not quite, but...

Grabbing her shoes on the way, she ran back to the Honda, jumped in, and pulled the smartphone from her purse. She typed the *S* word she'd thought of into the search engine then scrolled down the list—birds of North America, gemstones, fossils, herbs, horses... and there it was. She poked Will's number on the phone. No answer. Breathlessly, she listened to his clipped message and waited for the beep. "I figured it out!" she yelled. "I know who the killer is! Call Niome, and I'll meet you in five at my house." Having accomplished this important task, Emma peeled out of the Pinewood Lake parking lot as fast as the little car would take her.

EMMA ENTERED HER DOLLHOUSE with the intention of calling the police, just in case Will hadn't checked his messages right away. An ominous feeling overtook her, and a shiver roiled its way up her back. *What in the Sam Hill is* that *all about? I'm nowhere near a cemetery.* She checked her phone. Six fifteen p.m. Maybe the detective was done for the day, but there must be someone on duty she could talk to. She threw her purse and phone on the couch and called for her pets. Sir Toby was barking from the second bedroom, but no pets emerged. She called again, and the barking continued unabated. Puzzled and suddenly frightened by the barking and the creepy feeling, she went to investigate.

She saw Trinculo to her right on the dresser, flattened against the vanity mirror, spitting and snarling. Sir Toby was in the middle of the room, at the foot of the bed, tail rigid, front paws splayed apart, barking furiously at the navy bedspread that had been flung hurriedly across her bed this morning.

There, curling around one of her floral pillows, was a huge, hissing snake.

The point envenomed too?
Then, venom, to thy work.

—*Hamlet,* 5.2.315–16

Chapter 26

Emma sucked in a breath. The snake was huge, thicker than her arm and twice as long. It was striped with fat, vivid, black-and-red bands that undulated as it curled around and through her decorative pillows. She could see some of its belly as it raised its swaying head up and hissed, disturbed by the ruckus of the pets, legendary forked tongue flickering.

"Shhh. Sir Toby. Trinculo. Please," she whispered. She didn't want to move forward and grab the dog, which was much too close to the snake. She tiptoed gingerly to the dresser to put her hand on Trinky, and Sir Toby, who was not known for her skills at minding her momma, miraculously quieted. The snake stayed on the bed, still swaying and spitting.

Sir Toby backed up two steps, far enough for Emma to grab her tail and pull her back. She had every intention of taking her pets and fleeing, when the bedroom door slammed shut behind her, followed by the scraping of a chair wedged underneath the doorknob.

Emma picked up her sweet girl dog and, keeping her eye on the snake, backed toward the door. The knob turned under her hand, but when she pushed, nothing happened. She rattled it and pushed harder. Still nothing. She'd always thought that chair-under-the doorknob trick was another goofy horror-movie trope, but to her dismay, it really worked. Still conscious of the snake, she arched her head back, thinking. The windows in the room were on the left, but it was such a small room that Emma was afraid the snake would be on her before she could work the latch. Even the farthest window from the bed was only a few feet away from it.

"I'm sorry, but I'm soooo, so done. No one can learn to be nice." The voice floated in from the other side of the door.

"Rhiannon?" asked Emma. "Is that you?" *Oh my goodness. I should've called 911 on my way home instead of waiting to call Carl. I should've done that the minute I figured out Rhiannon was the one who killed Kisten and maybe Otto too. The second I remembered that Smithsonian book she was reading was a handbook on reptiles and amphibians, I should've done something more. My brain is rattling like a BB in a boxcar, and I can't believe there's a snake on my bed. We're gonna die.* Trinky and Sir Toby held still in her arms.

"I tried and tried to figure out a way to teach you all. I knew poison in the punch bowl wouldn't kill anyone, but maybe getting a bunch of people sick was a good way to make you think about being nicer to people. I spilled Diane's punch so she wouldn't drink it, but even the nice people can be bullies." The door shook as Rhiannon must've struck it with a fist. "Everyone needs to find a way to learn, but I don't think there is a way. You'll all look down on me forever. Just like my stupid, snotty mother, so beautiful and self-absorbed. Couldn't see my evil stepfather and stepbrother for what they were or how they treated me. They all should die. All you snotty women should just die and leave me alone."

Emma could sense Rhiannon leaning against the door. She tried to push on it, hold her pets, and watch the snake at the same time. The snake continued to move, raising its head to hiss then sinking back down to undulate around the throw pillows on the bed, seeming to favor the red one. *Maybe it's trying to match its own stripes.* Emma shivered and shushed Trinky and Sir Toby. *Cheese and crackers, I must be losing my mind. I'm contemplating decorating preferences of creatures who want to kill me, and the person outside my door wants to kill me, and I have to get out of here.*

The door rattled. "And now, Diane doesn't love me anymore," Rhiannon moaned. "I got to be her substitute daughter, you see. The one who took the place of the one she lost. And now she's gonna find out who she lost and what I did. She just came to my classroom, asking about snakes and Otto, and now she's gonna find out *I'm* the one responsible for who she lost, and she'll be gone too." Choking sobs filtered through the door.

"Rhiannon. Can you please let me out? We can talk, really talk. Can you..." Her voice rose. She pounded on the door again, eyeing the distance between herself and the snake, and then between herself and the window. *The snake's too close. I'm too far.* The snake was sliding out from under the pillow and looking like it was ready to slither to the floor. "Rhiannon, please!"

A thud and a swish hit the door, which she thought was Rhiannon's body slumping down against the other side. Her voice came through the door next to Emma's knocking knees. "Isn't it pretty? It's a coral snake, one of about five different snakes I have. My stupid stepfather was an amphibian vet, and he used to threaten me with snakes. So I learned. I learned to be around them and how to milk them so, one day, I could get back at him. I never could get back at him."

"Rhiannon, I can't help you if you don't let me out." Emma choked and squeezed her eyes shut like she could make the snake disappear. Tears leaked through and fell on Sir Toby. "This snake looks really angry."

"Anyway," Rhiannon said, and Emma could hear that her voice was getting weaker. "I let him bite me before I put him in there with you. I just... I just can't get you all to change. You can't understand how hard it is to be me, and now Diane, the one person who really tried to help and understand me, is gone too. I should..." Her voice grew fainter.

"Rhiannon, you let that snake bite you?" Emma cried. "Rhiannon! You have to let me out! We have to get help for you. Rhiannon!"

Emma strained to hear the voice that floated in. "It's best like this. I don't even deserve to be here, and you deserve it too much." The last sentence became a raspy whisper. "It makes sense, in a funny kind of way."

Hunter, Hunter... I need my sweet philosopher. Where are you? Emma pounded on the door. "Rhiannon! Rhiannon, wake up!"

Just as Sir Toby let out a heated bark, the snake lunged at her and sank its teeth into the back of her leg, up under her floral skirt. White-hot pain zipped up her leg. Emma yanked up her skirt and stared in mute horror at the bullet-shaped head now attached to her calf, half of its body still dragging on the floor. She jiggled her leg frantically, trying to fling it off. She struggled to cross the bedroom floor—with the snake still attached—to pound at the window. Emma tried to push it up and open, but the old house's old window frame stuck and wouldn't budge. The snake held fast, hanging from her leg. It hurt so badly. She screamed and screamed at the door, at the stupid old window, at Rhiannon, at a world that would let her and her beloved pets die in the middle of the day in the middle of her bedroom. She screamed until she passed out.

WHEN EMMA WOKE, SHE was lying across her tiny green couch, surrounded by worried faces. Above her head was Hunter, stroking her hair. At her side was Will Capshaw, who seemed to be stroking her arm. Emma didn't even want to think about the repercussions of being touched by these two at the same time. At her feet sat Leslie, who had propped Emma's feet up on a pillow and was now rubbing them, applying all the reflexology points that Rain had taught her. Sir Toby was next to Will with her paws up on the couch cushion, licking Emma's face.

"You're going to be just fine, Em," said Leslie. "Dr. Will already shot you up with antivenin."

Emma turned her head toward the doctor, who was not actually stroking her arm but rubbing it at the injection site. His face was set in anger. *He is madder than a wet hen. At me? For getting myself into the situation?* Her leg seemed heavy, and when she tried to lift it, she saw it had been wrapped in a wide white swath of bandages.

"Trinculo got bit too," said Leslie.

Emma gasped and tried to raise herself up from the couch.

Hunter urged her back down. "Shhh. She's going to be fine. Edward took her to the vet, but Will's pretty sure the snake used all its venom on you and Rhiannon. Trinky got a dry bite. She'll be fine." *He looks mad too. Because Will is here or because I got myself into the situation?*

"Rhiannon?" asked Emma. "Where is she? Is she all right? She sounded like she'd been bit bad. I know she wanted to die. She killed Kisten and tried to kill Leslie and maybe Otto." She considered everyone in the room, trying to read their faces. "But I don't want her to die." She dropped her head back down. "I don't want anyone else to die."

Leslie rubbed her arches. "Edward took her to the hospital. Detective Niome met him there. Dr. Belsing said it would be touch and go. She did have the venom in her for a lot longer than you did. But she'll probably be okay, and Carl will take her into custody."

Emma lay still for a moment, staring up at the ceiling. "You saved me. You all saved me." She shuddered. "Oh, that snake. It was so big, and all the hissin', and Rhiannon talkin' through the door like the angel of death. 'I don't deserve to be here, and you deserve it too much.' What does that even mean?" Her voice broke. "What brought you all here?"

Hunter coughed like it hurt to say the words. "Dr. Capshaw came first and saved you because you called him, remember?" He covered his eyes with one hand. "Leslie filled me in after school on the whole Simon Seymour aka Billy Barrows thing and the Diane and Otto family tragedy, so Edward and I got our detective thing back on. We felt like such failures when we were looking for Diane's journal. But we found Otto. So we were coming to let you know. We took some deputies with us to Rhiannon's house when we were out snooping around, which is where we all found Otto. Will had called the police right after you called him, and so he was already here, giving antivenin to you and Rhiannon."

Emma stared up at Hunter then sat up despite a chorus of protests. "You found Otto at Rhiannon's house? What? No, wait." She turned her gaze to Will. "I'm so sorry I called you instead of just dialing 911 the second I figured out it was Rhiannon and not Simon Seymour or Billy Barrows that killed Kisten. I should've gone straight to the police."

Will stood up and cracked his knees. "I need a chair. Can I have a chair?" He sat in the fat, striped loveseat. "Rhiannon lives by me. I didn't know her, see. Didn't know about all this that was happening at the school. I mean, I knew about it, obviously, but as far as all the suspects you were looking at, the last thing I knew was Simon Seymour aka Billy Barrows. Anyway, I came home from work, and all I really wanted to do was take a nap, but there were weeds growing in my yard about as tall as Jack's beanstalk."

Emma and Leslie made twin "Yes, and?" motions with their hands.

"Yeah, and anyway," he continued, "I was on my way out to pull the gargantuan evil greens when you called, and right then, I saw Rhiannon leave her house. She carried a big box, and I couldn't help noticing it looked a lot like those boxes we saw at the Holiness church service." He tilted his head at Emma, who nodded in agreement.

Hunter sat down next to Emma. "You two went to that service together? I thought you went alone."

"I *did* go alone. He just happened to have the same idea about Reverend Barrows that I did."

Hunter's eyes narrowed, but he clamped his lips shut.

I'm so sorry to you, too, sweetie. I'll find a way to show you later. "Go on," said Emma.

"She got in her car with the big box, and I decided to follow her on my motorcycle. I know your message sounded urgent, Emma, but I just had such a bad feeling watching her leave with that box."

"Yay! Will to the rescue!" said Leslie, clapping her hands.

She received a glare from Hunter. "But how is it Rhiannon had time to lock Emma in the second room and collapse in front of the door, and the snake had time to bite Emma, before *you* got there to save the day? You should have stopped Rhiannon at the door. Or better yet, you never should've let her get out of the car."

Will's head fell into his hands, and he talked to his knees. "I know. But I ran over something on the road and blew a tire about two miles back." He shrugged, sheepish. "No spare tires on a Harley, and the skid from the blown tire kinda... dropped me on the road and broke my cell. So I left the bike, and the phone, and continued in the same direction Rhiannon was heading, which was toward this house. I could have been wrong about where she was going, but"—he shrugged—"I don't know anyone else from this side of town. I wanted to check here first. Anyway, by the time I arrived, Rhiannon was unconscious and so were you. The front door was unlocked. Hasn't anyone ever told you to lock your door?"

Emma ducked her head to avoid Leslie's I-told-you-so glare. "I've been told."

"She didn't really want to die, Emma," Will said, "and maybe she didn't want you to, either. There was antivenin in the box. She must've passed out before she got back to it."

"So you ran here?" asked Leslie. She clapped again, ignoring another black look from Hunter. "Yay! Dr. Will to the rescue! Think about it. How strange is it that Dr. Will should be near Rhiannon right at that critical moment? Coincidence? Divine intervention? I'm starting not to believe in coincidence."

Emma regarded Hunter and Leslie. "I still don't understand what brought you *all* here. Leslie, were you running from the Pizza Hut again?"

Hunter lifted Emma's elbow, helping her up from the couch. Leslie held her other arm. "We'll tell you all about it," he said, "*after* we get you to the hospital."

Upon standing up, a wave of dizziness hit Emma, and she leaned on her friends. "Oooh. I guess that's fair enough."

Chapter 27

After a thorough checkup by Dr. Belsing and some pain-relieving needle punctures given to her by a nurse—she so didn't want anything sticking her right now, but the doctor had insisted—Emma was resting comfortably in an emergency-room bed. Well, as comfortably as one could in a gown with no backside. Dr. Belsing had ordered her to stay put until all tests were finished, but then, since there were no residual effects from the venom, she'd be allowed to go home.

Leslie and Hunter sat by the bed. Will Capshaw had said his goodbyes a few minutes earlier, but Edward had just arrived and sat on the other side of Emma's bed.

"Hello, ladies and gentlemen," he announced. "Is everyone here feeling shipshape?"

Emma smiled wanly. "Maybe ship. Not sure about shape. How's Rhiannon?"

"She'll be fine. Detective Niome has placed her under guard, and he'll take her into custody as soon as she's well enough." He frowned. "That girl is *not* shipshape in any way, shape, or form, though. She kept moaning that we should have just let her die."

Leslie sniffed. "Maybe she's right."

Emma poked her friend in the arm. "Leslie! She's obviously sick. Maybe now she can get help. C'mon. Spill. How did you three come to be approachin' my house at exactly the right moment? Did you say something about Otto?"

Edward nodded and patted her arm.

Ow. Now why would my arm hurt? I got bit in the leg. My gosh, I hope Otto's going to be all right. I can't imagine what Diane is already going through, having lost her daughter to Rhiannon, her surrogate daughter, all at the same time. How devastating.

"I checked on him too. He's up on the third floor, with a concussion and a broken leg. He's also dehydrated, but he'll be fine."

"A concussion? What happened?" Emma couldn't wait to hear this story. "Oh, I'm so happy he's still alive, now that we know he's not the killer."

Leslie leaned forward. "I saw Diane up on the third floor, too, with Otto. Remember how we told Diane to stop to see Rhiannon on her way home, to let her know the situation with her father?"

Emma nodded.

"Well, I guess she did that, and she told me she was all excited and emotional because their long journey was coming to an end. They were going to find Eloise. She just went on and on about it, but I guess Rhiannon acted really weird about the news, ya know? Like, not happy Simon was found, and I guess she did this bizarre shiver at the mention of Eloise, and then she basically shut down. Diane thought it was really strange, but you saw her when we sent her home. She was wiped out. So she went home and collapsed."

Emma rubbed the phantom pain in her arm. "I'm havin' a hard time connecting the dots, if you please. The snake bit my leg, not my brain, and I don't have a concussion. How'd we get from there to here? Go. On."

Hunter chimed in. "Diane woke up from her nap in a panic and didn't know how to get hold of you or Leslie, so she raced back to the school in hopes Abigail or someone would be there with phone numbers."

"A dream caused her to panic?" Emma asked. Boy howdy, did she know *that* scenario. "Was she dreaming about unreachable babies?"

Leslie looked at her strangely. "You remember I had to stay after school to tutor Kevin Rafferty? Well, he had just left, and I was cleaning up to go home when Diane burst in, babbling about bullies and necessary consequences. She'd been dreaming about Wendy—Wondrous Wendy and Wrinkled Wendy."

"What did she say?" Emma breathed. "Those paper shapes are possessed, I know it."

"Well, you're kinda right. In Diane's dream, Wendy was alive and talking, but in Rhiannon's voice. The voice said, 'Those bullies will have necessary consequences. Remember Alexa Champlain? She called me *fat,* Diane, and in front of students. It's only a force of nature that can smooth them out. They need to be smoothed out, Diane. Only a force. Of. Nature.'"

Leslie shrugged. "I guess Rhiannon spent a lot of their lunch periods, in addition to the search for Eloise, bemoaning her situation as compared to everyone else around her. She talked about how the girls in those two social groups—SSP and the cheerleaders—indeed, most of the girls in TJ High, including us, Em, were too perfect to be believed. Diane said no one ever said anything about the threatening notes. Kids don't really talk to her, and you saw those three and their lack of interaction with any of us. Maybe if she knew, she would've made the connection to Rhiannon and her constant grousing. She was focused more on how to make Rhiannon feel better."

"I'm still not landing on Rhiannon and snakes," said Emma. "Or Otto."

"I'm getting there," Leslie huffed. "You just lay back and recover, Grasshoppah, and let the story unfold." She raised her hand like she was going to pat Emma's arm, too, but then she just grabbed her fingertips and lightly held on.

Now it was Edward's chance. "Otto got his mail on Monday night, and the letter from Heritage Harbor said their investigators found out Eloise had been adopted by Tamara and Walter Hollis."

"Simon was a really, really devious guy," Leslie said. "He went through the whole name change and church denomination change after he stole Eloise, and then he pretended he'd found her—that she was left on his church steps, lo some mysterious morning, and he arranged for her adoption by Tamara and Walter, these parishioners of the church. Heritage Harbor did the same thing you were trying to do, Emma, and sort of travel forward from where Simon Seymour became Billy Barrows in order to walk backward to Eloise's birth and subsequent kidnapping. They—"

"Oh my dear Aunt Fanny!" Emma roared. For a moment, she sounded like Abigail on the intercom, but with a twang. "Otto and Rhiannon!" She grabbed Leslie's hand and yanked it back and forth. "Somebody tell me about Otto and Rhiannon, or I'm gonna have a dying duck fit right here on this hospital bed!"

Leslie and Hunter burst out laughing, but Edward's alarmed expression suggested he didn't want to see what a dying duck fit entailed. "Please don't get upset, Emma. Before I start, I just wanted to tell you how Otto's 4-H pin got into Leslie's room, because he told me this too. Don't growl, Miss Emma. Otto's so nice, and I just want to reinforce that. He is the one who brought the paint to help cover the message on Leslie's wall, that's why." He shook his fingers out. "That's all, that's all. He's just so nice. So, on with the story. No fits, dying duck or otherwise."

Edward took a breath then continued. "Otto took the Heritage Harbor letter to Rhiannon's house after school on Monday with the intent of showing it to her then bringing Rhiannon along to tell Diane because Diane would need much, much comforting when she found out Eloise was Kisten." Edward jiggled his hands like he was shrugging off a germ. "But Rhiannon didn't want to comfort Diane. She wanted Diane all to herself, and she already knew Kisten was Eloise. I guess she'd intercepted the original Heritage Harbor letter, or was doing her own investigation, or... I'm not totally clear on how she knew this. Anyway, she pushed Otto down her basement stairs. He passed out from the concussion and the pain, and when he woke up, he was hog-tied—"

"No pun intended, Farmer Otto," Leslie broke in.

"And his mouth was duct-taped. That's where we found him." He looked so proud. Edward to the rescue.

Leslie jumped in to continue the story. "As soon as Diane talked to me, I found Hunter and Edward, and we went to Rhiannon's house with the police. We took that Incredible Hulk officer that was guarding the crime scene last year, remember? Officer Ted. His biceps are as impressive as ever."

That Edward is such a sweet, earnest, crime-fighting Third Musketeer. He manages to accidentally help us all the time. "You still haven't told me how Diane figured out about the snake," Emma said.

"Oh, sorry, right. When dream Wendy talked about nature's consequences, that's what woke Diane up. She remembered something Rhiannon had said after the poisoning in the punch bowl at the dance. Rhiannon showed her the Smithsonian book and commented on the snake chapter as a possible way of making people sick—how venomous snakes could be a 'vicious consequence of nature' for the careless. Diane was so focused on finding Eloise and helping Rhiannon feel better that she simply nodded and patted her on the back then forgot all about it. She felt so responsible for missing it, with everything that's happened since. And I just have to say, we missed some really obvious things too. For instance, because *Diane* is so short, it never even registered that Rhiannon is decently short too—short enough to introduce her campaign of terror with the graffiti on the gym wall."

"The Smithsonian Handbook on Reptiles and Amphibians," Emma said quietly. "That was the *S* word I couldn't remember. I helped her pick it up when Alexa pitched that fit in her room and swiped all her stuff off her desk."

"Well," said Leslie, "Diane has been investigating her daughter's disappearance for sixteen years, and you've been... at least reading murder mysteries for that long. I don't know how you both missed

Rhiannon's book, or why we didn't spend more time on these two diminutive ladies. So I guess the dream, coupled with Rhiannon's odd behavior from earlier in the day, was the reason Diane went to find me for help." She squeezed Emma's knee—not the leg with the snakebite. "And look how responsible we were. We got all sorts of backup!" She waggled her eyebrows Groucho Marx style.

"How do you think Rhiannon hid all this from Diane and Otto?" Emma asked. "God, that's terrible."

"We're not sure," Leslie said. "That basement in her house had locks on the door. Maybe she told Diane and Otto it came that way when she rented it. That's what I would do."

Emma sighed. "I can't believe Rhiannon could do something so horrible, could terrorize a whole school, because of jealousy."

Leslie stood up and struck a pose. "'Beware, my lord, of jealousy! It is the green-eyed monster which doth mock the meat it feeds on.'"

Emma hugged herself. "'It is a monster begot upon itself, born on itself!'"

Leslie sat back down. "See, Othello killed because of jealousy and without really knowing the truth about Desdemona. People do crazy things like that. They don't understand that everyone has problems."

Emma thought back to Kisten's speech. "It's all about perspective."

Earlier, the nurse had brought paper cups of apple juice for all of them. Edward lifted his cup. "To perspective."

"Perspective!"

They drank. Emma stopped mid-gulp. "By the way, where is that snake?"

Leslie pish-poshed. "Oh, it's still shut up in your second room. The gal from Animal Control doesn't have the equipment or the training to catch the snake. A bear? She's on it. Coyotes? No problem. But this needs a different expertise, and since the snake's not a danger right now, Denver Animal Control can't get here 'til tomorrow."

Emma almost choked on her juice.

"But don't worry. I've got Sir Toby, Trinky's staying the night at the vet, and you can stay the night at my house. Plus, I think I've found a good long-term solution to get rid of said snake."

"I don't know if I can face school tomorrow," said Emma. "Maybe I could spend the day in front of your giant TV."

"I already called Nate," Leslie confirmed, blowing on her knuckles and wiping them back and forth on her shirt to go along with her I'm-so-impressed-by-me face.

Emma smiled. "I'll let you know what happens on *All My Children*."

Sound drums and trumpets! Farewell sour annoy!
For here, I hope, begins our lasting joy.

—*King Henry VI Part III*, 5.7.45–6

Chapter 28
Monday, September 28

Emma had slept for three days—she didn't like soap operas anyway—and on Monday morning, she showered at Leslie's house. Leslie's Ritz Carlton-esque bathroom had two sinks sunk in a marble countertop as long as two of Emma's countertops. The bathtub had a built-in spa and a shower head on either end, of which Emma was sure Leslie made good use. Oh, Leslie's ex-husband had paid dearly for his marital indiscretions, the most notable of which had been a personal trainer named Anthony.

Leslie had picked up one of Emma's ubiquitous floral skirts on her way home from school on Friday. She still wouldn't tell Emma how she got rid of the snake and continued to be more closemouthed than usual this morning.

"C'mon," pleaded Emma. "How'd you get rid of that nasty ol' snake? Did you get someone from the Pentecostal Church to come in?"

Leslie looked startled. "No, but that's a good idea." She grinned. "My way was more fun, though. You'll see."

"Oh I'll see? I'll see?" Emma said in a whiny voice. "I've had enough surprisin' in my life the past few days to last forever. Not the least of which was a giant serpent in my house."

"Oh hush. It wasn't a giant serpent. Actually, I think it was sorta small for a coral snake. I've been reading up."

Emma brushed on some mascara and blinked a few times. "Yes, tell that to its humongous fangs." She rubbed her leg with her other hand, which still felt like someone had taken a baseball bat to it. Repeatedly.

"I also found out how extremely lucky you are that Rhiannon had an antivenin. It's not really available in this country anymore. Something about expiration dates? Anyway, her psycho stepfather must've had some."

"Poor, poor Diane and Otto," Emma said. "They've been working so hard to find their daughter, and now they've found her and lost her all at the same time. It's gotta be so, so devastating." She capped the mascara and rubbed her leg with both hands, trying to rub out the horror. "Where are they now? Do you know?"

"They're gone." Leslie brushed the edges of her bob and kiss-kissed her reflection in the mirror. "They told Nate they needed to go away together to process their loss. They both went to the jail to say goodbye to Rhiannon, which is waaay more than I would've done. I don't think they'll be back. Diane asked me to thank you, though. Said she'd be in touch."

There was a knock on the door.

"Who is that?" asked Emma.

"Surprise number one for the day," Leslie replied sweetly.

Emma threw the mascara into her makeup bag. "Aw, wasn't I just complaining about the overabundance of surprises in my life? It's not Dr. Will, is it? Come to take us to breakfast? I told you, Hunter and I—"

Leslie led Emma to the door. "No, it's not Dr. Will. It is, however, a personal ride to breakfast." She picked up Emma's bag and handed it to her. "Come on."

Leslie checked her red sleeveless suit, brushed off some imaginary lint, and opened the door with a flourish. On the other side stood a handsome black man.

"Shawn!" Leslie said. "You're looking terrif."

He walked in, smiling with a mouth full of incredibly white and straight teeth. His head was smooth and bald, and he had a rakish, close-cropped goatee that was at odds with his conservative blue polo and Dockers. "Shawn, you remember Emma? Emma, Shawn. Shawn works at the junior high." Her grin was playful.

Emma shook his hand. "Yes, Shawn. From the junior high. Sure, I remember."

Leslie winked at her from behind Shawn's head.

"How did you and Leslie meet again? I forgot."

"It was the funniest thing," said Shawn. "We were playing one of those 'bonding' games at an in-service this summer, you know, where we had to work together to keep these balloons from falling off of this string network we'd made with our hands."

"Very conducive to the educational system, balloon games," said Leslie.

Shawn and Leslie smiled at each other.

"Anyway," he continued, "Leslie got frantic trying to keep this pink balloon from dropping, and she fell right into my arms. Lucky I was there to catch her, or she'd be sitting on one of those blow-up donut things right now."

Emma tried to roll her eyes for Leslie to see without Shawn's notice. "Lucky you were there."

Shawn tapped his thighs with his hands. "Leslie told me about what's been happening at your school. I thought I would drive you both there this morning, just to give you a break. And I've got multigrain bagels in the car."

Emma broke out her best debutante accent. "Oh, thank you, kind sir. I'm feeling much better, except for that whole lead-pipe-to-the-leg feeling. But y'all know, it *is* such a distance from here to the school that I just might swoon."

Leslie punched her in the arm, and they followed him out.

AFTER EXTRACTING A promise from Leslie to have lunch with him the following day—an extraction he didn't have to work very hard at—Shawn dropped the two off at Thomas Jefferson High. They responded to high-fives from a lot of the kids, and Caitlin Bauer was waiting for them in the teachers' lounge, along with Nate Farrar and Abigail Patterson. They all had hugs for Emma and congratulations to both for figuring out the killer. *Such as it was, education by ambush. Detection by accident. At least all the information we collected along the way will help convict her and Simon, who really is responsible for starting all this.* Even Alexa Champlain stopped in to say thank you.

"I really miss Kisten," said Caitlin with tears in her eyes. "But I'm glad no one else got killed. I'm thinking of starting a club, some sort of diversity club, a way to teach us all that we're not really that different underneath." She struggled for the wording. "I think people need a little more..."

"Perspective?" said Emma.

"Yes! That's it. Perspective. I'm going to do it in honor of Kisten."

Nate came forward. "You'll need a sponsor, of course."

Emma and Leslie laughed. "We'll help you, Caitlin."

Nate nodded. "Cool. Now let's have one good, threat-free day, yeah? Okay?"

With one more large-group bear hug, they were off to the English wing.

"Whoo, those were nice surprises, Leslie," said Emma. "Your new friend Shawn is very cute. I didn't get to talk to you about him at the in-service. Too much crazy. He's a bit of a Shemar Moore, isn't he? Remember that guy from *Criminal Minds*? I think he's got some other show now. Cutie patootie. With muscles."

Leslie licked her lips. "Yeah, succulently Shemar. But the surprises aren't over yet." She skipped through the hall to Emma's room and flung open the door. "Ta-da!"

Emma's classroom was filled with flowers. Jars of daisies, vases of lilies, and sprays of roses were on every available surface. The room smelled heavenly, and Emma thought she really might swoon. In front of the whiteboard stood two people, and Emma had to blink to bring them into focus, so out of context were they in this setting.

Next to her desk, she saw the small brunette woman with a face like hers, deep smile lines framing a big grin and happy lines fanning out from her mouth. She, like Emma, wore a floral dress. "Momma!" cried Emma. She ran to hug her. "What are you doin' here?"

Emma's mother hugged her tight. "Oh darlin'. It's so good to see you. I flew out the minute I found about the snake. I was so scared, but Leslie said you were gonna be just fine. You look wonderful! I am just as happy as if I had good sense." They hugged again.

Emma scanned to her mother's right. "Ronald! What are you doin' here?"

Ronald Talicky, her ex-husband, stood with his hands awkwardly poked into his pockets. He was tall, with wavy blond hair and the broadest shoulders Emma had ever seen. Emma could almost remember why she'd married him. But she immediately remembered why she'd divorced him too. *Danger. I really don't need it in my life, especially not in my love life.*

Leslie sidled over to Emma and bonked her in the hip. "Don't be mad. When I called your mom and mentioned that we were waiting for Animal Control, she knew right away he'd want to help."

Ronald gestured to a box sitting on one of the few desks not flower-laden. "I know you don't want me back, honey-pie. And tha's okay, really. I'm datin' a real nice gal back in Holly Hills. She's a trapper. We got lots in common." He flung a blond lock of hair. "But Leslie and yer momma knew I could help, so I came along."

Emma hugged him. "I'm glad you're doing well, Ronald. But what do y'all mean, 'help'? What'd you do?"

He yanked off the lid of the box and pulled out the snake that had bitten Emma. Emma gasped and recoiled until she saw its still and statuesque form. *Of course. My ex-husband, the taxidermist, to the rescue.* Its tail rested on a buffed wooden stand, and it rippled straight up like it was launching itself into the air. "I got it out of your house, Emma, and Animal Control finally got there to euthanize it because, a'course, it tried to kill you. So I stuffed it for ya." He grinned and swished his hand through the air up and down, displaying the multicolored bands. "See, it looks like it would look mid-attack. But I guarantee it ain't never gonna attack you or anybody else ever again. This way, you got a memory of all yer fine detectivizing."

She gazed at the snake trophy. Its skin had been polished to a dull gleam, and he'd worked some sort of superglue mojo on its mouth so it would perpetually bare fangs and extend a forked tongue. *Eww.* "It's... lovely, Ronald. But I'm not sure it really goes with the decor of this room. Do you think I could donate it to the science teachers? Surely they could use a reptile model."

"You can do whatever you want with it, sugar. I'm just glad I could be a help." He gave the stuffed snake to Emma, who gingerly handed it over to Leslie. "And, Emma?" he asked.

She faced him.

He winked and grinned. "Don't call me Shirley."

EDWARD POPPED IN TO take Ronald and Emma's mother on a tour while Emma got ready for class, setting the flowers all along the baseboards for a lovely floral frame of the room. *Much better than a snake frame around someone's face.* She was sure this was Hunter's work. A romantic gesture very much in keeping with her sweet philosopher.

Leslie poked her head back in, saying, "One more surprise..." And she disappeared.

Hunter came in, holding Trinculo in his arms. Emma snuffed, grabbed her pet, and held her tight, breathing in the smell of cat. "Trinky," she cooed. "Momma's so glad you're all right." Trinky lay in her arms like she was really tired but cozy and content. Emma grabbed Hunter with her other arm and smooched him. "I'm so glad to see her. Is it okay for her to be here?"

"Yeah, I asked Nate. He said he thought it was okay for this one day to have a non-caged, non-stuffed animal in here. Abigail said you're lucky no one in your classes has allergies—she checked—but not to make it a habit, though, since the custodians don't deal well with pet hair." Hunter stroked Emma's hair. "Do you like the flowers?"

Emma kissed him again. "I knew it was you. This must be your mysterious errand from Friday. They're beautiful. Thank you." She reached up to kiss his cheek. "I love you."

"I met your mother. She's sweet. The two of us have already arranged a reunion for Christmas break." His eyes searched hers. "If that's okay with you."

Emma cast her eyes down to the floor. "Of course it's okay. Why wouldn't it be?"

He shrugged. "I don't know. I just thought... Emma, do you want to see other people? I've been feeling like maybe you do."

"I really don't." Her eyes stayed glued down, because she remembered Will's brown eyes, and she remembered how he'd almost kissed her. But Emma knew what she wanted, and he was standing here with her now, surrounding her with flowers.

Hunter twisted the heel of his shoe into the classroom floor. "Hey, I know I'm not as interesting as Will Capshaw. I can see, as much as I hate to admit it, why you might be intrigued by him. I'd be loath to be the subject of resentment down the road because you didn't get to know him like you wanted to."

Her eyes crinkled. "You'd 'be loath' to be?"

He smiled. "I couldn't bear to be the motive for your malignity. It'd be excruciating to be the object of your execration. How'm I doing on the second-semester word thing?"

"You're doing great." She ran her cat-free hand over his cheek. "I think I got scared you didn't want what I want when we kept running around in circles over the meet-the-parents thing. It was silly. If we love each other, we just need to communicate better. I will communicate with you right now. Moving forward in our relationship doesn't mean I think we should run off and get married and make babies tomorrow, for Pete's sake. Just that we want to keep moving forward. And I won't deny Dr. Will turnin' my head. But I want to be with you. Is that okay?"

He leaned toward her. "It's extra super okay."

They shared a long, sweet kiss, which didn't end until Trinky started to struggle between them and until students started arriving for first hour.

"True hope is swift and flies with swallow's wings;
Kings it makes gods, and meaner creatures kings."

—*Richard III*, 5.2.23–4

Epilogue
Monday, April 6

Emma had come in early in the morning to meet with the diversity club and finalize their plans for Spring Fest, which ran all that week after school and served as a buildup to spring break the next week. She figured her favorite activity would be on Wednesday, a little ditty she called Hump Day Hugs. It involved a variation on Wrinkled-slash-Wondrous Wendy and ended with Nate Farrar, Hunter, and Edward going into a dunk tank. *Edward volunteering to get dunked in the water! By students! Imagine that.* She wandered around her classroom, dropping song lyrics on desks for her students' Creative Writing assignment.

Leslie swung the door open, posed with her hands up against the doorframe, and started to sing, "Daaaaaaaaay-oh!"

Emma stopped and stared.

Leslie belted out "The Banana Boat Song," a throaty celebration. She sashayed into the room, holding a pile of mail in each hand. She shook them like maracas while she sang the Harry Belafonte favorite. "Oh, baybee, take me on home!" She reached the desk where Emma stood and punctuated her notes by dropping the mail bundles on the desk. "Hayr-ee Bela-fon-tee is the King-oh!" She inhaled and blew out. "I had my ulcer-friendly diet sent to the resort. Are ya ready? All-inclusion? A week with Hunter and Shawn, you and me, baybee, lounging in the Caribbean for seven, count 'em, seven day-ay-ay-os and six nights in bee-you-tee-ful St. Lucia? Can ya dig it?" She dropped a letter from the top of her bundle. "Got your mail."

"I can dig it, Grasshoppah." Emma grinned. "Lookin' forward to fruity concoctions on the beach." She glanced down. "Ooh, look. Letter from Uganda!" Running over to her desk, she plopped down, sliding a finger under the flap. "I hope Diane and Otto are doing okay."

Leslie sashayed over. "Read it! Read it! Can't wait! We'll have to tell Edward. I'm sure he'd love an update on how it's going with those five laptops he bought and sent along to Uganda."

Emma whipped the paper open. "Edward's so great, always lookin' for a way to help." She started perusing. Her eyes stopped on a paragraph about halfway down the page. She looked up at Leslie, and her eyes had filled with tears.

"Read!" Leslie commanded.

Emma nodded, smoothed the page, and cleared her throat.

Dear Emma,

Otto and I have never, never learned as much as we are learning here in Uganda! We're working at an orphanage in a town called Jimba. There are 220 orphans here, most of whom lost their parents to murder or HIV. Did you know Uganda has over 2 ½ million orphans? They don't have anything, any of the creature comforts we take for granted, but do you know what? They still find a way to be happy. They still give anything they have even though they don't have anything. I've never seen anything like it.

The classes I'm teaching at the orphanage school are going well, and Otto's doing great, too, teaching the villagers about sustainable farming, but that's not why the letter, Emma. That's not why!

This is why. We've met a baby. There's one here at the orphanage, a little girl named Suubi. Her name is the Ugandan word for Hope, and that's what she is for us. She laughs at us even when she's crying, and I think our favorite thing to do together is cuddle up while I read to her. It's like we're in a permanent hug. Our court date is in one month, Emma! One more month, and we get to adopt her.

Emma's hand flew to her mouth. Leslie bounced on her toes like a kindergartner who'd just found out it was snow cone day.

"Go on. Keep reading!" Leslie grinned and planted triumphant fists on her hips.

Emma burst out laughing even as the tears glistened in her eyes. She continued.

Otto and I can't agree on how to spell her name—he thinks it should be Sooby because that looks more like a farm girl's name. But whatever we decide, her full name will be Suubi Eloise Kisten Seymour Henry, and this place and this family feel more like God than anything my father ever tried to teach me.

By the way, he's going to be in jail until he's at least 98.

I hope you're doing well, Emma. Please say hello to Leslie and Edward and the whole gang back at Thomas Jefferson. Otto helped Suubi plant a seed for each one of you in our garden. We'll send pictures when the seedlings come up. Take good care of yourself.

With Hope, literally and because she's right here,

Diane

Leslie met Emma's eyes. "Now *that's* a religion I can understand," she proclaimed.

Emma wasn't sure who started singing first. "Sooooo-bee! Soo-oo-oo-bee." Leslie began a sort of conga move in between desks, Emma grabbed her by the shoulders, and they continued to dance until students came in.

Dear Reader,

We hope you enjoyed *Poison by Punctuation*, by Kelley Kaye. Please consider leaving a review on your favorite book site.

Visit our website[1] to sign up for the Red Adept Publishing Newsletter to be notified of future releases.

1. http://bit.ly/SMYH1u

Author's Note

Are you interested in knowing more about war-torn African countries like Uganda or international adoption? Here are a couple of places you can look:

https://www.amanibabycottage.org/

http://childrenofallnations.com/adoption-programs/africa/uganda-adoption/

The end of the story was inspired by the real story of two of *my* former high school students: Morgan Daub Hansow and David Hansow. See their story in this documentary: https://www.youtube.com/watch?v=q-uxt5VbKqU

and learn about the business they created (Suubi!) to help a group of Ugandan mothers support their own children! I'm so proud of you, Hansow family!

The Wrinkled/Wondrous Wendy activity was modified from an activity by James H. Burns. To learn about other anti-bullying activities you could practice in your home or classroom, visit his Bully Proof Classroom here: http://bullyproofclassroom.com/great-anti-bullying-activities

Shakespeare quotes from *Shakespeare's Quotations: A Players Press Guide*, by Trevor R. Griffiths and Trevor A. Joscelyn, Players Press Inc., 1992.

Acknowledgements

To Red Adept Publishing and the Red Adept Acquisition Team: I'm so glad you liked where Emma was going for this second book in the series. It's again been an amazing experience! Alyssa Hall, I thank you profusely for being my Content Editor. I continue learning so much about the editing process and the challenges you face in helping this book be the best it can be. What a task you face! Jennifer Wadsworth, thank you so much for being my Line Editor, and Skyping with me so we could talk "face to face" about where to go with Poison by Punctuation. Thank you both for guiding me to a much better book than the one I started out with. Glendon Haddix—what a great cover! You create amazing visuals to complement the stories; I know it draws in readers because giveaway winners keep choosing my books based solely on the covers, and thank you Jessica Anderegg for making that happen. Thank you Mary Fan for being my Book Trailer Badass. I know, I should get you a cape. RAP Authors—you complete me. You had me at hello.

Thank you to Morgan and David Hansow, whose adoption story and successive international volunteerism inspired the "Suubi" story at the end of the book. I'm very proud of you two former students! Thank you thank you thank you.

To everyone who helps me with all the minutiae of putting this story out there in a final form that's much better than it was when it began: Melissa Fischer, Laura Kelly, Danielle Baldwin, thank you because I just need to talk to other writers sometimes. Michael Steven Gregory, Wes Albers, Jennifer Redmond, Claudia Whitsitt, Judy Reeves, Matthew Pallamary, Mark Clements, Jaxon Crow-Mickle,

Linda Rhoades, and anyone I might've missed at the Southern California Writer's Conference, y'all keep my battery charged like I'm the Duracell bunny! Thank you for being you. Shawn Clingman, Richard Lai, and Ken Khoury: thank you for keeping me questioning things.

Finally, to my husband, Jim, here we are—just another day in Paradise! You may never know what a gift you've given to me and to our sons as they experience support and encouragement from you for achieving our dreams. Thank you. I love you to infinity and beyond—to quote Buzz Lightyear, and because that is much farther than to the moon and back. Speaking of our sons, I want to acknowledge them here, because I can't believe I get to do that! I waited so long for you, Grey and Griffen, and you guys were definitely worth the wait. How long will I love you? That's right, always, forever, and no matter what. The fact that you are such wonderful little boys makes this job easier, too.

I will keep acknowledging my father, Donald Wilson Bowles, who died in 2012 but whose influence is still so present in my life. His love for books and the language and culture of books exceeded anyone else I have ever known. I can only aspire. I'd like to acknowledge him and my mom, Shelley Rochelle "Rachel" Frick Bowles, again, for being *those* parents. You know those parents—the ones for whom every achievement of their children, no matter how small, is placed on a stage and applauded and oohed and aahed over so much that those children will succeed no matter what. That kind of unconditional love and support is cherished by those children, every day. Thank you. I love you both so much.

About the Author

Kelley taught high school English and drama for twenty years in Colorado and California, but a 1994 diagnosis of multiple sclerosis has (circuitously and finally) brought her to the life of being a writer and mother, both occupations she adores and dreamed about way back when she was making up stories revolving around her Barbie and Ken dolls.

Kelley has two wonderful and funny sons and an amazing husband who cooks for her. She lives in Southern California.

75198701R00168

Made in the USA
San Bernardino, CA
26 April 2018